RENAISSANCE IN
PROVENCE

RENAISSANCE IN
PROVENCE

a cycling story

John Mugglebee

This is a work of fiction. Names, characters, places and incidents either are the product of the author's imagination or are used fictitiously, and any resemblance to any actual persons, living or dead, events, or locales is entirely coincidental.

This book was printed in the United States of America.

To order additional copies of this book, contact:
Xlibris Corporation
1-888-795-4274
www.Xlibris.com
Orders@Xlibris.com
25351

To Pierre Escoffier, farmer-at-heart, father and friend.
He was good at the little things in life, cleaning and
pitting a cherry or clinking a glass of chilled champagne.
His favorite word in the language of Shakespeare was "rabbit",
which his Pagnolesque tongue butchered like ground beef but
which his joie de vivre served up like sirloin.
He proved that the devil in the details
can be a dapper dude.

COUNTIES OF PROVENCE:
The Bouches-du-Rhone and The Vaucluse

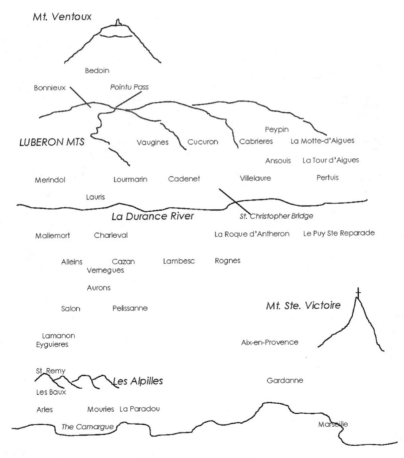

Mt. Ventoux

Bedoin

Bonnieux   Pointu Pass

Peypin

LUBERON MTS   Vaugines   Cucuron   Cabrieres   La Motte-d'Aigues

Ansouis   La Tour d'Aigues

Merindol   Lourmarin   Cadenet   Villelaure   Pertuis

Lauris

La Durance River   St. Christopher Bridge

Mallemort   Charleval   La Roque d'Antheron   Le Puy Ste Reparade

Alleins   Cazan   Lambesc   Rognes
Vernegues

Aurons

Salon   Pelissanne   Mt. Ste. Victoire

Lamanon
Eyguieres   Aix-en-Provence

St. Remy
    Les Alpilles   Gardanne
Les Baux

Arles   Mouries   La Paradou

The Camargue   Marseille

The Mediterranean Sea

SUMMER

I

The view east, albeit behind bars, is unbeatable. Mount Saint Victory rises off the argillaceous plains, a lone tooth on a bloody gum. A fervent sunlight beats like a band conductor against the red clay rooftops of old-town Aix-en-Provence and its villas and chateaux fanning out across the valley. Closer to his position, swallows draw notes around an orchestra of bell towers, sooty chimneys, and terraces spilling over with red and white geraniums and yellow pansies. Provence, he decides, is visible music.

Russell Stone lets go of the window and drops back into the toilet. He is on the last floor of a condemned 17th century private hotel, without the protection of an attic or insulation. The summer swelter descends in ripples from the roof tiles and beams. He unbuttons his grimy shirt and flaps cool air against his sweaty chest. Then, he takes a pen and notepad from his knapsack and starts writing.

> *Dear Penny, it's my coffee break, so I thought I'd whip off a note to say I'm in better spirits. I hired on this morning with a construction crew. Destruction, actually . . .*

"Hey, you, the American—"

An Algerian man, Stone's circumstantial partner in labor, is squatting in the rubble where a wall used to be, extending a cracked thermos top of strongly scented mint tea. "You want some?"

The Algerian's gritty hands are so gnarled they look like pretzels, and he's missing an index finger. Years of demolition have driven his eyes deeper into his skull. The man's sledgehammer probably weighs more than he does, thinks Stone, figuring the Algerian for 110 pounds including the mummifying layer of white dust that covers him and clouds the collapsing corridor and comes out sticky in Stone's spit.

"*Merci*," says Stone, taking the cup. "Just the smell of mint is a comfort." The liquid goes down nicely, taking with it the taste of destruction.

"My son, he is about your age. Got him a computer repair business in Marseilles. Why a young guy like you do this shit? Why you not work in Silicon Valley?"

Stone hands back the top and swabs at the sweaty plaster in the corner of his eyes. He knows that it throws people to see a white, 30-something, butter-haired Californian, fit and apparently straight in the head, doing manual labor in the South of France. He should be vacationing in Provence, not laboring alongside back-broken illegal workers.

"The Stones," he answers, knowing that the pun has no chance of success. "Stone is my last name."

But the Algerian is waiting for a serious answer. "You want that I talk to my son about you, maybe get you a good legal job?"

"No, this work suits me fine."

The hour gongs from nearby Saint Sauveur Cathedral, 10 blows that hit the hollow building like gunshot blasts. "Well, back to work." Relieved to escape the man's questions, Stone picks up his sledgehammer and returns to the Turkish water closet to finish demolishing it. Chunks and shards of porcelain and ceramic litter the floor. A stream of sunlight pours through the bull's-eye window, illuminating flies and dust. Until an hour ago, the window was boarded up. A fellow laborer once told him that a window tax existed during the French Revolution. He wonders what other secrets are concealed behind these walls.

Before he has a chance to find out, whistling peels up the four flights of stairs. It is the job foreman's signal to get out. Stone drops his hammer and hits the corridor running. The Algerian is already bolting for the stairs, yelling over a shoulder: "The police!"

The main stairway is a mistake because they will never make it down in time. So Stone heads in the opposite direction, down a condemned hall where the walls are so warped they seem to undulate. He busts into what was once a servant's chamber, ghosts waiting for dead madam's ringing, silver saucers and fine china cocoa. He pops outside onto a small terrace which he cased out yesterday as a possible escape route, and shinnies down a drain pipe to another terrace, another building.

Down on the street, the miserable blue van of the labor police blocks the entry. Lawmen are verifying the laborers' working papers. Stone appears three doors away on the opposite side of Rue Chabrier, trying to dust himself off and look nonchalant. He passes the shakedown without a hitch. He is invisible. Tall, fair-skinned Americans are blind spots on French construction sites.

The Algerian is being detained roughly in the hotel doorway. Stone catches his eye, then bows and keeps walking. He can kiss another job goodbye.

*   *   *

Newspaper in hand, Stone goes among the cafés of the Cours Mirabeau, Aix's most famous thoroughfare, and settles in the oldest and most famous tavern in town, *Les Deux Garçons*. He knows the name refers to waiters, but he prefers his own translation: The *Two Boys*. Stone is thinking of the one he used to be and of the child Peter Terrell who didn't live to see his eighth birthday. Stone orders a coffee, which becomes his odic, penance-quenching collation to innocence.

He smoothes out his newspaper on the table and gets busy checking the want ads.

In the months he has been in Provence, Stone has done all manner of manual labor. Laid brick, mounted dry wall, painted, installed electricity, sandblasted the pollution-wasted facades of Aix-en-Provence. Occasionally, he moonlights as a store detective for the sex shop opposite the train station. He has no working papers. His employers are always a certain kind of person, the sort willing to hire him *au noir*. Most stints last a day and finish the way the latest job did, running from the police.

An interesting job proposal jumps off the page. A watchman is needed to look after an old farmhouse and its lands in the Vaucluse countryside to the north. Room, board and salary provided. Stone goes into the café and rings up.

The gentleman on the other end is huffy, audibly short of breath and not very forthcoming. Stone finds it tough to glean much practical information out of him, except the name of his village: Lauris.

"What experience have you?" asks the gent.

"I'm a store detective in Aix."

"Speak up."

"I said I'm a sort of store detective."

"A sort? What sort?"

"Well, there's this sex shop in town."

"You mean that you order flushed faced men with erections to stop pawing over porno magazines?"

Stone sees the job slipping from his grasp. "I also know how to get rid of them."

"Be in Lauris tomorrow at 11:15 sharp."

Stone barely has the time to catch the owners' name and the meeting place, before the line goes dead. The man has hung up without the customary au revoir. He opens his pack and removes a map. The village of Lauris is situated in a river valley, in a fertile area halfway between the twin towers of Provence: Mont Sainte Victoire and Mont Ventoux. At least, he muses, it is in the middle of somewhere.

II

Stone gets an early start, setting out by bike. He relies on his bicycle to get from place to place. It is a top-notch racer, carbon frame, state of the art components and wheels. The day he bought it, he telephoned Penelope from a phone booth in Aix. It was 6 o'clock in the morning Los Angeles time, and she was mystified. "Russ, why are you waking me up to tell me this? A bike's a bike."

"I'm excited and wanted to share it with you. I plan to ride, ride, ride."

"Honey, you're lonely. You're not made of stone, even if it is your name. Stop putting yourself through this and come home."

He wants to tell her that no one ever goes home. "No, not now, not yet. Be my watch person for a while longer, would you?"

"You've lost your confidence."

"Five thousand smackers."

"Pardon?"

"It's what I paid for the bike."

Silence on her end, then: "I don't understand you! That's the price of a car! If you had a car, wouldn't your life be easier there in France?"

"Penny," he heard himself say as if to a child, "I didn't buy a *bike*. I bought myself some therapy. I don't want to get anywhere fast any more, and I want to do it in style."

"Right. And hasn't it hit you yet?"

"Hasn't what hit me?"

"The paradox of buying a racer to go slower?"

He bounces up cobbled Rue Gaston de Saporta to the ring road and leaves town via Philippe Solari, climbing north out of the bowl that Aix sits in.

At the top of the hill he passes the gray ruins of Entremont, a Ligurian settlement overrun by a Roman line of such numbers that the first Legionnaire was striking a defender while the last was still debarking in Marseilles harbor 20 miles to the south. A fight that started and finished at the same time.

The road flattens across a vast agricultural landscape. Melons, lettuce, squash. Men and women are stooped in the fields, filling wood crates under a windswept sky as generous a blue as Stone has ever seen. The west wind is rising. He works against the breeze and is in fact a little thankful for the burden. A powerful rider, Stone knows that the temptation to go faster remains, as ever, a sweet poison.

Before coming to France, he did not equated Provence with wind. He knows better now. It is a land of Sun White and the Seven Drafts, of Mistrals, Tramontanes, Southies, Easterlies, Siroccos, Alizés, Zephyrs and sea breezes. In the three months he has been here, Stone the rider has experienced every air movement that Aeolus can blow at him. Gales violent enough to lift his wheels, furnace simouns hot enough to melt the tarmac, glacial aquilons fusing his fingers to the handlebars, south-wind drenchings, north-wind slappings, and westerlies working in cahoots with all the others. Sometimes, he sets out against one wind and finishes fighting another, and has no idea whether he is coming or going. Little wonder that the Celts named the highest mountain in Provence, Mont Ventoux, after ventilation.

Stone's mother grew up in the shadow of the Ventoux, which she referred to as *Le Geant de Provence*. She said that, in her region, the four corners of the earth were called the Four Winds, he who sowed the wind harvested the storm, constipation was *vent de cul* or ass wind, and pride and vanity were the property of the winds.

As a rider, Stone does not care for wind and its invisible force driving at him, impinging his progress. But not liking wind is not the same as wishing there was none. Biking against a stiff wind is a punishment, certainly, but wind also has redemptive qualities. It sweeps away his pain, at least momentarily. It is both a challenge and a cleansing process, an event and a lesson learned, a season unto itself, a miraculous equation of air and physical suffering equating to a temporary amnesia. It allows him to forget that he is riding, thereby creating a dynamic that no longer needs him. He can lose himself and, for a few hours, know freedom from the images that oppress him.

He makes a steep descent into a valley of pink villages and farmlands, France's vegetable basket. On the valley floor, a river, the Durance, meanders along the foot of the Luberon Mountain range, as round and convoluted as the fatted flanks of cows. The road moves through vast sloping vineyards and fields of sunflowers growing taller than he is. He follows the river to the St. Christopher Bridge and crosses over into the County of Vaucluse. He can see his destination across the valley, 15 kilometers away, a village sitting on a promontory shooting 300 feet straight up, a perched village ready to spring. Lauris.

The final road into town begins brutally, every bit deserving of the chevron it received on Map #84, meaning an eight to 10 percent grade. The first kilometer steals his remaining energy and he knows much suffering up the last kilometer. The village bells toll eleven times. Four minutes later, he pulls over to the ramparts and dismounts, breathing heavily.

As he steadies himself against the wall and pumps oxygen back into his depleted body, he notices a sign. It tells him that he now stands in a place constructed in the 13th century by knights of the crusades. Jerusalem to Lauris, a holy trek of 4000 roundtrip miles.

He leans over the ramparts. The drop is straight as a plumb line, though, if he were lucky, some trees and bushes might break his fall. Down on the valley floor, a rich sunlight turns the cadre of crops into a brilliant patchwork of chartreuse, reds, multiple greens and yellows. Khaki canvas-bedded trucks and red Massey Ferguson tractors inch along the private dirt roads running along the fields.

Stone smiles. Everything within his view is owned. Every farm is framed, every rise hammered, every ledge sculpted, and perhaps every minute claimed in the area. A perfect purgatory for someone like himself.

A moment later, a tired and battered blue Citroen truck turns into the village service station across the road, cuts its motor and coasts to a stop. A short rotund man in his sixties steps out wearing filthy work clothes and dancing moustaches. The gent takes a wide circling trajectory like a dog might to have a glance down the road.

Stone rolls up, the gravel making rhythmic pings against the alloyed rims of his wheels.

"Monsieur Sorbin?"

The man, perhaps one too many problems on his mind, looks through the American as if he weren't there. He stuffs his hands into the pockets of his soiled trousers, squares his shoulders, and keeps perusing the road. The man's attention is obviously attuned to cars, not a bicycle. True, Stone didn't mentioned that he would be arriving by bike.

If biking has taught him anything about the French, it's that the French are fairly oblivious to bikers. Pedestrians look his way and still step into his path, while motorist check for other cars, and then pull out in front of him. Purblindness? Rampant individualism? Too much strong coffee? Whatever the cause, he has learned not to take incivility personally.

Stone seizes the chance to study the farmer. He is as short as a morning shadow, and no doubt contemptuous of any correlation between stature and status. Despite the patchy clothing, there's a rough dignity about him, about the way he stands, firmly rooted as if he had grown out of the road and not just happened to be using it. His silver moustaches are bushy but trimmed, his thinning gray-blond hair is slicked back, and his sharp blue eyes are pressed into a ruddy head like imbedded jewels in a lump of dough. His face is clean and shaved with a surplus of cheeks. He seems jolly and personable but, judging by the scowl on his face, also quick-tempered and easy to annoy.

Stone reaches out his hand. His instinct is to hug the hard-hearted bastard.

"Monsieur Sorbin?" he repeats.

The man starts as if from a deep sleep. His eyes widen with latent comprehension. "Oh, right, there you are." There's more intelligence than patience in his regard. "On bike you came.

Pardon me, I am a little hard of hearing." His cheeks lift and a note of mischief sparkles in his moustaches. "You are on time. That is a point in your favor. Where is your watch?"

"I don't own one."

"No watch?"

"No, sir. I threw it away when I left America."

"Then how do you know the hour?"

"I use the church bells and steeple clocks, if I must. Even without them, I have acquired a pretty good feel for the hour."

Sorbin frowns. "This does not speak in your favor."

"No, I guess it wouldn't."

"*Bon*, let's be off to the house. Can you keep up?"

"If you don't drive too fast."

"I do not drive at all, if I can help it," Sorbin answers gruffly.

The farmer gets in and starts his hoarse engine, then guns it and speeds from the village, leaving Stone stupefied.

The descent is winding, so Stone is able to keep an eye on the vehicle coming out of the lower bends in the road, the truck's weight balanced on two thin tires screeching. In the valley, it turns up a shady lane into a wood.

Stone reaches the turn-off, a much-neglected road, its ancient cobblestones humped and split by the roots of gnarled plane trees. Further on, he comes to a narrow ravine, which the road chooses not to cross. On the far bank and through a flank of trees and thickets, appears a large property enveloped in summer light. A crusty two-story stone farmhouse shines white in the sunlight, with dark splintery shutters. Its once orange roof tiles, now gray and cracked, hang like marcescent fruit too willful to stop clinging, and too dead to know it.

He crosses a narrow arched bridge of moss-covered stones joining the two banks. Nailed to the trunk of a linden tree are three signs: "Private Property", "Keep Out", and the more auspicious "Elysian Farm".

A carpet of rich uncut crab grass and purple wild flowers fills in a circular dirt drive with no other sort of adornment. Sorbin's truck is parked crookedly between twin cypress trees. The farmer, unapologetic for having left him in the lurch, is setting a liter of beer and two glasses on a large wooden trestle table dragged up against the side of the house. Under the table, an elderly bitch of wire blond hair lies twisted over its own hindquarters, nipping at ticks.

"You got here. That's a point for you. Say your name again for me."

"Russell Stone."

"*Roussel*, you say? Well, come sit down."

Stone pulls up a wicker chair. "Some place you have, Mr. Sorbin. You must be a large family."

"There is only me," replies the farmer, pouring the beer.

"Oh, really?"

"The house, this table. They are for me and me only." Sorbin elicits a peculiar hoot, whether of pain or amusement, Stone cannot say.

"Well, there is your dog." He hopes to sound encouraging.

With a grunt Sorbin reaches for the animal, fingering its thin coat. He torques a tick, displaying the blood-gorged parasite between callused thumb and forefinger. "Old Dora here is not mine." He presses the bug till it pops. "She belongs to Maurice."

"Maurice?"

"You will meet him later. So, you are an American, *Roussel*?"

"Yes, sir, I am." He waits expectantly for the man to follow-up this opening with other questions, or at least to comment on his ability to speak good French. But Sorbin seems to have reached the limit of his interest in Stone, for now. He rises.

"Come to the house."

The farmer walks with a gimp to the entry. "One passes through the kitchen, as in most old houses," says Sorbin. Inside, the temperature drops considerably. The kitchen is like a cave, with its high round ceiling made of rock and its mustiness. But the blue, ceramic, counter tiles add some light there. They continue down a dark corridor to the living room, elongated like the nave of a church and buttressed by one continuous arch of stone, three feet thick. A massive white-stone fireplace heads the room, beside a granite staircase heading both down to a wine cellar and up to the higher floors. The décor of naked stone is somehow exactly as Stone pictured it, crypt-like.

"Believe it or not," shares the farmer, obviously pleased to present his home, "this room was an animal stable back in the 17th century. Made of Rognes rock. Very spongy, you see. Ideal against heat, cold, and wind."

"And time," mentions Stone.

"Say again?"

"I said it's an insulator against time too."

"Time, you say?"

"No, nothing."

Going upstairs, Stone bangs his head against the ceiling, which, for some reason amuses the farmer. "My house is not so good for people tall like you."

"Yes, I must make a note of that one."

The second floor is much warmer than the ground floor. The thirsty shutters are fixed open, and an intense sunlight floods the rooms and warms the terra cotta floor tiles. From the bathroom window the American can make out the southern fields spreading across uneven terrain. There's an abandoned sunflower plot. Its rows of wilted plants look like the desiccated cadavers of soldiers killed upright. To the east of these fields, Stone spots a trailer home and an old man leaning over a bench, repairing beehives. "Is that Maurice?"

"Yes. He used to be a supervisor here, back when the farm was still working."

"What does he do now?"

"Makes do. Just like all of us."

"What exactly do you expect of *me*, Mr. Sorbin?"

"I receive *visits*."

"And my job is to dissuade your *visitors*."

"The rumor is that I have gold buried on my land."

"And is there gold?"

"Wait, wait, not so fast! Do not go faster than the music, young man."

Sorbin takes longer to descend the stairs than to mount them. Bad left knee, farmer's knee, he explains. They exit the house and Sorbin hobbles across the side yard to the barn, which is longer than the house and perpendicular to it. Its huge, double-sided barn door, a splintering wreck, holds itself up with leverage applied equally—its hinges have come out of the wall. They move aside a piece of door and enter.

The interior of the barn is a clutter of ancient farm tools and conserve-making utensils. Mallets, demijohns, awls, pitchforks, cogwheels, a rusted tractor, mud-caked plow, and several ribbed barrels of black nails, tins of wax and glue and hermetic jars with orange rubber washers. A horse-drawn wagon from another century goes almost sight unseen under a stack of sallow mattresses.

"A wagon?"

Sorbin confesses that he no longer has a horse to pull it. "But, for sentimental and practical reasons, I try to keep it in good condition, oiling the chassis, lacquering its wooden wheels, tongue and breast yoke, and lathering the hitch reins and traces."

"What are the *practical* reasons?"

"In case I never want to drive a goddamned motor vehicle again!"

Stone, somewhat stunned by the outburst, concurs: "I know what you mean."

The irascible fellow will have nothing of platitudes. "You know nothing of what I mean, monsieur! Do you have a gun?"

"A gun?"

"Yes, a gun. You do know what a gun is, don't you."

"Mr. Sorbin, me and guns . . . ."

But the farmer ignores his reservation and barrels on: "I did have a .12 gauge shotgun, which I could have lent to you. But it got stolen, too."

"I can't become involved with—"

"It's true that I still have my .19 caliber. Peashooter, really. Can't put a hole in a dormouse. Knocks them off the eaves and I have to finish them off with the rifle butt."

"What I want to say is—"

"Wait! I almost forgot! What about my great grandfather's musket!" says Sorbin, suddenly animated by the prospect. "You're in luck, *Roussel.*"

"I'm trying to tell you that I will only watch . . . ."

"Are you willing and able to shoot at trespassers with a ball and powder?"

"No, I . . . ."

"Then it's done. You are hired. Start when the night jar sings."

III

Sorbin gives him a lift back to Aix-en-Provence to collect his things. The rusty Citroen truck has no passenger seat, so Stone must sit on the floor, using his duffel bag and some wine crates as a backrest. "I suppose you need the extra room for hauling, Mr. Sorbin?" The noisy engine and the farmer's bad hearing force Stone to rephrase his comment. "I was just saying, you removed the passenger seat to have more room for loading, is that right?"

"Nonsense! And a turtle? A snail? How many seats does it need? I have one seat because I am one, *et voilà!*"

The farmer lights his fourth cigarette of the trip. Through the haze of Gauloise, Stone cranes for a look at the countryside whipping past. Countryside has been the extent of it for the past 20 miles. Nothing but trees and hills and rivers. No cities, scant few villages and, for that matter, only an occasional house, yet there is nothing feral about the place. The Provencal countryside is one big French garden.

"Is all this land privately owned, Monsieur Sorbin?"

The farmer, manning the steering wheel with little apparent regard for anything beyond the windshield, throws up his hands in frustration and puffs. "Bah! It's owned by those with damn little knowledge of tending to it and tended by those who do not own anything! And call me Osiris."

"Sorry?"

"Call me by my first name. Osiris." The gusty fellow's choler has settled into chumminess; he plays his emotions aloud.

"Isn't that the name of an Egyptian god?"

"For the past 63 years, it has been the name I go by. It was a nickname given to my great grandfather, you know, the owner of the musket. He fought in Egypt in the Grand Army of Napoleon Bonaparte. Elysian Farm is his doing. He got it started."

Osiris draws a last lungful of cigarette and tosses it out the window. Alongside the road, the discarded butt continues to smoke itself for a few more minutes, proving, Stone doesn't know what. Maybe that living is an act that doesn't just stop with dying.

Ten minutes and another cigarette later, they are back in the village of Lauris. The iron belfry makes a dramatic snapshot in the side window, and stays there, as they stop in the heart of town. Sorbin pulls the parking brake, a sound like shattering glass, and invites the American to follow him. "Let's go for a drink, shall we."

Stone steps from the truck, unaware that Sorbin has parked in the middle of Main Street. A car comes at him, swerves, mounts the sidewalk, sideswipes a plastic café chair and speeds away. The car has passed so close that Stone can smell its metal.

The farmer smiles mischievously, seeing little harm in his action. "Careful, you risk catching a cold," he hoots, oblivious to the growing line of irate drivers being blocked by his truck.

"You're parked in the middle of the street, Osiris!"

But the man is already gimping towards the curb.

They enter an establishment called the *Bar des Remparts*. It is a gloomy, smoky and somewhat garlic-pungent chamber of suspicious men and women, villagers who, in perfect contrast to the sun-seeking tourists who invade from the north, wait out the heat in dark closed places. Most of the patrons are seated around small card tables, holding a midnight wake of Tarot in the middle of the afternoon.

A voice rises among the congregation of laborers in filthy overalls standing at the bar, announcing Sorbin's entrance. "Oo la la! My dear friend Osiris!" Calls out another: "Come, let me pay you a round!" Other offers come from the tables. Sorbin makes the rounds, shaking hands and exchanging pleasantries, but he accepts no one's drink. These patrons' welcome has little positive effect on Osiris, who whispers to Stone: "Pay no attention to these louts. If it means a shot at the gold, they'll claim to be your best friends, too."

There is one man present with whom he refuses even to shake hands, a town-dressed guy drinking alone at the end of the bar, with one foot up on the shining boot rail. The man, in his 30's, resembles a weasel in more ways than anyone should, being puny and chinless, beady-eyed and gray-nosed. He wears yellow suspenders, a polka dot supermarket tie, and the shoe he is showing off has a permanent plasticized finish to it.

The man takes no apparent umbrage at Osiris' slight, on the contrary he seems inured to it. He tips a brown felt hat in salute, exposing a bony pate of black oily hair. Stone feels compelled to nod at him, but regrets it immediately. The man throws a coin on the counter, picks up his drink and slides over.

"So, Osiris, still pining, are you?" The weasel looks furtively at Stone.

"You must be referring to the tree that always straightens after a wind," Osiris retorts with little humor.

"Ha! Of course," laughs the man, snapping his suspenders, his bluster intact. "But pines grow together because deep down in their roots they know that standoffishness offers little protection against wind and illness."

"Pines grow where they grow, Sabag, and the only thing a pine *knows* is that the fastest arriving company is usually the thuggish thicket."

"Still more royalist than the king," chuckles Sabag, gnawing on his glass.

"We haven't had a king in 200 years. Maybe had you gone to school, you would know that fact."

"Why, you are our king, my dear friend. To your health!" Sabag raises his glass in tribute to be joined by others. Stone notices what gives the man's nose its permanent shadow: a thick covering of ingrown blackheads.

"Bah, you talk to say nothing," growls Osiris, dismissing the man and his discourse.

"And who is this stranger?"

"A stranger," barks back Osiris, efficiently killing the conversation.

The weasel draws back to his end of the bar to scrutinize Stone from a distance.

The countertop is an unholy pulpit of cigarette ash and sticky stains. Osiris calls across it for someone named Jean-Jacques. Through a curtain of clacking beads comes the bartender, a skinhead tattooed in red and black. The barman's eyebrows are stitched with a multitude of tiny rings. Fleshy pincushions. He and Osiris shake over the counter.

Osiris gestures for the barkeeper's ear and whispers in it: "Anything new?"

"Same bullshit," whispers back the skinhead. "People dreaming and making plans on a comet."

"You just keep listening to these connivers," he says, slipping the skinhead a sum of paper money in the handshake. "They will talk. If there's one thing they cannot stop doing, it's to blabber. One of them is behind the trespassing. Oh, this is *Roussel.*"

Stone quickly sizes up the barman. Same height as him, a little over 6 feet, though the barman is heavier. He is a poker-faced, hard looking man, probably violent. Definitely duplicitous. Which means little, Stone must admit, in a society where being constantly on the make is a way of subsisting.

"I met one or two *Amerloques* in my time." Jean-Jacques' aggressive Midi accent, deep and hard on the syllables, shortchanges any effort at amiability. "When I was in the Foreign Legion. Let's see, there was Rick from Florida and, what was the other guy? Snake Boy from Arizona. Nobody had real names. Maybe you heard of those guys. Like I said, Americans, like you."

Osiris answers for him: "When you're a detective, you get around."

"You're a detective?" The earrings in the barman's eyebrows start twitching.

"A watchman."

Osiris cuts in. "Keep it to yourself. Enough of the small talk. Serve us up a couple of little yellows."

The doser fills with the clear alcohol of Pastis, which Jean-Jacques pours into tall glasses. Water turns the concoction cloudy. Osiris picks up his glass and toasts Stone's arrival. "Welcome to Lauris, *Roussel*."

After a few sips, Stone inquires about the weasel. "Who's this Sabag fellow?"

"Bah! Every farmer's favorite rifle target!"

"What do you mean?"

"Bastard complained to the police after I shot at him. Foolish laws we have in this country! Imagine, they came and confiscated my shotgun in exchange for not taking me to jail, while that *putain* of a poacher there goes Scot free. *Putain*, if a man hasn't the right in France to defend his own property!"

"I thought you said you lost your shotgun?"

"Never in life did I say such a thing!" lies Osiris, oblivious. He steps brusquely away from the counter. "Feel it?"

"Feel what?"

"The earth rumbling."

Stone is lost.

The farmer throws back his drink, says come on, and limps back outside the bar.

Stone joins him on the pavement. A blinding light penetrates the afternoon haze. Yes, now he can feel it. The sidewalk is shaking, as if a subway train were passing underfoot.

"What is it? An earthquake?"

"Earthquake, my ass!"

On the western ramparts, behind Lauris castle, a dust cloud is rising higher than the iron bell tower, dropping a fine precipitation of sand into the Durance valley. Along the parapets a stout policeman wearing a navy-blue hat is running towards them, shouting to no one in particular: "Another section of catacombs has caved in! Collapsed like a wet crêpe! Where will it stop? China?"

Three gendarmes squashed inside a tin car look on disinterestedly as village folk stream between the orange plastic boundary posts cordoning off the castle's west courtyard. Osiris takes Stone by the arm through the barriers to the lip of an enormous crater. They peer over the edge. The hole seems to have no bottom.

"Drops all the way to hell." Osiris seems more irritated than awed.

A hundred feet down the hole, a mangled backhoe is lodged on a subterranean ledge, threatening to plunge much deeper.

Stone looks at the disgruntled farmer, his burnished face shining with alcohol and despair. "Water and Power did this to me," laments Osiris.

"Did what to you?"

"If it were not for this pit, I would not have those crows descending on my property. But I will not be intimidated, no monsieur! This is not about any damn treasure. This is about my patrimony!" He spits into the hole. His moustaches gleam with the spittle of indignation. "If they want war, they will have it!"

"I don't see the connection between this hole and your . . . ."

"Well then, let's be off," Osiris interrupts, another sudden change of the wind of emotion. "A chill comes to the valley earlier than in the village and we must latch the shutters and prepare for nightfall."

IV

Osiris shows Stone to his bedroom, more an area than a room, located on a half level between the ground floor and the upstairs. "The Music Hall," the farmer calls it, though there is nothing present in the hall to connect with music. "*Ma pauvre femme*, may she rest in peace, played piano, you see. They carted that off, too."

"Who are *they*?"

"Carted off everything else of value, too, except this." Osiris points out a ponderous floor-to-ceiling oak cabinet from the 18th century. The furniture is missing its 10 doors. "Priceless, even without the doors."

"What happened to the doors?"

"They could not move the cabinet, so they stole the doors."

"You keep saying *they*. Do you mean those people in the bar? Sabag?"

"It could be any of them."

"The barkeeper as well?"

"Jean-Jacques? I trust him about as far as I can throw him."

Stone is pleased to hear it. "So, it's not only digging around your land for gold. Someone is actually breaking into your house as well."

"They're capable of robbing me blind. Put your things away. I'm going upstairs to get myself ready for the night."

Stone rolls his bike into the room, stands it in a corner, and throws the duffel bag on the bed. He has to chuckle at the bed frame, which probably fits Osiris but is too small for Stone to sleep on. He hauls the mattress onto the floor, to use as a sleeping mat.

The Music Hall is not a bad setup, he decides. It has a tall window offering a wide view of the west fields, and in two shakes, he can jump outside. But to do what exactly? Aiming at someone with a fucking Napoleonic musket?

Osiris has left his great grandfather's gun in the room, its polished wooden stock propped on a metal box full of slugs. Within a beam of direct sunlight, the rifle shines burgundy.

Stone would never admit it to Osiris, but he had in fact shot a similar weapon, a couple of years running, on deer-hunting expeditions in the Rocky Mountains. A colleague of his owned a lodge, and there were all sorts of rifles, including a Civil War model U.S. Army cap musket.

From upstairs comes the sound of running water. Stone unzips his bag and starts placing his belongings on the shelves of the door-less cabinet. He notices a picture hanging on the near wall. An old black and white photograph of a husky dark-haired man standing in front of the farmhouse. Sleeves rolled to his elbows. A determined, no-nonsense sort of character, bigger and burlier than Osiris but definitely family.

The shower stops and the creak and clatter of closing shutters begin. The farmer isn't going to bed now, is he? It's only five in the afternoon. To Stone's relief, Osiris makes a painfully slow descent and slides into the room in slippers and pajamas.

"Right, that's better. We will have daylight well into the evening, so you go take target practice while I prepare us some dinner."

"Osiris, about this gun business . . . ."

"Go try it out, I say."

"I was wondering. Who's this man in the picture on the wall?"

"My father. Marcel Sorbin," he declares proudly.

"He looks like a man's man," offers Stone.

"*Pardi*! A man like Papa does not come along every day." And he shuffles out of sight to the kitchen.

Stone opens the metal case. All right, he'll humor the man if it gets him off his back. He takes a handful of bullets, grabs the rifle and slips outside via the glass door.

The same blond dog from the morning catches up and lopes beside him. Dora. Stone makes a mental note to have a crack at Dora's ticks with a proper veterinary product. They go together to the barn where he searches for something to shoot at. He empties rusty nails from two varnish cans and carries them into the field behind the barn. He sets down the gun and tells the dog to sit there and advances roughly half a football field and places the cans upright. Fifty yards should be okay, he tells the dog, because such a gun can deliver a slug on target at 100 yards.

Stone pats the hound and then busies himself with loading the rifle. He tamps a ball with the steel rod and clicks the gunlock into place. Levels the barrel and takes aim at the left can. It's the first time he has had anything in a sight since . . . . Probably just as well Osiris didn't come. In case the gun implodes. Wouldn't want to be responsible for the old man's death, too. He braces his shoulder and presses the trigger.

A staggered coughing explosion spews a cloud of bittersweet powder into the air. The sound strikes a false note against the multi-chromatic countryside, and seems silly and useless compared to the sharp crack of modern ordnance. Dora, who still has not budged, seems less than impressed.

He puts the smoking rifle down and retrieves the can, which blew about 20 yards back. The inspection turns up a 3-inch gash in the metal. It amazes him that such a period piece is so well balanced and true. More amazing is the fact that he managed to pull the trigger. The act seems a sort of sacrilege and exploit all at once. The gun's muffled fire seems to have broken the glass of time.

He shoots it another five times before taking it back to the house. Osiris is sitting outdoors on a block of granite placed under an acacia tree, dicing zucchini into cubes and knifing the cuttings into a saucepan on the ground between his feet. Chiseled into the rock between his thighs is a Provencal saying: *Pasto tems, lacte resto. Time passes, the act remains.*

"My favorite place to sit. Every man should have a rock of his own to sit on, eh, *Roussel?*"

The farmer makes a rather tragic-comic figure, peeling vegetables in his old striped pajamas and all this verdant land around and no one to share it with. The guy must miss his wife. Stone asks him if he has any children, but Osiris apparently doesn't hear him.

"Does it shoot well, the musket?"

"Very true indeed."

"Fine, it pleases me to hear it."

"I'll just take it inside then. Oh, I was hoping to go for a little stroll with the dog, if I have the time."

"Make yourself at home."

In the kitchen he cuts two pieces of Reblochon cheese, which Osiris left on the stand. He gives one to Dora, before heading out.

In the west field behind the barn, he quickly arrives at the first obstacle: a tree-tall wall of thickets. Inside its thorny web of branches is a row of cedar trees, all dead and petrified. Stone is beginning to understand that Osiris' problems go deeper than a rash of robberies. The fields are no longer being cared for. The orchards have been abandoned. What does this Maurice fellow do anyway? And if he cannot handle it, why doesn't Osiris hire someone else to clear and prune? Why has the farmer allowed all this beauty to go to seed? It's a mystery every bit as intriguing as that of the supposed gold.

"Well, maybe we can do something about these prickers," he says to the dog. She doesn't care; she's simply delighted to have her chin scratched.

Stone returns to the barn and pries a pair of shears and a scythe from the clutter of old utensils. He starts into the high grass and the dog tags along so closely that he can feel her body heat through his pant leg. He attacks the thickets with the scythe, hacking left and right with moderate strokes. The dog lies down beside a rotted log and watches him patiently.

He cleaves a passage into the heart of the hedgerow, where he discovers juicy berries clustered like black cotton among the thorns. Now this is what I call treasure! He plucks them off and stuffs them in his mouth. The blackberries, hairy and dry on his tongue, break apart against his palate, filling his mouth with sugar and sunlight and the easy memory of Penelope's tongue.

He carries berries in his purple stained hands to the dog. She lifts her wiry head, but rejects the offering. "Dora, you don't know what you're missing. This is the stolen sugar of murdered plants. These berries are a kind of sweet revenge, don't you think?" The animal prefers to lick the salt of his flesh.

A grunting sound comes through the breeze. He stops dead still to listen. There it is again, a coarse throaty cant that should rouse Dora but doesn't. She remains as loosely relaxed as putty. Bitch must have ears like Osiris.

Stone raises the scythe and whoops: "Heeya! Heeya!" But he scares only the dog, who starts a high-pitched howl from the depths of her barrel chest, echoing across the acres like the screeching brakes of a car that cannot stop in time.

"Shut up!" he screams. The dog stops abruptly, and stares, now unsure of him, unsure of what he wants of her. Scythe in hand, he treads back into the prickers.

Five yards in, he is blindsided, knocked off his feet and sent flying 10 feet into the thorns. The hard landing steals his wind, and as he struggles for breath, he catches a glimpse of an enormous pig working its way back into the hedgerow. Stone rises, feeling sick to his stomach. He can map the pig's escape by the snap of the brittle stalks and the sway of the tops of the cane.

Back at the house, he sheds his shirt and stands before the bathroom mirror. His back is welted with thorns, some of which are still stuck in his skin. He thinks of himself as being physically nailed to his past, and swears out loud. He swears again, this time to see himself speak. It has been a long time since he had the courage to look at his face in a mirror. A boyish face, marred by torment, stares back at him. He looks at once younger and older than he remembered, and quasi unrecognizable to himself. Two thorns start from the base of his scalp, and he decides that this is only right, for he is a sort of devil wreaking havoc on his own psyche. Emotionally, he has been like Osiris' farm, going to pieces in a fast way. He brushes off the thorns and throws cold water on himself.

Osiris is raging in the hallway. "What in hell's name possessed you to start gardening!"

It dawns on him how cavalier he was. He should have asked permission to use the man's tools and hack at his land. Maybe Osiris is the kind of guy who resents a helping hand. Farmer's pride or some such thing.

"Berries," he calls back. "I just wanted some berries."

"*Foutaise*! You're not much good to me broken up." Jesus, if only he knew! "And don't drink the tap water in there." The man's sharp tone is worse than the thorns.

"Yes, you told me already. Who owns that pig?" But no answer comes. The farmer has already turned and gone.

The two men eat dinner in silence. Zucchini, lentils and Toulouse sausages cooked in garlic. The farmer loves garlic, which he chews whole at the table like radishes. A fresh baguette lies in front of Stone's plate, while Osiris prefers the day-old loaf. Osiris has put down a half bottle of the local red table wine. They each have a linen napkin, originally both of the same scarlet set, though Osiris' has been worked pink, because, he says, he likes using the same one over and over and washing it.

Stone clears the table and Osiris starts in on the dishes and Stone stiffly retires to the couch in the salon. He hears Osiris bolting the kitchen door, and a few moments later the farmer slides in his brown leather espadrilles across the tile floor. Osiris' crusty disposition has completely melted off his face; his demeanor is pleasant, almost cheery.

"Do you want me to call a doctor?"

"I'll be fine, Mr. Sorbin."

"I told you to call me Osiris."

At day's end, Osiris is most at peace with himself. He's a man who enjoys his day only in its final five minutes before sleep calls.

"Then, *bonne nuit*, and pleasant dreams, *Roussel.*"

"Same to you, Osiris."

"By the way, that pig belongs to Sabag," he says, prefacing a pun with a smutty wink, "and rumor has it that their relationship is swinish."

V

Mid-August brings the lavender harvest, the bee-swarming buckboards stacked with fragrant bushels carted to smoking distilleries, the plant's essence infusing the high plains and dales of the Lesser and Greater Luberon Mountains and the Vaucluse Plateau to the foot of the Giant of Provence. The daytime temperature stands at 90 degrees, but the nights are no cooler. Stone recalls what Osiris said about the cicada: it will not chirp if the thermometer drops below 80 degrees. Stone checks his watch by the light of the stars. It's two a.m., yet the insect drones on.

He's been at his job for two weeks now, and still there's been no sign of an intruder. It could well be that Osiris' gamble has paid off, that introducing Stone to the patrons of the *Bar des Remparts* was enough to scare off the scoundrels. Then again, maybe Osiris has only managed to give the crooks advanced warning, and they are using the lull to develop a different strategy. Only time will tell.

Then, a pair of headlights spills into the western fields. The visitors have come. Stone will need to get closer. He takes the swath that he cut in the hedgerow to the floor of the dark ravine and follows a swampy obstacle course of felled and rotting trees to a position lower than and 25 yards from the intruders.

A small sporty car idles in a clearing, lights blazing, trunk open, and three guys removing shovels and pick-axes and trying to get organized. They argue in marketplace tones, voices sharp as gunfire, town kids. Only a heavy sleeping, heavy breathing farmer hard of hearing could fail to notice these galoots.

None of them bears the port or profile of the polecat Sabag. These are young guns, confident and cocky. A stocky North African, probably the leader, is trying to understand the paper in his hand while barking at the other two. A second figure is Caucasian, taller than the others, wiry and head-shaven. But it is the third who grabs Stone's attention. The kid is wearing a white satin athletic jacket, the trademark Nike swoosh stitched large across the back.

A simple and emphatic gesture will probably succeed in chasing them away. Stone, who never takes the gun—he takes up his watch only after Osiris has retired—cups his hands about his mouth, ready to call out. But before he can sound a word, a thwack of gunfire reverberates round and round the brindled hills. The sound of a .12 gauge pump shotgun. Panicked, the young men jump into their car. The driver presses too hard on the gas and the car goes spinning nowhere. They get straightened out and wheel out of there.

Stone arrives at the spot, the dust of a mad exit settling within the beam of his flashlight. They've left behind their cheap shovel. Better still, he finds the document the stocky one was studying. It's not a paper but a very old-seeming parchment, a map of some kind inscribed with hills, a river, some trees. There are symbols as well, triangles and circles enclosing what looks like a kind of animal with horns. He scratches his head and stares back out at a circumference of darkness to wonder who fired the gun and what kind of crazy game he's gotten himself involved in.

Osiris is taking his breakfast in the yard the next morning, scooping sardines out of a can with a fork. A chunk of the previous evening's bread, now two-day's old, rests on a jar of black olives, next to a flagon of wine from the co-operative. He chews as a man does when his teeth are bad.

Stone sets the abandoned shovel against the table. "You had a visit last night."

"I know. Maurice told me."

"How would Maurice know?"

"He heard your shooting, I suppose."

"*I* didn't shoot. Does Maurice own a gun?"

"Do not be daft. He would not touch a gun to save his own life. If Maurice were capable of that, I never would have put the ad in the paper."

"Also, I found this." Stone sets the map on the table. Osiris opens a booklet of crossword puzzles to the page marker, his glasses case, and slides out his bifocals. He gives the parchment a moment's perusal, before taking off his glasses and grunting. "You would agree it's a map," says Stone.

Osiris shrugs. "So it seems."

"Of this farm?"

"This farm or El Dorado, who the hell can tell."

"Can you understand any of the symbols?"

Osiris refits his glasses on his nose. It takes him only a second to reach a categorical conclusion: "No. Pure gibberish, if you ask me."

"I'd like to know what's going on here."

Osiris is evasive, he refuses to meet Stone's eye. "There should be coffee in the kitchen."

The cool morning casts an easy light across the dewy yard. A sweet earthy odor hangs in the air. August, the richness of parting beauty.

"Osiris, don't get me wrong. I'm not looking to get involved any more than I have to. But I do think I need to know a little more about . . . ."

"You just keep shooting at trespassers!"

"I told you I didn't shoot!"

The farmer rises menacingly and rounds the table, coming at Stone as if to box his ears. Instead, Osiris claps him on the shoulder, father-like. He makes a remark the meaning of which escapes Stone. A humorous comment, by the way his moustaches dance. "Come, *mon ami*, it is time you met Maurice. And bring this," he says, tapping the map.

The two of them keep to a gradual incline leading from behind the barn to a higher field. "The east fields," Osiris relates, "were for artichokes, carrots and leeks." His morning voice is clouded by regret and nicotine congestion. "Madame Sorbin loved these fields."

They cut across an adjacent field of desiccated lavender plants. "I don't care about the lavender. The plant is beautiful and fragrant, but it brings wasps, vipers and trouble."

"What happened? I mean, to your farm?"

"You should have seen it in my father's day! Three hundred and fifty hectares to tend. One heard the drone of tractors from sunrise to sunset. My father drove me to school on a tractor. It was a slow happy drive to the village. Slow and happy as childhood."

"How did things go sour?"

"Mother's family were town folk. Merchants, mayors, council people and the like."

Talking with Osiris is tough going. The man, Stone realizes, is not deliberately disingenuous but merely impermeable to Stone's style of straight talk.

The trail winds around an abandoned vineyard. Vestiges of petrified vine stock stick out of the tall wire-grass like the exposed claws of giant birds.

They come to three towering acacia trees. Their large roots make a natural staircase down a steep bank. Osiris' knee does not bend very well, so Stone offers his shoulder for the descent. The farmer leans on him and Stone can smell him. He smells clean of the brick-sized bars of *Le Petit Marseille* olive oil soap stacked two feet high and a foot deep inside a cupboard in the downstairs bathroom. Remarkably, maybe even miraculously, the man's skin and clothes have no residual stink of nicotine.

Stone tries a different tack. "That guy Sabag, he doesn't seem the most honest of men."

Osiris' jowls jounce. "Ah, that one! He makes fire with any old wood, as we say. Nothing is too shady or slimy for his hands!"

Finally getting somewhere. "You mean he could be the thief."

"*Could be*! Angrier men than I have attacked him with mallets for his fraudulent schemes. He barters and always has something *cheaper* to trade for or to sell. I am not the only farmer who has shot at him as he tried to steal truffles. *Tiens*, his pig! It's no pet! That's a truffle-stealing pig!"

They enter a small pasture, and almost immediately a downwind breeze batters Stone's nose with the pungency of animal waste. Up ahead is the trailer home that he glimpsed from the second-floor window of the farmhouse. The trailer's rusty carcass is mounted on bricks. The ground around it is clawed into a packed-earth plot of bleached bones, dry feces and crusty slops. Blue flies hover over a pail of chicken parts and water-bloated bread. Dora is snoozing in a ditch, but ambles forth for a scratch when she sees the two of them. She lies at Osiris' feet, legs up. Osiris' habitual anguish leaves his face as he bends over and brushes her sad sick underbelly, purple udders drawn and scarred.

"This old hound has had pups recently," observes Stone.

"Dora! Ha! Dora puts down a litter twice yearly."

"What happens to the pups?"

"Maurice takes them to the river in a sack."

"Why doesn't he have her spade and be done with it?"

With obvious pity for the American's naiveté, Osiris shakes his head. "This is the countryside, my boy."

A hard wave of human urine reaches Stone, driving him a step back and calling his attention to the plastic bottles piled under the trailer. Wine bottles, olive oil bottles, sunflower oil bottles, vinegar bottles—all filled with urine. Maurice does his pissing in bottles.

Sorbin calls gruffly: "Wake up, you old fart, and come meet *Roussel*."

A bony old man, with long strings of pepper gray hair, emerges from the trailer, still buttoning his britches. "Hold your horses, there's no fire as I can see."

"*Teh*! You couldn't see it if there was one, you."

"You're one to talk. At least I could *hear* it coming, which is better than I can say for some."

Stone understands why Maurice is useless for farming and surveillance. He's geriatric! Must be 80 years old. That, and the fact that it is only an hour after dawn and he already stinks of booze. It hangs over him like a fog, and the odor of it will stay on Stone's hand all morning, from the moment he reaches out, reluctantly, to shake Maurice's hand.

Maurice's face is a sun-wrecked scrap of flesh. His teeth are rotted beyond repair and buggers dangle from nostril hair. His long crooked nose is something out of Grimm's Fairy Tales. But, unlike Osiris, he has a hard-earned patience in his gray eyes, as well as an easy disarming manner.

"So, this is the detective!"

"Watchman," corrects Stone.

"I heard your shooting last night. Did you hit anything?"

"He did all right," interjects Osiris. "The nail on the head. Look what they dropped." He hands the parchment to Maurice.

"So it wasn't just a rumor," says Maurice.

"He demands to see what he's shooting *for*. Go on and take him."

"*Avec plaisir*."

Osiris, without a further word to either of them, starts back for the house.

VI

Maurice pulls a 50-foot section of steel rod from between his bottles of piss. "My poking stick," he explains.

"Poking for what?"

"Snakes, rats, millipedes, whatever might be ahead of us in the cave."

"There's a cave?"

"*Pardi* there's a cave! It's on the map. Here—" pointing out the circle of symbols and the horned creature.

"How would anyone know that's a cave?"

"Well, I suppose you wouldn't, unless you already knew there was a cave." He gives Stone a chummy clap on the shoulder. "If this map here is authentic, and I'm not saying it is, then it's only fitting that no words are written on it."

"Why is that?"

"Because in the Middle Ages even noblemen didn't know how to write. Writing was for the religious orders."

Stone follows the curious old peasant into the west fields, the rod dragging behind Maurice like an extended tail. The rod swishes through the tall grass, causing an army of gray grasshoppers to pop up like hot corn. The geezer proves quite fit for his age, hauling 50 feet of steel and still managing to tax Stone, whose legs are a little sore from yesterday's bike ride.

"I am told you are from America. That explains it then."

"Explains what?"

"That you're a shooter."

Stone grimaces.

"You know, youngster, you and I have something important in common."

"What's that?"

"We're both foreigners here."

"You're not French?"

"I am not *Laurisian*. I hail from another village."

"Oh? Which one?"

"Cadenet. Maybe you know it? With its statue of the little drummer boy who saved Napoleon Bonaparte at the Arcole Bridge?"

"I've been through it on my bike. It's only four kilometers from here. That doesn't make you much of a foreigner." Stone thinks the man is having him on.

"In Provence," says Maurice, deadly serious, "four kilometers is a world. So tell me, how is it an American like you speaks our language so well."

"Because French was my first language. My mother was French. We lived in the States, but she made it a point of honor never to speak anything but French to me."

"You don't say! Your mother, French. Where from?"

"North of Avignon, actually. A whole whopping 80 kilometers away!"

Maurice ignores the tease. "Where does she live now?"

"She doesn't."

"My condolences."

"She died long ago." As if that meant something.

"Condolences all the same, youngster. When it concerns a mother, there is no such thing as a lapse of time."

Stone gives the old man a closer look. Despite his hillbilly appearance, Maurice seems somewhat educated, book-learned at any rate, more culturally versed than Osiris. But before Stone can ask him about his schooling, the brittle little man sneezes into his grimy hands, then sneezes again, and smears the contents across his dirty trousers.

"You see, I'm still allergic to Osiris' plants, even after 45 years of working here."

"Forty five years. That's a stretch. What about your own family? Do you have children, grandchildren?"

"Dogs and fleas have been my family since my brother died some 20 years now."

"Maurice, about that shooting last night. I didn't fire a weapon. And I take it that it wasn't you."

"Ah no! I won't have anything to do with guns, me."

"Then who else could be shooting at trespassers?"

"Maybe other trespassers."

"Have you ever seen a young man in the village who wears a white nylon jacket with a black *Nike* insignia?"

"Nowadays, all the young men wear coats with names."

"Yes, but this was a distinctive *Nike* coat."

The old man shrugs and, after a few moments reflection, asks innocently: "What sort of thing is it, this *Nike?*"

They come to a milky field, rippling like a wind-battered sail under the sun's reflection. Maurice stoops to show Stone the white snails clinging to each blade of grass. Seen closely, the shells are the color of dried ash.

"Are these snails still alive?"

"Some are, some aren't."

"How can you tell?"

"At night, only the living move."

They cross the barnacled field, making cracking sounds with each footstep. On the opposite perimeter rises a tree, but one so great in height and girth of branches that it looks like a thick grove of many trees. They must bend and crawl through a robe of branches to reach the trunk.

Stone finds himself standing in a dark sanctuary, inside the chill enclave of a natural living church.

"Welcome to the Grand Oak," announces Maurice. "The Old One. The king of trees! A monument of nature, no?"

Sixty feet above their heads, the branches arch, span and weave against a rose window skylight. Underfoot is moist mush, the humus of time untold. As for the trunk, five men, arms outstretched, could not have encircled it. At some point in history, a bolt of lightning rent it, though neither half died. The left section grew straight and tall while the heavier right branch bowed under its own weight to the ground, burrowed into it, popped back out of the earth half a century later and 5 yards away, and shot back up, the resurrection of an indomitable time-defying tree.

"How old is this tree, Maurice?"

"Folks say different things. Marcel Sorbin, that is to say, Osiris' father, figured that the Grand Oak first saw light during the eighth Crusade, which makes it, what, 700 years old, and the same age as the village. It split probably sometime prior to the discovery of your own country by that Italian mapmaker. This tree was already a monument before Louis and his bitch lost their heads." Maurice strips a small piece of bark and sticks it in his mouth. "Try some, it will keep you young."

"But no one official has ever verified its age?"

"Verified? Pshaw! Who do you want to verify anything? The visitors, yes, they would like to verify everything." Maurice turns the bark with his tongue like a cough drop. "Poor Osiris, he already has enough trouble without calling it in. What people don't know won't hurt them. Alas, they know everything already."

"Do you know who these visitors might be?"

"Everyone in the village is suspect," Maurice answers unhelpfully.

"Sabag would be the number one suspect, no?"

"*Bof!* He's too lazy to bend over for the truffles his pig digs up."

"So you'd rule him out?"

"Never rule Sabag out of anything dirty. But his ribs are stretched out from lying on his side so much, you see? Lazy as a Corsican, he is. I mean, if he was involved, he would pay someone else to do the labor, though Sabag wouldn't pay anybody anything, being stingy as he is indolent."

"What happened here, Maurice? What happened to the farm? Why have things gone bad?"

The question seems to stun the geezer. He stares incredulously at Stone, as if the American had just insulted his descendants. His look is cold and resentful.

"One is better off not tending to other people's business."

"I'm sorry . . ."

"Your *maman* should have taught you that in the country one does not ask too many questions about other folks' business."

"I asked Osiris but he avoided the question, and I never know if it's on purpose or if it's his hearing."

"He hears what he wants to hear, that fox," hoots Maurice, losing his sternness.

They part the tree cover and come out on the far side of the Grand Oak. Maurice points towards a spread of wide-open grassland. "That's where we're headed, you see there, where the land rises slightly and the hawthorn bushes are thickest in a row?"

They advance through a water-gorged meadow that Maurice explains is swelled from an underground wellspring. They arrive at a wall of briar bushes and dwarf oak, a mass of vegetation as effective as barbed wire. On the other side of the prickly hawthorn row, is the ravine and, further on, the spot where last night's trespassers had been.

"What are we looking for?"

"This," announces his ancient guide with dog-like playfulness. "It's what they're all after."

Maurice gets his wiry arms around a pile of dead branches and pushes it aside, revealing a small passage, no larger than a foxhole. The pencil thin man, wearing his blue overalls like a hanger wears a suit, kneels before the hole and finishes clearing it. At last satisfied with his efforts, he asks for his steel rod. He plunges the tip of the rod into the hole and, hand over hand, forces it down like an elf tamping a cannon.

"I'll scare out whatever snakes are in there, though I reckon even the vipers have packed up and gone because of these fools who come ferreting through here."

When no snakes appear, Maurice reels in the rod. Stone stands over the old man. His hair has not been washed in some time. Whole cords of it are tangled into unsolvable knots like mop strands.

"What is this hole?"

"Have you read of the Knights Templar?"

"Can't say I have."

"They were mercenaries from the Crusades. Hired to protect the temple in Jerusalem, especially the treasure and booty hidden within. After the wars, these parts became something of a stronghold for them, especially Lauris. They built a network of tunnels from the village castle to the abbey and out to the river and then some. Well, last month, Water and Power made that crater in the village by mistake, and that's how the Knights' catacombs got uncovered."

"Catacombs? You mean tombs?"

"Goddamn hour did not go by before folks were pitching ropes and descending and scavenging through the burial objects. Then, the rumor got started. Somebody tells somebody else that somebody found a Templar treasure map with booty located in a cave on Sorbin land." Maurice's pruned face puckers into convergent wrinkles. "*Oui*, this fool map here says that Templar gold is buried under your feet, youngster."

"What, you mean this hole is the cave?"

"Come see for yourself."

"No man can squeeze down there. I doubt your dog could get down it."

Maurice winks, and then begins squirming into the hole. He is swallowed bit by bit until Stone sees only the soles of his shoes and then that image, too, disappears. His voice calls out from the bowels of the earth. "Your turn."

He sets down the map and gets on all fours. It's a fight just to get his head inside. His face is flush against the soil. The sharp smell of earth is overpowering, and steals his breath. He gasps and takes in a mouthful of dirt. His nostrils are quickly caked with clay. "Maurice, this is crazy!" As he strains to gain an inch, panic wells in him—he'll be stuck, lie trapped under a field, under a thousand tons of land, buried alive by his own devices. And what of it? Isn't he already living in an emotional tomb of his own making?

Then, suddenly, he is moving freely, feeling that the passage is no wider, but he has narrowed, his corporality has shrunken.

His ribs join like fingers in prayer. The two sides of his rib cage interlock to make a chest cavity one half its normal size. By consequence, his shoulders droop, his hips liquefy, and he is becoming some kind of underground creeper of the human variety.

He breaks through the ceiling and finds himself staring into an underground chamber about the size of a choir. Maurice is standing upside-down, ankle deep in water, flashing his light at the walls and ceiling. The cavern, thick with dark moss, crawls with translucent bugs. The old man has a good two feet of headroom. Stone continues wriggling until he falls headfirst into the cave, catching himself on his hands and immediately sinking to the elbows into a thousand years of ooze. Up ahead, another such cavern extends into the dark.

Maurice leads the way into the second chamber. Stone searches for large stones to walk on, to keep his sneakers dry, but eventually gives in and sloshes through the bog. He looks for gold in the beam of Maurice's flashlight, but sees none.

"So, where's the gold?"

"That's the point, youngster. There isn't any. The map shows a cave, but the gold is somebody's wishful thinking."

Stone scratches his noggin. "Well, wouldn't it be simpler to bring in a backhoe? Excavate this cave and prove to people, once and for all, that the gold thing is a hoax?"

The old man snaps his index finger back and forth. "Oh no! That would make a bad situation worse."

"I don't understand."

"Because of the government."

"What's the government have to do with this?"

"Look."

Maurice shines his lamp at the north wall, and the cave suddenly springs under the rumbling stampede of fauna long since disappeared from the region: antelope, mammoths, great woolly rhinos, and long-toothed tigers. The limestone's natural bumps and bosses give movement to these black and ocher figures.

"Cave paintings!" Stone reaches to touch them but Maurice grabs his hand.

"They must not be touched. They are too valuable."

"You're right." He borrows Maurice's lamp and scrutinizes them. "They're beautiful, man. Damn, when I think I'm looking at art dating from . . . well, how old do you think they are?"

"Beats me," says Maurice. "All I know is this hole is a hell of a place do such pictures."

"Well, unless this cave was once above ground, I doubt they were meant to be seen."

Maurice scratches his scalp, unconvinced. "Youngster, what artist doesn't want his art seen?"

"Prehistoric ones. My guess is this was a secretive place, a place of ritual and testing. A place where someone who did something terrible came to exorcise his demons."

"Penance?"

Stone shrugs. "So, what exactly are Osiris' options?"

"*Eh beh*, it is simple. If Osiris shows his cave, the CNRS confiscates it and his land becomes national property. If he doesn't show it, the gold rumors subsist. *Et voila!*" declares Maurice, throwing up his arms and bowing to the fatality of the situation.

"And only you, Osiris, and me know the truth?"

"And Mathilde."

"Who's Mathilde?"

"Mathilde Sorbin. Osiris' daughter. What, Osiris didn't tell you he has a daughter?"

AUTUMN

I

Each morning a cock crows from somewhere on the property. Osiris won't say where, only that it does not belong to him or Maurice. Stone replies that a wild rooster is something rare. His irony is not lost on Osiris who retorts sass for sass, it's called a cockle-bum-to-you-too. The farmer's sternness weakens and cracks and he enjoys his own joke till his cheeks are a couple of russet apples. "Anyway, that cock is a damn fine clock."

And Osiris makes a better one. The rickety farmer clunks downstairs in pajamas and a cardigan, wheezes emphysematously through Stone's "bedroom", and jump-starts his day (and Stone's) banging pots and brewing coffee in the kitchen. As the water heats, he has himself a pee and leaves the door open and his urination sounds like stacks of spilling quarters. Flushes then fetches a coffee (thick as mud) and farts back to the water closet for a long sit-down with yesterday's newspaper and the first cigarette of his two-pack day.

Osiris is always showered, shaved and dressed by the time Stone staggers bleary into the kitchen, his five hours of sleep begging another two. The mysterious cock is just starting to crow, and *voilà* Osiris, sitting at the corner fold-out table, before a breakfast of smoked sausages, tins of sardines, a jar of olives and a bottle of red table wine.

This particular morning, Osiris looks up with some concern when he sees Stone enter the kitchen, dressed for biking.

"You are meeting me in town later?"

"Absolutely. I just thought I would get a ride in this morning."

Osiris' worry devolves to mild panic. "You must be on time. The *affair* does not last long."

"The square. Eleven forty five sharp. I promise to be there *on time.*"

"Well, sit down and eat at least!"

"*Merci*, no. I'll get something later."

It is leaf-burning season and decks of smoke hang about the farmlands, little inclined to dissipate but gradually diminishing all the same. The air waxes heavy with winemaking. His tires hiss from the stickiness of mashed grapes on the tarmac. The growl of tractors, combines and grain trucks has replaced the summertime whir of the cicadas. Dirt clods clutter the country roads.

Eastbound, he cycles into Cadenet, Maurice's natal village, and stops at the first bakery on the way. He pays for a lemon tart and asks the baker the same question he has been asking the Lauris shopkeepers. "By chance you wouldn't know of a young Arab kid who wears a white Nike coat?" The man's face collapses into wrinkles of puzzlement, his shoulders rise above his ears. "Coats, they come, they go"—adding, with a racist edge—"unlike the Arabs, who only come but never go."

About what he expected. Such flimsy information got him nowhere in Lauris either. As he comes from the bakery, he could kick himself. Going around asking strangers about a kid in a coat! He was hired to watch a property, and now here he is, conducting this silly manhunt. Definitely, inexorably, he is slipping into something much more complicated and unwanted than mere surveillance.

Stone takes up his route through the sleepy stone villages on the southern flank of the Luberon: Vaugines, Cucuron, Cabrieres, Peypin. Between towns he passes clanging herds of dog-tended sheep, tractors churning the sprawling earth, produce wagons plying the roads, and pickers bent over the vines or standing in ladders pressed into trees. Farms at work everywhere, except for Elysian Farm. Only Osiris' land is stuck in standstill, decaying daily for reasons only the Sorbins and Maurice know.

It's a pasty morning. A tepid sun makes dabbled splotches across the ocher hillsides. The vines have gone a blood red. There is precious little evergreen or perennial in Provence. The country wears an old coat of leaves. Stone turns downhill between columns of yellowing plane trees. He zips up his windbreaker, sticks his nose to the handlebar, and gives himself over to gravity. *A rolling Stone*, he chuckles. He shoots down a spotty forest of wild oak. Forty, 50, 65 kilometers an hour. The Canal de Provence winds like a silver ribbon through the land. Grazing stallions feed headless in the high grass. White clouds cap the mountains, while south, the horizon is lavender, beautiful, menacing. The smell of rain.

Stone rolls into the Lauris village square with 20 minutes to spare. No sign of Osiris yet. Instead, a civil wedding ceremony is taking place on the steps of the town hall. Well-wishers are crowded deep into the square, listening to a village notable bandoleered in a blue, white and red sash. Tranquil beams of autumnal light transverse the heavy branches of the plane trees encircling the place. A southern breeze has heaped dead leaves into the far corners. Rustling poplars dull and shine in the wind. The numbers of onlookers, awed to silence, only adds to the restfulness of the square.

Stone winds through the crowd to the third bench, leans his bike against a tree and, as per Osiris' instructions, plants himself down to wait. A moment later, Osiris pushes through the wedding party, looking like one of the guests. The usually tatty landowner is wearing a smart green corduroy suit with matching vest, a beige shirt and brown tie, suede shoes with tassels, and a felt fedora with a small pheasant feather stuck in the band. Round and ruddy and grizzled and charming, Osiris is the picture of the gentleman farmer. He is even carrying a bouquet of lilacs. Meeting his daughter obviously means something to the man.

Osiris is winded upon reaching the bench. He drops himself next to Stone, who feels the man's heaviness, his girth of inertia.

"You shouldn't have," Stone says about the flowers, but the joke falls flat; the farmer is preoccupied and either has not heard him or has chosen to ignore the quip. Osiris lights a cigarette and blows resentful smoke in the crowd's direction.

"You don't like weddings, Osiris?" he says flippantly, regretting it immediately. He knows so little about the man and ought to mind where he puts his foot.

Osiris answers with a curt weather report: "South wind. Means rain tonight."

After a moment of silently shooting the celebrants with his critical eyes, Osiris can no longer restrain himself: "Bah! Later on they will be racing their cars and tooting their horns and destroying the country quiet."

"So, this is where you see your daughter." Stating the already known seems safe enough.

"I did not pick the place. It's her idea."

Just then, a woman's hand alights on Osiris' right shoulder. "*Bonjour*, Papa."

"Ah, there you are, my dear, *bonjour*," says the farmer, hurriedly crushing out his smoke underfoot and rising. "Right on time."

Stone is surprised both by her height—she is much taller than her father—and her complexion. Unlike her father, Mathilde Sorbin is not fair-haired but dark. Her eyes are as black and round as brook stones, placed in a face as white as eternity. Dressed as she is in black, she makes an aggrieved sort of fortuneteller. A classic pullover, formal pleated skirt, and flat-soled dress shoes. His daughter, according to Osiris, always wears black to their weekly meetings.

Father and daughter embrace expeditiously, more from ritual than affection, though maybe there is some of that too, unspoken, poorly translated, but, nonetheless, some caring seems to transfer from one to the other. He hands her the bouquet, and she places a butcher's package in his hand. That evening the two men will enjoy her pâté made of various parts of a pig's face, called *fromage de tête*. Stone wonders which pig did the honors.

As they converse, Stone gets a better look at her. She strikes him as cold, with her helmet-shaped hairdo and aloof tilt of the head. Hers is a long high-boned face, full of charm, maybe even beautiful but a bit lifeless, inert, like a broken light bulb. She has small pointy ears like her father's, and a very attractive neck, long and pale above a body-fitting black cardigan. A gold chain seems to tie her to something, the earth perhaps, much the same as her large breasts, the rotundity of motherhood without its caring. Her jet-black hair is thick as mohair, worn as the tortured had worn theirs a millennium before, clipped expediently. Placid hands are crossed in her pleated lap, as she sits straight and proud, unmistakably her father's daughter. She has exquisite hands.

"You are the detective?" Her words are curt, brittle, and critical. Is she worked up against him? If so, why? Maybe simple mistrust, wondering what kind of rogue he might be.

"No, I'm the *watchman*."

"The town is talking about your shooting at people," she says matter-of-factly to the open square, her voice husky and assured.

"I didn't shoot at anyone. I didn't shoot period."

In profile, she smiles wryly, obviously content at having gotten his goat with her first barb. "In fact, no one is talking about it. Papa told me."

Stone reclines on his side of the bench, determined to make himself small and let the two of them have at whatever it is they do during their 15-minute encounters. Beats him why Osiris wanted him here. It is none of his business if the farmer and his daughter meet once a week in a public place, shunning the comfort of their respective homes.

But neither father nor daughter is much inclined to let him blend into the background.

"I'd say your association with your detective is doing you some good, Papa." There is an ambiguous restraint in the way she addresses her father. Then, less guilefully: "You do look better," she says, her voice tapering off. "Calmer."

"*Roussel* has my confidence."

"But of course! Strangers are easy. It takes a saint to deal with one's own family."

"He is working for *us*, my girl. Both me *and* you."

"You don't say!' she sings with mock surprise. "And what exactly is he doing for me?"

"The farm will be yours, when I am gone."

"But you know I don't want it, Papa."

"So you have said."

"It is out of the question that I ever have anything more to do with the farm."

"Why are you like this?"

"You very well know!" The subject of the farm is obviously a well-tread argument, and one that she wields like a club against him. "Did you tell him why we meet here?"

"*I myself* don't even know why we meet here!" he bellows.

"Don't be obtuse!" she scolds, apparently too caught up in her own truth to notice that the man is being sincere.

"Well, tell me then. Why do we meet in this public place rather than at the farm?"

She isn't quite sure how to tackle his direct approach. In the end, she settles on a frontal attack. "Because *here*," her arm casts a graceful arc about the square, "you must recognize *me*. At the farm, I'm," she hesitates, evidently not wishing to go too far, "invisible."

"Oh, here we go again! Invisible! As if *you* could ever be invisible."

"Invisible, insignificant, call it what you want. At the farm I'm less tangible than a ghost."

"You say?"

"I *said* I'm less real than a certain ghost."

Osiris coughs in exasperation. "If that were the case, my daughter, why would I make the effort to see you at all?"

"That's just it, Papa! You would not make any effort to see me if I were at the farm."

Stone realizes that both of them are using him as a sounding board to tune an old song. The proof comes when he tries to excuse himself to leave.

"Sit down!" they both thunder.

The tolling of noon bells breaks across the square, and a flock of applause lifts above the heads of those congregated in front of the town hall.

Out of the blue, a talking fit overtakes Osiris. "When my father returned from the Great War, he wed my mother there. Eight hundred guests! A 20-piece orchestra! A flood of champagne! Uncle Jules drove a motorcar all the way from Orange, 90 kilometers away! Back in 1919, it might as well have been Siberia!"

Sorbin's soliloquy flows and Stone keeps glancing at Mathilde who seems as dumbfounded as he by her father's sudden desire to discourse. Mathilde clearly holds something against her father and it is this resentment that holds sway over her behavior.

"The Devoses, that is to say my mother's side, are one of the oldest families in Provence. Why, a Devos has lived in Lauris ever since the crusades! *Tiens*, take Mathilde Devos' crypt. Oldest tomb in town, and old as anything they dug up in that hole this summer."

"In the cemetery?" asks Stone.

"Of course not in the cemetery! The village cemetery dates only as far back as the 17th Century. No, you must look in a scraggly bit of field just outside of town. If you dig through the weeds, you'll find a flat crypt, a crumbling patina-coated tomb with little claim to a form. That's where she is buried. Born in 1281. Executed—murdered rather—in 1304."

"Hearsay, Papa! She was not murdered."

"I say she was! Her father married her off to a wealthy Knight of the Order of the Temple. That rogue Pope there in Avignon, Clement Idon'tknowwhat, he had Mathilde tortured on the orders of Philippe Le Beau, because she knew the whereabouts of the Order's treasure."

"There's no documentation . . ."

"Documentation smockumentation. I know what I know! Mathilde Devos was murdered over gold and everyone knows it and that is why I have trespassers today!"

"You have trespassers because people are as gullible as you about history. I'm surprised at you. You're starting to sound like the very fools you're trying to run off the property."

Her brutal words silence him instantly. The fragile mood of nostalgia is broken. But Osiris has told Stone more about himself in two minutes than in the entire two months of their improbable relationship.

Osiris reaches inside his jacket for his pack of cigarettes.

Abruptly, she rises. "I'll leave you to you butts. *Au revoir et merci pour les fleurs.*" As if taken in a gust, she's gone. Stone watches her cross the street and enter the bread shop.

Osiris shakes his head. "I've never understood that girl."

"She seems unhappy."

"*Bof!* What does happiness have to do with anything!" He gets to his feet and, unlit cigarette dangling from his mouth, totters into the crowd.

Stone sits a moment by himself, and then goes to his bike. His bike gloves are still wet from the ride, the helmet band is sodden and very disagreeable against his forehead. "Forgive me . . ." He's so startled that he doesn't realize he is hearing English spoken. He looks around. Mathilde Sorbin is cradling her bread, pressing her belly against the bench. "I was rude. I don't like to be like that. We're a little rustic, we country folk."

"No problem. I was, how do you say in French, a hair in the soup?"

She smiles. A most becoming light that was not there in her father's presence, shines from her face, giving it a religious-like radiance. Looking at her, he can understand a Renaissance painter's rapture and inspiration.

"That's Papa and me, we won't change, I'm afraid. Anyway, I have to go now, but I'd really like to know about you and where you come from, if you have 5 minutes some time."

"Sure, I'd like that."

"I work at the town hall. Please come by when you can."

She reaches out, shakes his hand and walks away. Something indescribably sweet and more than a scent lingers about the bench. It's the odor of memory, the rapture of childhood infatuations, the humid flesh of summer meadows, the sweat of kids you played with, something long forgotten to him. She goes back across the main street and turns down a small alley beside the castle.

Stone takes the cemetery road to avoid the wedding traffic. It's a narrow broken avenue behind the town hall. Suddenly, his back tire goes flat. He dismounts beside the cemetery gate. That is when he catches sight of Osiris.

The poor fellow, befuddled, disoriented, turns round and round among the tombstones like a dog seeking the right pissing angle. Stone almost rushes in to aid him. But the situation suddenly clarifies. Osiris is seeking the necessary bend in his bad knee to allow himself to kneel properly in prayer before a certain sepulcher, probably that of his defunct wife.

Stone regrets taking the road and being a witness to this. He doesn't want Osiris thinking that he followed him. He flips the bike onto its saddle, unlocks the rear wheel, and tries to lose himself in the business of changing the inner tube. When at last he is ready to roll, he glances back into the cemetery. Osiris is gone.

Curious, Stone enters the cemetery grounds and sets the bike down on the finely raked gravel path. He duck-walks in bike shoes along a corridor of ornamental crypts. Photographs of the sleepers' mortal coils tell him that he has journeyed into the neighborhood of the recent dead, meaning the past century. Old or young or somewhere in between, what they all share in this neighborhood is the age of celluloid.

He hunts around until he finds the spot where the gravel has been pushed around by Osiris' painful genuflection. The Sorbin family burial vault, seven souls in all, most not much beyond middle age when their clocks stopped ticking. But there is one picture that stands out from the others, and not simply because it has color. It is the face of Osiris, minus 40 years. That of a blond, blue-eyed teenager, bearing the smile of a bright future. Stone goes to the inscription.

Jean Horace Sorbin, 1966-1985
Beloved son and brother

Osiris had a son? Mathilde Sorbin, a brother? At that moment, Stone starts to comprehend the possible complexity of their mutual antagonism.

II

An October rain, pushed by the South Wind, batters the Music Hall window. Osiris has gone to bed. Stone is sitting on his mattress, reading a paperback novel that Maurice lent to him. Maurice's caravan is stuffed to the roof with all kinds of books, fiction, non-fiction, histories, science, as well as magazines, some dating back several generations. Stone saw a pre-World War II *Paris-Match*. Maurice may piss in bottles, but he's a well-read fart.

The telephone goes off like an alarm. There is only one apparatus in the house. It's a daisywheel dating back decennia, with an appalling apple-sized bell producing a horrible clang. In the past, Stone has noticed that four rings change the pitch and yaw of Osiris' stentorian snore. The game is to grab the receiver before it wakes up the Egyptian God.

"You made it." Penelope's seductive voice makes sensuous music in the receiver.

"I must be getting good in the dark," he says, reaching for the kitchen light switch.

"You were always good in the dark, handsome. So what were you doing?"

"Reading."

"Not *Playboy*, I hope."

"A whodunit. Great for a rainy night."

"What's it about?"

"Okay, it's your nickel. This guy comes back to his native village in Provence and starts taking down his family farmhouse stone by stone to discover why his entire family was murdered when he was a baby."

"What a surprise, a man on a mission. You can relate to that. So, how goes the investigation, Inspector? Found your Nike suspect?"

"Not yet. The trespassers could be from anywhere."

"Hired by 'His Ring'."

"His Ring? Oh, *sa bague*, I get it. Clever. I don't have any proof that Sabag is ringleader of anything, but it sure would make sense. Anyway, nobody's been back since, and that's what counts."

"I don't like the situation, honey. You're not in your element."

"Relax. Once I find them, I'll pack it in."

He notices that his right sleeve and pant leg are finely dusted in white powder. The stone walls are downy with saltpeter. He and Osiris will soon be amusing themselves in the barn, fashioning gunpowder with the "salt of stone".

"And the other guy hasn't been any help?" she continues.

"The barman?"

"The skinhead."

"He's working on it."

"Yeah, sure, a regular full-blown inquiry."

She grows quiet. He is not immune to her worry and unhappiness. It's just that each time it only manages to pull him closer to his own self pity, and it is only by focusing an ear to detect movement from upstairs that he manages to remain beyond it.

Penelope, too, has a remedy for snapping out of her sadness. She teases him. "Want to know what I'm wearing?"

"I can think of nothing," he teases back.

"Don't be so direct," she scolds coquettishly. "Besides, I'm at work." She sketches her skirt, and the latitude at which its twice-stitched hem crosses her thighs. The sun is streaming through her window, touching her inner legs higher than the hem. Panties? What panties?

"That's easy enough to claim seven thousand miles away."

"Hey, the rut is in the smut," she comes on.

While midnight mice chew, oblivious, behind Osiris' cereal cabinet, Penelope's teasing settles into his trousers. Stone stands at the kitchen counter like a ruttish hickory dickory, indulging in short shots of her plastic, her curves and bust and sunny freckled smile and all the ephemeral dynamic of flesh and material that keeps the male world groping for air. He revisits his first come-on, which she met without resistance. Lovemaking started underground, in parking lot C, in her Maverick. By the time they came up for air, the fling had become a thing. But no love affair, not as far as he was concerned. She didn't touch him in any essential way. His eyes could love her up, but his heart remained numb to the relationship. She accused him of being aptly named. He was made of stone, he had calculi circulating in his cold blood. He remembers her sitting on the edge of their bed, watching him pack his bags for France, distraught and remonstrating. "Why are you punishing me for what happened?"

"It has nothing to do with you. I need to go look for answers to questions I don't even know I have and wouldn't be able to formulate even if I knew them."

"Bullshit. You're running away from me."

He kept packing.

"At least admit it."

"All right, I admit it. I'd go poor and eat horse shit for the rest of my life if . . . ."

"If if if! Time heals, Russell, it doesn't punish."

"I've forfeited my rights to those kinds of illusions, Penny."

"You don't have to do this to yourself! It's the job, Russ. Maybe they're right and you just weren't cut out, emotionally speaking."

"Damn it, there's a difference! This aint burn out! A boy should still be walking this earth, growing pubic hair, eating popcorn, having his first wet dream, sprouting pimples, getting laid, smoking a joint, seeing Star Wars."

"Star Wars isn't much of a loss. Or the pimples." Her wet cheeks shone. It was the moment when, if there is love in a person's heart, it must rear up. He should kiss her, jump on her, push his prick between her hot kidneys . . . stay. Instead, he wiped her tears and finished packing his bags.

What started as a loin-kindling memory finishes by extinguishing his fire; the only thing hard in his hand is the phone receiver.

"Penny, did you receive my photos of the cave paintings?"

"Sure, but it's tough to tell their authenticity from snapshots, Russ. The best thing would be to have an expert examine the cave."

"No can do. Osiris would freak out if some big shot from the CNRS started poking around his fields. Like I told you, he wants the story kept under wraps."

"And if the big-shot were me?"

His response is too slow for her swift sensibilities. "I see you miss me as much as I miss you."

"I miss you, Penny."

"Hey, don't try so hard, dude. I'm not dumb. I know the score. But I wouldn't mind checking out those cave paintings all the same."

"I'll run it by Osiris."

"In the meantime, see if you can brush off a sample and send it to me for testing."

"I wouldn't want to damage anything."

"Right. Well, do this—get me a soil sample from what's below the painted wall. That way I can try to analyze the pollen particles and maybe get an answer there."

"Penny, I've been meaning to ask you. What specifically was the god Osiris supposed to be good at?"

A moment of silence. "Resurrections, Mr. Stone."

III

Indian summer overflows into deep October, ideal for *bricolage*. He and Osiris have cleared out the barn, hauled a ton of rubbish to the junk yard, repaired and refitted the barn door, and sanded and painted the house shutters. Stone himself has put some order to the eastern and western fields, uprooting thickets, dead roots and barbed shrubs. The yard work has cost Osiris a weed-buster, three tractor blades, two hand cutters, an ax handle and two shovels, and Stone four T-shirts, a pair of jeans and acres of good skin.

Maurice helps them wheel two hundred pounds of disease-deformed pears and apples to the barn. "Now you got your whole bloody winter mapped out for you in here making conserves and liqueurs," heckles Maurice, piling another crate of pickings beside a stewing vat.

Osiris is prickly when it comes to what he does and doesn't do. "You are one to talk, with all those books piled taller than you inside that contraption you live in."

"*Pardi!*" agrees Maurice, who owns no known vanities; breaking his thick skin is a lost cause. "Staying busy, that's what counts. Youngster here does not know that yet, being too young to think about anything other than his pecker."

"Leave my pecker out of this," warns Stone with a smile.

"*Eh beh,*" continues Maurice, "if Osiris here didn't have something to do during the winter months, he would go crazy."

"Oh shut up, you!"

Maurice winks at Stone: "Staying busy, that's the trick."

Osiris goes indoors and twists the knobs on the oven clock. The already shortening days lose an administrative hour. The hillsides throw a chill shade over the property by mid-afternoon. Night will descend around five p.m. Dinner at six.

Meals with Osiris are mostly long passages of silent chewing, linked like sausages to brief opinions on vast escapist subjects with more questions than answers: war, terrorism, disease, political and corporate corruption, cyber porn. Osiris takes refuge in the distant and superficial. The farmer either cannot or will not speak about his dead son.

As for his daughter, Osiris responds to Stone's curiosity with irritation. "She is a *woman*. Need I say more? A Sorbin through and through."

"What does *that* mean?"

"It means she does not have her tongue in her pocket, that's what!" Osiris seems to hold as much against her as she does him.

What Stone has learned thus far is that Mathilde Sorbin is 32, childless and divorced.

"And her husband? What was he like?"

"A Parisian!" barks Osiris, as if that says it all. "*Enfin*, one cannot hold that against a person, I suppose. Anyway, he was not a bad sort. Just over-educated. Some kind of big shot architect in the capital. They met up there, at a highfalutin school—don't ask me which one, she took care of her own affairs. Always has." The farmer's chubby face reddens with resentment. "She gave it all up when she moved back here."

"Any idea why the marriage broke up?"

"*Bof*! She never speaks to me of that! But I'd wager good money that she ran him ragged. A bit of a shrew, my daughter."

"Yes, I caught your drift. Don't you have anything nice to say about her?"

"Why, of course! She's my daughter, isn't she!"

"That's a point."

"*Pardi!*" he roars. "She makes a mean mutton, too! Used to, anyhow."

Stone takes their plates to the sink—it's sunk into a Herculean slab of Cassis stone—and empties the scraps into a dog dish he bought at the market. Osiris lights up at the table, gets puffing and making smoke. His chair is never actually turned towards the table. He eats and smokes twisted, as if he cannot even get relaxed enough to sit like other people. The Osiris Posture: fanned pelvis, hunched back, buttocks balanced on the edge of the chair. In fact, it's not really sitting but crouching, shoulders turned 3/

4s to whomever he's addressing. The Thinker with a Thrust. And of course the cigarette. The ubiquitous butt.

"I'll tell you this," mentions Osiris, torqued in a cloud of his own making, "my Mathilde means what she says and says what she means and in this *putain* of a world, that, my boy, is a rarity indeed."

Stone goes to bed feeling like an egg, full of burgeoning mass stuffed inside a shell. He is back in one of his recurring nightmares. Back in the hospital. A wall clock reads 11:04. A hospital intern shows him down a long corridor to a locked room. Taped to the door is a poster requesting vital organ donors, plus police photographs of people shot to death. The door swings open to a room with three beds. A woman and a man lie in the first and third beds, stretched out on their backs, blanketed to the chin and wired to large machines borrowing their blood. Between them, in the second bed, making a waning form under a blood-soaked sheet, reposes a third figure, covered from head to ankles, a cadaver taking up less than half the bed. Only the soles of his small feet are visible.

The 7-year-old boy, says the intern. His parents are emptying their blood for him.

But he's dead!

His mother is from France.

What does that have to do with it?

The boy's name was Pierre Pierre. That means Stone Stone in French. Isn't that funny? Stone Stone.

Stone escapes down the corridor, seeking a side exit that does not exist. The passage runs into a metal door. He pushes through it, and finds himself inside a full courtroom, peopled by his past. In this dream, Osiris joins the mosaic.

You are to be your own judge and jury, *Roussel*, pronounces Osiris. Can't say I like your chances.

Stone declares himself guilty and condemns himself to living out his days inside a subterranean cave. Not as a man but as something one-dimensional, flat, and smeared on the wall, a concocted image, a mere rubbing of a man extinct, biking in place ad infinitum.

He wakes briefly, then sleeps badly for the rest of the night and rises late in the morning at 9:35.

The kitchen door opens, closes. Someone is fumbling about in the hall closet. Stone gets up and flips on the hall light and is surprised to find Osiris wearing mourning dress, a glinting black suit taken out of mothballs. He is holding a black hat and umbrella, and looks so wan that he could be going to his own funeral.

"I came back for these," he explains, raising the hat and umbrella. "It's wretched out. Only a duck could appreciate such weather."

"But why are you wearing that suit?"

"Because we are the first of November."

"Sorry, you've lost me."

"My God, have you no religion in America? Today is the holiday of the dead. One goes to the cemetery on All Saint's Day."

Stone jumps up and throws on yesterday's clothes. "Give me a minute and I'll go with you."

"You must eat first."

"No, really, I don't care about eating."

Some color returns to the man's peeked face. "All right then. Of course. As you wish." Stone suspects that his coming back for the umbrella was a ruse to get Stone to go to the graveyard. The farmer may finally be ready to talk about something other than the weather and the land.

At the cemetery gate, Osiris pays a flower lady a small fortune for chrysanthemums, grumbling to her about death being a damn good business for some. A chill drizzle hangs in the iron-colored day, fully in keeping with the triste occasion of the holiday. Mourners, mostly the elderly, are out in numbers, umbrellas popping open like sprouting black flowers.

At the Sorbin family vault, Stone removes the umbrella from Osiris' shaking hand and holds it over the farmer as he sets his floral offering on the marble cover. Osiris dabs his eyes with a hanky and makes silent peace with relatives who have come and gone. With trembling fingers he caresses the letters of his son's name. He takes a step back and staggers. Stone catches him and realizes that he is fighting for air. "Take your time, Osiris, lean against me."

"It does not get easier with time," gasps the farmer, falling silent until they reach the car.

"Was he your son, Osiris?"

But Osiris is still too choked up to speak about the subject. "Not here."

Back at the farm, Osiris tells Stone to follow him upstairs. His bedroom is a stuffy chamber pared to the essentials like a monk's quarters, that is to say, the head monk. Osiris has few possessions, but they are large and sturdy. A four-poster birch bed, a deep, rustic pinewood dresser taking up most of one wall, and a floor-to-ceiling walnut wardrobe shined to a glassy finish. Osiris warbles processionally to the left side of the bed—judging by the way the mattress sags, Stone surmises that the man uses only one side, as he uses only one napkin. Either from habit or out of respect to his dead wife. Or both.

Osiris suffers his bad joints into bending and sits on the edge of his bed, a dark-clothed miserable underworld person on a sallow bedspread. The day is dull and not much light comes through the windows. He switches on an antique desk lamp, takes a framed portrait from the bedside table and signals Stone to approach.

"My son," he says, looking at the photograph as if for the first time, before relinquishing it to Stone. Osiris' face glows with a sort of reverence; he has turned a fallen child into a deity. "It is my favorite portrait."

His son, seven at the time, is shot in ¾ profile, chin lifted to better catch the kitsch light, in hindsight more funereal than celestial.

Stone looks at the photo and feels his resolve break. His hand starts to tremble, and he quickly turns it over and hands it back.

"I have others. Would you care to see others?"

Stone doesn't have the heart to oppose. Osiris slides some snapshots from the table drawer: a fair-haired youngster nestled knee-high between his grandparents in front of the farmhouse; a smiling lad sitting on a tractor with a much younger Maurice; a handsome teen with his school friends making ghoulish faces in the kitchen, covered to the elbows in baking dough.

"I have none of Jean-Horace and me together. It is a tragedy."

The farmer starts talking of his son's life, an outpouring of emotion that the man will repeat throughout the evening and for days thereafter, in stops and starts, in sentences that never end or fall suddenly from cliffs. Every other word is accompanied by a 'you see', as if the tired and world-weary farmer were pleading with Stone to help make some sense of the cruel meaninglessness of the loss of a son.

"I was, you see, too involved in the running of things here. Too involved to spend much, you see, time . . . time with him. He knew what he meant to me. I hope to God that he did. You see, when he was little, I tried to keep him on the farm. To protect him. I was always scared, you see. Then . . . . well, you drop your guard as you become older, *they* become older, adults. When they need you the most, you have forgotten how to protect them."

Jean Horace was the last male descendent, the keeper of the Sorbin name. He would have taken over the farm, maintained its success, then married, fathered children of his own. Grandchildren, descendents. Keepers of the name.

"He grew up too fast and then he was gone, snapped off the branch. How does it happen?"

"What, Osiris?"

"How does thieving time manage to sneak in and make off with your children? Turn your back, gone is the baby fat, the call from the toilet to be wiped, the need to be bathed, the desire for hugs and kisses. No more whining. No more tears the size of walnuts. No more hairless cheeks. Wake up one morning, they are taller than you, then taller by a head, and then no longer even the same people! Almost strangers, in fact. But you carry on loving them anyway. Then they're off to university. How do your kids go from babbling to business school without you seeing a thing? Why don't they stay at home, your children, *Roussel*? You can protect them better at home, *Roussel*."

"I don't know, Osiris. But, you can't hold on to them. It would be a disservice even to try. It's fate. There's nothing anybody can do about it."

After class one Friday, his son, girlfriend and best friend booze it up at a party and start back with the best friend at the wheel.

"I was long since gone to bed. It was the girl, you see . . ."

"What girl, Osiris? You're not making much sense. His girlfriend?"

"No! Mathilde!"

"What does she have to do with it?"

Osiris catches his breath and lights a cigarette. Stone notices the absence of a daughter portrait on the bedside table. There are no snapshots of her in the drawer, either. It dawns on him that he has seen no daughter pictures in the house at all.

"Friday nights, she drove him home. She was younger but already had her driving license while he did not. She should have driven him home. If only . . . ."

These words, their relentless drip, have probably carved a valley through his heart. The farmer has probably made his daughter pay in petty incremental doses for an accident that she really had nothing to do with. Osiris would be as oblivious to his hurtful comments as he is to his own emotional erosion.

"She was the one who woke me up. Papa, come, she says, and disappears before I can lift my head off the pillow. Why didn't she just tell me? Why did she make me hear the news from strangers? I checked my watch. I remember the hour, the minute: 23:04."

"Eleven oh four?"

"Yes. Why?"

"No, nothing. It is, I don't know, a strange coincidence."

"What coincidence? Are you feeling bad. You look bad. Sit down."

Stone sits next to Osiris and closes his eyes, waiting for the malaise to pass. "Sorry. I'm all right. I was just thinking of something. Please, go on."

"Well, I got from bed and into my slippers and followed her downstairs. Two gendarmes were standing in the door, failing to speak plainly or maybe speaking too plainly. I didn't catch a thing at first. Three in the car. Two dead. He was, you see, uninjured."

"Who was uninjured? Jean Horace?"

"No! That bastard friend of my son's who was behind the wheel. He caused the accident but had not a scratch on him."

Stone bows to the paradox.

"Some months later he came by to ask for forgiveness."

"The friend?"

"The killer of my son!"

"What did you do?"

"What do you think! I slapped his face, of course! I could not bear that he was still alive, my Jean Horace dead."

"It's a terrible thing to live with."

"He got what he deserved."

"What do you mean?"

"Three years to the day after he killed my son, he was killed in another car accident. An irony, to be sure."

"Maybe not," mumbles Stone. "It was probably a sort of suicide."

"I don't give a damn what it was! He wasted my son's life, then he wasted his own. And what are we left with? Not even a name to carry on. Where's the sense? What am I . . . ."

Osiris cannot continue. Stone puts a comforting hand on the farmer's twisted shoulder and quietly leaves the room.

IV

Stone takes to the damp roads for a short ride. It drizzled last night, and the weather is still uncertain, the sky low and gray. He cycles north to Merindol, crosses the Durance River to Mallemort and climbs into the shrubby foothills above Alleins. The sharp-climbing shoelace, known as the Calvary because of the wayside crosses at each road bend, brings him to the 12th Century village of Vernegues with its 360-degree view of the region. Despite the cloud cover, he can make out the Alpilles, the Luberon, Sainte Victoire, and the Etoile range. There is the chill odor of rain in the breeze. To the east a fine gauze obliterates the hills, spreading across the valley and down to the sea.

The road drops through a vale of cherry groves and sloping vineyards, foliage gone brown, air redolent with the odor of overturned earth. At Cazan he crosses the highway, and pedals fast for Charleval. He climbs the stiff, two-chevron pass from Charleval to Lambesc. At the summit, the horizon is black as night. He catches sight of the Rain God's crooked staff cracking across the spiked back of the eastern Etoile range. The thwacking of thunder. Here goes a drenching!

He races into the storm. A steady pelting clatters against his helmet and blurs his orange sunglasses. Water comes at him in all directions. His feet are soaked, his ass and saddle on which it sits are sodden, and his shoulders ache with the penetrating humidity. Frustration makes him miserable. For Stone, a ride is an exercise in voidance, but this rain is bombarding him with thoughts he does not want. He can't get Osiris' story out of his mind, both the death of his son and, more troubling yet, the suicide of the son's friend. Stone pulls over and seeks shelter from the downpour in Lambesc, sharing a bus stop vestibule with a passerby and his poodle.

He arrives back in Lauris an hour later, soggy, cold and glum.

"You ought to have your head examined!" hollers Osiris over a clap of thunder. "Are you crazy, riding in this storm!"

"It wasn't raining when I left."

"Bah, you are not serious!"

By nightfall a cold has settled into his chest. Maurice brings by a jar of honey from his hives, plus a paperback novel. Osiris makes him some blue tea from the Isope plant which "not only holds the land in place but is very good also for any and all ailments from hangnail to gout." It tastes like shit.

His condition worsens. He coughs through the night and runs a high fever. Osiris comes downstairs periodically to see how he is making out. Stone tells him to go back to bed, and Osiris uses that as an invitation for more diatribes against cycling in the rain and cycling period. "I cannot think of a more useless pursuit."

"It is anything but useless," he argues weakly, futilely. "It keeps me going."

"*Ouais*, just look at you go now! Bah! I will make you more tea."

"No thanks, it just makes me piss."

"Pissing is good, it cleans you."

"Not 14 times per cup. I'm too tired to play a siphon."

"*Ouais*, but you are not too tired to ride in the rain!"

Oh brother!

It rains all the next day with a jazz-like tempo of hysterical downpours and dreary letups. The oldest pantiles crack under the percussion. Osiris' upstairs bedroom leaks. The following morning, he steps outside to see an amazing scene: Osiris on the roof, standing on the edge upon slippery tiles, trying to replace the damaged ones. No safety belt, nor even a cap to shield his head from the whipping rains. "Don't move! I'm coming up!"

Osiris hurls admonishments upon him, but Stone mounts the ladder anyway. He arrives at the level of the eaves and prepares to get a leg up, but Osiris is livid.

"Go down, I say, and back to bed!"

"No, I won't let you walk around on this slippery roof by yourself."

"Look, you, I was changing tiles before you came and I will be changing them long after you have gone. Now, get back in the house."

"Osiris, we can stay here and argue in the rain or you can accept a hand and finish faster."

In twenty minutes they are back inside. Osiris heats some wine and starts in on him again, telling him he deserves to catch pneumonia. Stone answers that his illness is only partly viral, and an insignificant part at that. The real sickness is in his head. As he waited on his bike at the bus stop, he could not rid himself of the idea of boys playing in timeless fields. The suicide of the friend infected Stone like a virus. The emotion struck so close to home that it brought his health tumbling. In short, he fell sick *with* the storm, not because of it.

But Osiris cannot understand a word. "Your gibberish is proof that you run a fever!"

After three more days of rain, Osiris himself comes down with a cough, aggravated by his smoker's lungs. He is up and dressed at 6:30 a.m. anyway, but can barely walk. Stone offers to make him some blue tea, but the farmer throws the idea back in his face. "I don't drink that shit."

Stone drives him into town to Doctor Guillot's, where they join a packed waiting room of patients. It is the sick season in Provence. Flues, chest colds, ear infections, sinusitis, colitis, gastroenteritis and every other "itis" in the working vocabulary. Stone believes the diseases are timed to go off in people's heads at the first sign of lowering temperatures. Nothing depresses a Provencal like a lack of sun. A week of low sky and rain is time enough to drive a region of hypochondriacs to hospital.

They have an hour's wait ahead of them, so Stone steps out "to run an errand".

He walks across the square to the town hall and inquires at reception for Mathilde Sorbin. A middle-aged woman directs him down a short corridor to an office opposite the mayor's. There, the door is inscribed in gold letters: *Secretaire Generale, Mme Sorbin.* Osiris' daughter is the second most powerful political person in the community, and the farmer never mentioned a word about it.

He's a little apprehensive about seeing her; who will be seated at her desk, the shrew from the bench, or the Madonna from the bakery? He has his answer straight away. Mathilde, smiling warmly, steps around her desk. She is wearing an attractive aquamarine dress suit and is professional and elegant. They shake hands.

"Papa says you were ill."

"Just a cold."

"You must learn never to downgrade a cold, Russell! On the contrary, a Provencal builds it up. Instead, you say: 'I had the death,' even if it is only a sniffle."

He chuckles and uses her example as a transition. "Actually, I'd like to look into being more Provencal. Just out of curiosity, I was wondering what it takes to obtain proper working papers."

"I have a meeting in ten minutes, but please . . ."

"I can come back."

"No, sit down. The ten minutes are yours."

As they both get comfortably seated, she asks him what his current immigration status is.

"Tourist visa is all I have."

She picks up the phone, calls someone in the building, explains the situation and jots notes on a pad. "It's a bit complicated," she says, hanging up. "French administration, you know."

"But not impossible?"

Her pessimistic grimace says everything. "You'll need a contract to obtain a working visa and a working visa to get a contract."

"Catch 22."

"Pardon?"

"Getting the run-around."

"Were you thinking that my father would declare you legally?"

"No. I mean, I don't plan on staying very long. As I said, just simple curiosity."

"Well, don't give up so easily. If you like, I'll gather the relevant documents and pass them to you via Papa."

"I'd prefer to come back for them."

She's quick. "I understand. I'm his daughter, remember." She makes her apologies for having to cut short his visit, and walks him to the door. "I hope he's not driving you out of the house."

"Nothing like that, no. He's a guy who likes to impose his opinions, but I can handle it."

"Well, thank you for your patience," she responds in English. "I have not seen my father this calm and cheery in quite some time."

"If you call this calm and cheery, what must he have been like before!"

"You can't imagine!"

"Anyway, the good is reciprocal," he smiles, letting down his guard. "I'm feeling better myself."

"Ah, then all is for the best in this best of possible worlds." The parting note of sarcasm seems to escape her through no volition of her own, a reflexive slap in his face. A shamed color rises into her cheeks. Suddenly, the lamplight that is her face extinguishes, leaving a dull disappointment lingering. There is as much bitterness as beauty in this woman, he thinks to himself. He wishes to say something but hasn't a clue where to begin. So, he turns and walks down the hall.

V

Osiris returns visibly peeved from his weekly meeting with his daughter. "What are you two plotting behind my back?"

"How could you think that?"

"Because I know her scheming ways, and when she says you can go by and pick something up but won't tell me what, it tells me something is going on!"

Stone explains his interest in acquiring papers but can't do much against his own abashment for having concealed the step from Osiris.

"So, I take it you do not trust me, is that it?"

"Not at all, Osiris . . ."

"Then why did you not come to me first?"

"I don't know. I didn't want you to feel . . . I . . . well, I wasn't even very sure myself."

"As usual, I do not understand a thing you are trying to say!"

"That makes two of us. I'm sorry."

Later the same afternoon, Stone takes a ride into town. The heavens are still menacing, so he packs a parka. What he fails to take is a flashlight. A misty rain begins to fall. A pea soup fog sets in, obliterating his view. Good sense has him get off and walk his bike up the hill into the village.

Mathilde is in a meeting, which drags. Stone occupies a bench in the corridor, and watches the paucity of daylight, framed in the town hall doorway, squeezed out of the village square like juice from a citrus. Darkness comes before she does.

Her greeting bears little resemblance to the last one. Today she is distant, standoffish, and Stone hopes the cause is a work issue, not him. They go into her office, the lingering alchemy of perfume on flesh, making gold to his senses. Something starts in him and he looks to the source, but her mien is as devoid of light as the day. She hands the folder across her desk and does not ask him to sit down. "Residency application forms, le voilà," she says without raising her eyes. He was planning to discuss her father's resentment towards her, but it is definitely not the time. He thanks her and leaves.

Outdoors, on the road without a light, he feels colder than the actual air temperature warrants. Loneliness is a great thief of calories and reason, and he chooses to cycle rather than walk. The overcast night obliterates stars and moon and he cannot see the road and can barely make out his own front tire. He might as well be navigating through ink. His parka glistens with humidity. The stinging smell of night brings tears pouring down his face. The air rushes past his ears. A compelling sensation of fear takes over. He becomes caught in titillation, exhilaration, but also powerlessness and chaos. He comes to the realization that being out of control means it is already too late to do anything about it.

At the bottom of the hill, where the road bends sharply, a car appears suddenly. Stone is going too fast to stop in time; he brakes but his tires lock and skid. He hits the front bumper head on, flips over the hood and lands against the windshield, smashing his head. The dry burn of cracking vertebra, the cool numbing of his limbs. A broken neck, and the dark beyond.

A car, a foolish biker without a light, another senseless death in an all but senseless world. Russell Stone, dead, wormy, rot, ash, gone.

It is a self-destructive, self-pitying scenario that never happens thanks to a webbing of light burning in the hulking headlands, troglodyte dwellings inhabited by people seeking tax shelter. The caves have doors, potted plants, clotheslines and, above all, electricity. Handy land marks for a fool biker plying a dangerous pass. Stone slows long before the car careens into the bend. The car passes. Stone is still alive. But to what purpose? His life benefits no one, least of all himself. He tells himself to stifle such self-indulgence. To stem the taps of thinking, he concentrates on the hissing turn of his tires.

*   *   *

Penny phones. She, too, is upset at him. He hasn't taken the time to call her in over a week. "I suppose you've been too busy seeing Osiris' daughter about paperwork." She is having a tough time accepting Stone's decision to seek residency status in France. Her frustration has found a home in jealousy. "By the way, when are you gonna waltz *her* by me? I don't know anything about this Mathilde. Osiris has dancing mustaches and smokes for an hour in the toilet. Maurice pees in bottles. And Sabag may or may not be poking his pig. I know these things, but nothing about Mathilde. Why is that? It was your idea, my being your watchperson, so volunteer some info, boy."

"What do you want to know?"

"What's she like?"

"Mistrustful and moody. Real moody."

"And *physically?*"

"Normal."

"*Normal,* he says. That means what? Is she pretty?"

"Drop it, Pen. You're barking up the wrong tree."

"Yeah, well I'm sure you're sniffing up the wrong leg!"

"I said drop it."

"You've been getting it on, right?"

"Stop it! Having residency status doesn't mean I have to stay."

"But you do like it there and you will stay, because you LIKE BANGING THE FARMER'S DAUGHTER!"

"Look, all right, yes." He hears himself say it and cannot believe he is doing it. He tells himself to shut up but he proceeds anyway, victim to the same self-destructive impulse that made him imagine being killed on his bike. "I didn't want to tell you now, but, yes, I'm involved with Osiris' daughter."

"That *was* your intention all along. To find someone else."

"No, I never intended to get involved. It just happened."

"And you weren't gonna touch a gun again, either. How long were you gonna leave me suspended, Russ?"

"I never asked you to suspend anything, Penny."

"Fuck you!"

The line goes dead.

Stone goes to bed that night anguishing over his lie and wondering just what he does feel for Osiris' daughter. She attracts him in some way, though not necessarily in a good way. She is infuriatingly stubborn, mysterious and unreliable. He doubts he wants to get to know her. He has no energy to expend on such a complicated person, when he himself is so emotionally bankrupt.

The next morning he wakes up looking into Osiris' face. The farmer is bending over him, shouting angry accusations about a door.

"What is it, Osiris?"

"Damn it, the door has disappeared!"

"What door?"

"The *only* door! It's volatized! And you slept through it!"

Stone dresses and hurries to the kitchen. The doorway is a gaping mockery. Maurice, standing in the empty doorframe, conducting rainwater down his slicker and heedless of the sizable puddle he is making indoors, studies the theft from all its angles, as if the bare hinges hold a clue to what happened. A steady cascade of runoff pours over the roof tiles, splattering the stone threshold and throwing specks of mud inside the kitchen. The right side of the refrigerator grabs Stone's attention. The intruder has smeared a message in mud to them. Not words, but images of some sort.

Osiris is still grumbling. "My so-called watchman slept through this!"

"So did you," answers back Maurice. "That's what we all did."

"Yes," scowls Osiris, "but only one of us was getting paid for it!"

The farmer gets on the phone to his daughter, putting her in the picture and knuckling with furious impatience the blue ceramic counter tiles.

"This time the bastards took the door! . . . that's right, *the kitchen door* . . . No, we haven't gotten that far yet, we haven't been out looking, if that's what you mean . . . it's pissing down rain here same as in town . . . I don't know, I haven't had a chance to talk with him yet. All I know is that he slept through the whole damn thing!"

Stone, feeling subdued and awkward, throws on a slicker, draws the hood over his head and steps through the curtain of water. He doesn't believe that the vandal has transported the stolen door very far. He stops beyond the laurel hedges, listening for the door's speech. Its several individual panes of glass speak in more coded splats than the ticking of the rain-peppered plants. There it is, the door's voice calls to him from the cherry orchard.

Maurice helps him carry it back and set it on its hinges. Osiris, his face drawn with anger and age, slaps coffee grains into a filter. Stone stares quietly at the muddy message on the refrigerator, trying to think things through. Meanwhile, Maurice makes enough chatter for three people.

"If my memory serves, the last time we had so much rain was the autumn your *maman* died. I thought Jehovah himself was pissing inside my trailer home." Maurice addresses Stone. "When I was about your age, I had already been a carpenter, mechanic, mason, game warden, poacher, garbage collector and chimney sweep. My old man called me a soft gonad, good for nothing but bouncing between a pair of thighs!"

As Maurice regales himself, Osiris fills three small porcelain cups-on-saucers with his hot muddy brew, and the three men loiter about the sink stand, holding their drinks daintily, almost lady-like, in their rattling hands. The odor of wet vegetation invests the kitchen, but that green pungency is not the only smell accentuated by the rain; Maurice reeks. Osiris once confided to Stone that Maurice's baths came like the seasons, four per year.

"Got to say, it's been ages since we drank coffee in your mother's kitchen, out of her good cups. Fifteen years, maybe. Time shoots by like a fart in a gale, doesn't it."

"Bah, it doesn't shoot!" contradicts Osiris, still boiling over the door incident. "We dissolve in it like damn fizz tablets!"

"A curious philosophy," nods Maurice, puckering at Osiris, winking at Stone.

"*Putain de merde*! What will they take next? The shitter?"

The idea moves Maurice to whooping laughter. "That would surely mark the end of your reading anything."

"Not having a shitter hasn't stopped you from reading."

"I'll give you that," chortles the old man, looking even scraggier when wet.

"*Pardi*! Damn right!" Maurice's banter has managed to restore a semblance of good humor to Osiris. "Why, if I were to go by the facts, I'd say defecating beside a dog twice a day agrees with book reading," teases Osiris, tossing a wink of his own at Stone.

"Try it before knocking it. Your father must have taught you that much."

Osiris' ill will towards his watchman has passed. "It's nobody's fault, son."

"That's for damn sure," concurs Maurice on cue.

Stone ignores their clemency. "You both noticed that there's no sign of an infraction."

"One of us forgot to fasten the kitchen shutters," shrugs Osiris.

"No. I heard you close the shutters before going up to bed last night. And I didn't touch them afterwards."

"So how did they get in?"

"The person was already in the house, hiding, when we closed up."

Osiris, stunned, then incredulous, cannot see the point to that. "The gold, as far as they know, is outside in a cave."

"Whoever broke in here knows there's no gold."

The two peasants gape like a couple of guppies.

Stone steps to the side of the refrigerator, exhibits the muddy doodling. "This mess here, you know what it is? It's the cave paintings. Our burglar has been in the cave and seen the paintings. He knows the gold story is a hoax."

"But why take my door?"

"Because he's warning you."

"Warning me?"

"He's letting you know that he can blow the cave painting story wide open, and he wants you worrying about it. Just like you're making him worry over something. Who are you worrying, Osiris?"

VI

Forty years before, a bowlegged man in a wrinkled suit came sauntering onto the Elysian property, calling to the farmer cleaning his tractor. The farmer had already seen him from afar, and, between sweeps of the rag, watched his approach with suspicion. The thin stranger wore a fat bow tie and one of those stiff, striped dress-shirts with a solid collar like something a Ferris wheel ticket seller might wear. And there was something funny about the suit, the way it hung off his bony shoulders and the fact that the bottom of his pants wanted nothing to do with his ankles and let them fend for themselves. The stranger stopped beside the farmer and addressed the tractor: "Japanese kit model," he hummed, rubbing his chin. "Very varied. Converts from a tractor to a plow with a simple twist."

"State your business, stranger," said the farmer.

"I'm looking for Sorbin Marcel."

"You've found him."

"*Bonjour*. My name is Maurice Combes." He extended a hand and Sorbin shook it, though Sorbin found the man shifty and maybe too sure of himself. The stranger, ostensibly to swat a mosquito, maneuvered such that the sun was now to his back and Sorbin senior had the difficulty of scrutinizing him. "Monsieur Gerard maybe spoke to you about me."

"Monsieur Gerard, you say? You must mean his son."

"No, I mean the father. The son is dead since last week. Carried off by a sickness in his genitals."

"The father is dead, too, long before the son," pointed out Sorbin, lifting the sleeve of his soiled T-shirt and scratching his biceps where an agricultural tan drew the line between two opposing hues, like the coloring of two distinctly different arms.

"That's right. Last year. They're both dead now. Did he speak to you about me?"

"O *fatcha*! You're not the handy man he told me about!"

"That's me. I can do about anything. All I ask is a modest wage and roof to sleep under."

"My young son Osiris. He's a father now and his wife's not well and he needs to spend more time with his family. I want someone here on a permanent basis, who isn't afraid to work and won't go catching a hand in a combine or running off."

"I'm your man. You offering insurance?"

"I have not given it much thought since I last saw Monsieur Gerard. He didn't say in would take you a year to get here."

"He probably didn't say he was going to die either. I didn't know anything about this job until his son's funeral. A cousin of mine put me in the picture. If the offer still holds, I'm available. And I'm dependable, just ask anybody in Lauris or Cadenet."

"Monsieur Gerard's word was good enough for me."

Marcel Sorbin found the mobile home in Cavaillon. The private seller, as if to undermine his own affair, explained how dangerous it was in a wind, swaying back and forth. "You can feel it ripping the ass-end out of your car. It'll jack on you faster than an up-yours." But Sorbin did not intend to drive it, only park it and turn it into a home. "Oh, then for parking, it is a good caravan."

Sorbin put the caravan under a plane tree beyond the lavender fields, so that Maurice Combes could have some privacy and also because Madame Devos-Sorbin did not much care for the cunning look of the new man, him being a little too forward, too talkative, too overtly pleasant, a veritable child of the country, and she trusted none of them.

Maurice returned that week, driven by his brother who owned a motor repair shop in Cadenet. He was wearing the same suit and hauling three suitcases, none of which Sorbin could lift. The angry brother said that none of the suitcases contained a suit, or any other clothes to speak of. "Fucking books, is all they are."

"He will have time to read—" Sorbin wasn't taking sides, just stating the facts—"in his caravan *after sunset.*"

"Yes," concurred the brother caustically, "he always finds the time, even if he doesn't have it. Forty three years old and still a jack-off."

"He won't loaf here during working hours," promised Sorbin. "What he does on his own time is no affair of mine."

That spring was a good one for crops, with much rainfall, then heat. During the summer, at the height of the fruit-picking season, Marcel Sorbin had recourse to cheap labor, drawn from that particular breed of comer and goer called "people of passage", for the most part *Kalés*, gypsies originating in Spain and Portugal and parading across southern Europe in dusty convoys.

By mid-July the region was experiencing one of its worst heat waves on record, with temperatures holding above 100 degrees for ten straight days. With barely a tree for shelter, the melon fields were furnaces, and the air cracked with the sound of splitting cantaloupe. To re-hydrate themselves, the hands took 30-minute rest breaks every two hours under the Grand Oak.

"At the time, a well existed near the Grand Oak," Osiris stresses to Stone. "We tapped water from the underground stream that runs through the cave there in the west field. I had to condemn the well when the groundwater got polluted by the septic tank runoff from the likes of that riffraff Sabag."

One late afternoon, after work had stopped for the day, Maurice got to the well and found a young nomad woman, alone, filling flagons. He wouldn't have given her 20 years of age. She was dark-skinned and hairy with a fine down on her cheeks and lip. She had a manly sort of face, sharp at the edges, eyes black as beetles. Without nearly as much discretion, she stared at him with no uncertain calculation.

Maurice always found melon picking a sensual enterprise, working his hands over the round fruit fleshed by the earth and made wet and juicy by the sun. But a full day's labor in that torrid heat had left his mind as empty as her jugs, and no untoward thoughts came to him as her eyes set upon him.

"*Ooh lá lá!*" she sighed, tying her skirt up and exposing her legs to the mid-thigh. "What heat!"

"It is not cold."

And not even then did he react, when she bent over the well, shifting her backside, as if only to replace one ponderous jug with another. "Are you in a hurry, Monsieur?" she asked from behind her own fanny. "Because if you are . . ." A virginal politeness. Overdone. Phony, of course. He couldn't see her face.

"O no! Only a fool could be in a hurry in this heat. Take your time. There's no fire, except what's in the air."

The moiling of her own day's efforts stuck to her skin. Her skirt was a dirty print rag that nomad women worked in because their men folk, and maybe they too, preferred it that way as it made cravings easier to conclude, allowing those concerned to get on with their crop picking; it clung between her legs and drew out the general shape of a body that already showed signs of a heavy future. She went on filling her flagon from the runoff, which poured at only half the normal speed. Everything in the July heat worked at half speed.

He saw that she was struggling under the weight and gave her a hand, lifting the second jug, having to reach around her to do it. He felt something static escape her and enter his blood like an electrical charge. She smiled this time, an unmistakable smirk of a mission accomplished. "*Merci*," she said, setting a firm dirty hand on his arm.

Faster than any of her jugs, his sex filled with his own coursing blood, until he thought he might pass out from the sheer displacement. He shot out a hand and latched onto her, catching himself. She shivered like a viper, and her mouth rent but no words came out. But her eyes talked up a storm, a dark looming cataclysm, as she went about transfusing her poison in him. He paid that no mind. It was too late for worrying. This would be a delicious doom.

They tore at each other, coequal in their shabbiness. She smelled of stale clothes and a week's worth of sweat, as did he, only worse. He pulled down the melon-picker pants that hadn't been washed since he started the job two weeks prior. She lifted her rag and he lifted her. He bent her over the well, and her head and hairy arms dangled in the void and his good sense told him to drop her down that well and let that be the end of it. No, he wasn't one of those kinds of criminals, and maybe it's too bad he wasn't because it would have saved everyone a lot of trouble and grief. Instead, he let her teeter on the edge, while he reveled in everything that was water and wetness and heat. Her ripened fruit was by far the sweetest he had known, of a texture and temperature that defied foolish comparisons, and afterwards, when she had taken her jugs and left him, his rut had hardly abated.

Her men folk turned up that evening, as Maurice knew they must. Four of them, each one nastier that the previous, claiming to be brothers but without papers to prove it. They seemed produced by the shadows, and stepped silent as nightmares into the light of the dining porch and demanded over a table of half-eaten victuals and near-empty wine bottle the whereabouts of Maurice Combes of Cadenet village.

Marcel Sorbin rose angrily from the table, demanding an explanation for their impertinence. Madame Sorbin bellowed a sickened "*Oh mon dieu!*" when confronted with their accusation of rape.

"The business was settled by morning," says Maurice. "Or so we thought. They lit out in their dusty clunkers with doors that didn't sit right and couldn't close and had to be held shut, with a curse from Marcel that he'd kick their asses all the way to Spain if they showed up again for work."

"What did they extort?" asks Stone.

"Some money, certainly not what they expected. Marcel was willing to give them something to get shot of them. A few thousand *sous*, which, of course, he deducted from my pay. As they drove off, you remember what your Papa said to me?"

"*Pardi!* He said the next time you wet your wick with a person of passage, he'd light it with a blow torch."

The memory has the two Frenchmen crackling nostalgically.

"Never saw your Papa any angrier than that!"

But wait. Their problems weren't fixed by a long shot. Hoping to milk the ugly business some more, she of the well, calling herself La Suzon, turns up the following year, this time without her pimps, but not alone either, holding a package she claims belongs to Maurice. It's a child. The age fits, more or less. Her clan had thrown her and her infant out to fend for themselves.

All right, he says, he will accept his responsibilities. But his fool gallantry only riles her.

"I want no money from any dirty good-for-nothing like you!"

"Then what is it you *do* want, La Suzon?"

"Land! Half an acre."

"Don't be a fool. I have nothing of my own. I am only an employee of the Sorbins."

"They gave you a piece of land and a trailer. They can do likewise for me."

"Sure, and maybe this baby here will grow up to be President of the Republic! Look, you hoodwinked me once, and so much the better for me, for the lesson it taught me. But hang me if I fall twice into the same trap. I do my share of pig labor, but that doesn't make me hog-dumb."

La Suzon went away, that time. But the next year she was back, a little stouter, a little harder about the eyes, a little more determined, holding the walking child by the hand. She threatened Maurice with a paternity suit, "having talked things over with someone of the profession even to know the word paternity," adds Osiris.

But Maurice, neither resentful nor impertinent, explained to her that, paternity or no paternity, she would obtain no Sorbin land. She answered that, if he refused to help her in her designs, she was prepared to drag the younger Sorbin into her suit. "The one called Osiris. I'll claim before a judge that Osiris Sorbin took part in the rape."

Maurice slapped her. Unfazed, she grabbed him and shoved him over the trailer table, like a man would. He jumped up but thought better of tangling physically with her. La Suzon was stronger than he was. "Come on," she taunted, "and I'll brain you."

"I know all about your tricks, woman! It's common knowledge that gypsy whores such as you own ointments that can drive a man mad with lust."

She laughed in his face. "You bet I have magic! And I will curse you until the sky collapses in an orgy of water and death, I will! You and the whole Sorbin family! If I don't get satisfaction, I will hex all of you! You'll know only tragedy! I don't care how long it takes. If it takes till the end of time, I will be here, waiting, till I obtain satisfaction!"

La Suzon took to living in a lean-to at the river, feeding that child of hers with trout and watercress and small land creatures, and pressed on with her outrageous claims. But the Sorbin-Devos clan was too powerful, too well established in the area, to be hurt by the groundless accusations of a hard scheming gypsy. She didn't care.

"Sorbins," she spat at Maurice, "they come, they go. Remember my malediction."

A few years later, Marcel Sorbin drove his tractor into a ditch. The rear wheels spun naked, catching only air. When he got down to have a look, a sudden chill passed through his left ear. Overcome by pure fatigue, the rugged farmer sat down on the tractor step, then lolled over.

"We took him home and he died," says Osiris, eyes misting, yesterday's pain approaching on quickened feet. "He was 68."

"It was a beautiful death," Maurice reminds him, "a farmer's death, and one to be envied by any man."

"Yes, may I be so lucky as to go like my father."

The woman was still there eight years later—making 16 years total of pestering—hips twice as wide, mustache more pronounced, and determination redoubled as well. She was making a living investing certain bends along the national road, posed to attract feckless truckers, the only sort of prostitution accepted by the French authorities.

The autumn of '77, during the great rainstorms of October, Marie Devos-Sorbin succumbed to lung-rotting tuberculosis. The day of her funeral, the weather worsened until, by nightfall, it seemed there was no air, only water, as if the whole continent were submerged in sea. But neither funeral nor tempest stopped La Suzon. She stood outside in the deluge and pelted his trailer with rocks until he threw open the door and told her to get in.

The inside of his trailer wasn't much drier than the outside, what with the storm finding holes throughout the leaky contraption. But she hadn't come for comfort, only crowing. "I demand my due, now that there are no more Sorbins or Devoses in the town council. It's a fact that the new mayor and his machine never thought much of the two families. Looks like hard times for those who always hid under a Sorbin-Devos skirt!"

"What do you expect me to do about it?"

"Arrange a meeting between me and Osiris, and I'll see to the rest."

"Sure, and then I'll arrange a meeting for you with the Pope."

She was right about the hard times. Old enemies of the Sorbin-Devos clan used the gypsy woman to settle scores, and she used them to strike at Osiris, who didn't have the political reach or clout of his father.

"I wasn't helpless," explains Osiris defensively. "I defended myself and the farm against her slander."

"*Pardi* you did at that!" seconds Maurice.

"So what happened?" asks Stone.

The two farmers shoot each other a look, the identifying regard in a brotherhood of failure.

"You mean she won anyway?"

Only Maurice has the courage to continue speaking. "We were afraid, after . . . ." His unfinished sentence runs to infinity.

"After what?"

It is Osiris himself who breaks the impasse. "After Jean Horace was killed."

Osiris' eyes fog and Maurice, with less the need for the appearance of control actually does sob once, a hard gasping emission that sums up his own attachment to Osiris' son. "I saw that child born. I watched him take his first steps. I gave him his first tractor ride. No offense to you Osiris, but I was more available to him than you were."

"No offense taken."

"It's normal, what with running the operation and also fighting off that she-wolf and her lawyers."

"And I much appreciated the time you spent with my son, that's a fact."

"I loved that boy, I loved him more than any I could imagine having and certainly more than the one I was accused of begetting."

Stone is commiserating, but he still does not understand the point. "What were you afraid of? I don't see the connection between the accident and her slander campaign."

"We did not know what else she might do," says Maurice.

"You mean what? Legally?"

Maurice shakes his grizzled wet head. "*Magically.*"

Stone is floored. "You're not telling me you believed her nonsense!" Their silence fans his exasperation. "The two of you, two grown men, believed Jean Horace was the victim of a curse?"

Both storytellers shrug. "I wasn't going to take the risk," answers Osiris. "Not with my daughter."

The subject is like religion; Stone sees that a debate will lead nowhere. "What," ventures Stone, putting the topic on a more concrete surface, "did La Suzon get out of you?"

"Her half acre!" shouts Osiris, silencing everyone, himself as well, though it is only himself he meant to upbraid. More quietly: "At the north end beyond the woods, there's a plot of land. It's far enough away from here as not to warrant her taking the same road to town as me."

"You signed it over to her?"

"Leased it. A 20-year lease."

"Which, I take it, is coming up for re-leasing."

"This coming spring."

"And with Mathilde now General Secretary of the Mayor's office . . . ."

Osiris nods grimly. "Yes, La Suzon knows her gypsy luck is running out, and I think she'll try anything. But it's not just her."

"Who else?"

"Sabag, that's who."

"What does he have to do with any of this?"

Neither of the Frenchmen answers at once, which leaves Stone the chance to formulate his own answer. "Wait! You're not saying that Sabag is her son? Maurice's alleged son? The child of the well?"

Maurice, as if reading from his own epitaph, mutters: "For all my failures in love and war, nothing, absolutely nothing, can touch my execrable record in the fathering department."

VII

Now Stone is sure that Sabag and La Suzon are behind the shenanigans. There is their motive: to stay on the property. And the proof: the gun blast he heard no doubt came from Osiris' former shotgun, which Sabag now owns. But to confirm it, he will need to get inside their house. First, he must find the place. He can't ask Osiris for directions because, skittish as he is, the farmer would only nix the initiative. That leaves Maurice.

"Cut through the woods," says the old guy. "You will know you are on the right track when you run into twin persimmon trees standing in a clearing like a couple of done-up Christmas trees. This late in November, they will be leafless and bowed almost to the ground with more fruit than you can shake a stick at."

Stone finds the trees and understands Maurice's holiday simile. The fruit's orange and red persimmon bulbs, stocked with autumn's last light, make the dull wood dance.

But he is not alone. Sabag's pig is squatting in his path, champing on fallen fruit. He hasn't seen her this close since she ran him over four months ago. She's a hefty 300-pound creature of curious hue, more violet than pink, with dark brown patches about the haunches. Her pendulant gray teats attest to an admirable longevity. But Stone already knows that this animal was never destined for pork chops. The swine serves a lower purpose.

"Truffle sniffer," said Maurice, scratching the grains of whiskers peppering his jaw. "Why, with all the woodlands around here, that pig is good for 20 pounds of truffles a night. That's eight million *sous*, eighty thousand francs of black fungi, at the open market in Apt."

"Twelve thousand dollars for a night's labor is not too bad."

"If poor Osiris had even a small percentage of the profits from what Sabag and his pig have pilfered from around the Grand Oak alone!"

"So there is real gold on this property. Black gold."

"*Pardi*. How do you think Osiris lost his shotgun?"

"He told me. The police confiscated it because he shot at Sabag."

"Shame he missed, if you ask me. Except then Osiris would have gone to prison. Damn police don't care! They say, and maybe rightly so, that Sabag has a right to walk across the property to get home without getting shot at. But he was walking home like I'm clean-shaven. The funniest thing is, who do you think now possesses the very gun they confiscated?"

"Not Sabag!"

"*Oui, Monsieur*! The fool bought it at a police auction."

"Does Osiris know?"

"I didn't have the heart to tell him. Predators, that's what they are, Sabag and La Suzon! Deforciants! They think everything Osiris has is theirs to take. Anyway, forget about that. For the moment, stolen truffles have cost him only his rifle. Those cave paintings mean the loss of his farm."

The pig spots him and turns in his direction. Stone lifts a stick, waiting for her to charge. But the animal makes only a dismissive snort and lumbers off in the opposite direction.

He places his faith in brute nature, hoping that the animal is on its way home. Stone follows it down a tree-sheltered trail into a windy field almost completely overgrown with hawthorn trees. The pig has no more desire than he does to attempt a passage through the wall of thorns, so she circumvents the problem, climbing a contiguous hill in a meandering smash-up through dead, wet branches.

Another short rise and Stone comes into a land of scrub brush, rocky soil and steep headlands. Sabag territory. In the distance he can make out two dwellings, a fixed-up troglodyte cave and, to the lower right of the bluff, a dismal attempt at house construction.

The thin daylight, somber setting, and silence accentuate an air of willful disregard hanging over the half-built house. Its tar-black roof is nothing more than corrugated strips of pestiferous asbestos sheeting. Its unfinished porch has no roof at all, but consists of pillars abandoned halfway, with rusty iron girders poking out like wart hairs. None of its four crooked walls has a coat of stucco. Rather, the composite clay bricking, the cheapest and most uncertain of building materials, lies as exposed as a tailless dog's ass. In lieu of windows, yellow plastic panels clatter in the wind. Neither the structure nor the rusty cement mixer behind it looks like it has been touched in quite some time.

A full clothesline angles away from the cave. Undergarments of both sexes plus those of a small child, twist and dance provocatively in the wind. Stone steps onto the lot, watchful for the owners and the unpredictable swine, which has gone over and plunked down beside a door-less automobile on blocks.

The path to the cave dwelling passes through a gaggle of chickens, ducks and, lo and behold, the phantom cock which has heralded the dawn for the past four months. "Nice to meet you at last, Master Rooster."

An actual door, with brass knob, is built into the cave entrance. It flies open, and a grimy ragamuffin first-grader is standing there in her underwear, leaning on the door jam and staring dully at him. He lifts his sunglasses.

"*Bonjour*, mademoiselle."

She says nothing in return.

"Is Mr. Sabag around?"

Still no sound.

"How about Sabag's mother?"

The child is so unaffected by his questions, he is beginning to think she is deaf. She is a brown little thing standing on stick legs, barefooted, her forehead hidden under dirty ringlets of black greasy hair. She has a white smile and a tired regard. The bags under her eyes look like thumbprints.

"Mama and Papa are gone to town," she says all of a sudden, but without the slightest emotion.

"Oh, La Suzon and Sabag are your mother and father?"

The question goes unanswered, and he realizes it was stupid to pose it. "They left you all by yourself?"

"I'm old enough to fend for myself."

"I believe you are. How old are you?"

"Six." As proof, she displays the appropriate number of fingers.

"That's pretty big."

She likes hearing that, or so he assumes from the fact that her eyelids move. She asks if he wants to come in and play.

The cave is a pitiful, frowsy scratch of human subsistence, furnished with every shiftless bit of furniture one can drag from the refuse yard down by the Durance River. Electrical wires litter the floor with scant regard for safety or the legal consequences—Sabag has tapped illegally into a power pole 50 yards south of the area.

"Okay, what shall we play?"

Tiny but dexterous hands, black with grit, shuffle a deck of cards. She is not a handsome child. A thick down blackens a trowel-shaped face, from its protruding forehead to its receding chin. But he sees in her ruddy Bohemian cheeks the survival cleverness of an entire race, from its origins in northwest India 3500 years ago, pushed to Persia in the 10th century, blown to Byzantium in the 14th, then France and Spain in the 15th, deported to colonies in South America, the West Indies, and even Virginia and Louisiana in the 17th, chased away because of physical appearance and poverty in the 18th, feared and discriminated against in the 19th, and gassed by the Nazis in the 20th, 250,000 murdered, or a ¼ of their population in Europe, according to a book Maurice lent him.

While she deals, Stone takes quick visual inventory: a half-eaten, mushy bowl of cereal, a pillow and a blanket on a leg-less sofa, one bed, a television and combo DVD/VCR, recent and maybe stolen, though he doubts it; even the trashiest and tortured fringes of society will pay the price for a tubed window of dreams.

"Do you sleep on the couch?"

She shakes her head. "Papa sleeps there. I sleep with Mama, except when she gets mad and kicks me out and I go with Papa."

"What's your name, sweetheart?"

"Sonia."

"Sonia is a pretty name. I'm Russell." He decides to get about the business that has brought him there. "I'll bet you know where your Papa keeps his rifle."

She opens a cabinet and pulls out the .12 gauge shotgun. Stone takes it away, quickly verifies that it is unloaded. Further inspection turns up a small gold plate on the stock reading *Osiris Sorbin*. It is the rifle used to scare off the Nike bunch.

"Go on and play your hand, honey."

As she studies her cards, he loosens the firing pin and sticks it in his pocket.

Sonia quickly gets ahead of him. At one point, she flashes her cards, to give him a chance, and her expression is so full of coquetry that he is remind of an adage: boys must learn what girls come knowing ready-made into the world.

"Sonia, this is not the first time you have seen me, is it?"

She goes back into protective mode, disappearing behind the dull expressionless mask she showed him at the doorway.

"You saw me at the big house, didn't you?"

She shrugs and looks down, revealing a crooked hairline.

"You were hiding inside Mr. Sorbin's house, the night it rained so hard. You sneaked in and hid and then when I went to sleep you opened the door, right? Go on, you can tell me. I won't get mad. It's only a game."

She hesitates. "Papa will beat me if I tell."

"Does your Papa beat you a lot?"

The light leaves her face. She is downcast.

"It's okay, honey. Listen, I have another game we can play. Can you keep a secret? When I leave, you can tell your parents that the American came by, but you can't say you let me in, okay? Say that I left right away. Can you do that?"

She nods.

As he leaves the cave, Stone hopes for Sabag's sake that he does not run into him, for fear that he could break every bone in the profligate's scrawny hide.

VIII

Osiris toils the day long in the barn, pitting and boiling fruit in wine and sugar to make conserves. He takes breaks outdoors, squatting on his rock under the acacia tree, enjoying a smoke.

In the middle of the afternoon, Stone fetches a pruning pole and ladder from the barn. On his way to the orchards, he passes

Osiris on the rock. The farmer is hunched over himself, elbows on knees, the only difference in his seasonal garb being the red-checkered long-sleeve shirt, which has replaced his red-checkered short-sleeve shirt and suspenders of warmer times. Still the same faded blue trousers, though. Constant washings with hard lards have stolen the structure from the crotch; Osiris' sagging testicles make a breast against his left thigh.

He looks harassed. Stone has come to believe that his boss is not so much weary from work as pursued by an obsession to think up what next to do, to self-motivate before acting, to know exactly what awaits when finally he does lift his tired self off the stone. All part of the routine, repetition being a religion unto itself for the farmer.

Osiris looks up. "Where do you think you are going with those things?"

"I thought I'd pick those persimmons I told about."

"Not even a moment do I have to myself!" he grumbles.

"No one's asking you to get up, Osiris."

Another drag on the cigarette. Ash drops on his old boots, straps barely holding to their eyelets. Osiris rubs his thinning pate, hair combed by the wind, as the French say. His face is a tortured map of irritation. Furrows of failed responsibility. You'd think the stone were sitting on him, rather than the other way around.

The farmer stands and sticks a shoulder into oppressive gravity. The desire to keep moving. "All right, let's have at it."

The autumn sun passes, never managing much height above the eastern ridge. Later in the afternoon the property lies in shadow, but the two of them have filled ten wicker baskets of unripe persimmons the size and texture of a baseball.

"They will soften before Christmas," assures Osiris, pouring a Pastis on the porch table. The air has a bite to it. They raise their glasses, clink and drink. Osiris quaffs his and, wasting no time, tends to the logs burning in the stone furnace.

The man cannot sit still for a minute. Between sunrise and bedtime, Osiris is always peeling some vegetable, repairing a wire, plastering a wall, cutting grass, treating wood for worms and termites, cementing leaks, changing broken tiles, trapping dormice and any other manner of rodent nesting in the eaves, removing hornets and wasp nests, dusting out spiders and small scorpions, pruning the acacia trees, clearing leaves off the surface of the spring, burning branches, priming pipes, sweeping the chimney, painting the shutters. It is true that he must attempt to stay one step ahead of tasks threatening to cave in on him. But it is also true that the man has to be busy every instant, as if a moment's peace might cause him to sink into some suffocating self-truth.

Stone watches him roll dough onto a powdered board. Osiris ladles homemade tomato sauce from a bowl and spreads it around, lays on slices of mozzarella cheese, sprinkles out oregano and other herbs, and slides the pizza into the outdoor furnace by way of a long-handled spatula.

He's a meticulous bastard, Stone will give him that.

As he studies his boss, the Pastis goes to Stone's head.

"Have you ever traveled anywhere, Osiris?"

"What kind of a question is that? I've been all over the South of France. I did my military service up north in Nancy."

"Have you ever left France."

"*Ouais*, on a cruise."

"Really? Where to?"

"Corsica."

Stone has to sit on that one for a moment. "Look, I have an idea. Would you consider taking a trip with me to California?"

The question stuns even the questioner. Stone himself cannot say why he thought to ask. A moment of . . . what? . . . gratitude? Grateful for the healing he's known these past months on the farm? Grateful for being renewed, rebuilt, or just plain rested with each passing day spent in the countryside, on the farm, in the company of this man who, despite his flaws, is dignified in adversity, and whom he respects in a way he has respected no other mentor, not even his own father, no especially not him. Stone never had a proper father-son relationship with his own father.

Anyway, he could have saved his breath. The farmer does not take the trouble even to grunt in Stone's direction, but sends the sound into the inferno with the pizza. "Bah, do not talk to say nothing."

Osiris would no more consider separating himself from the farm and his daily routines than from his arms and legs. The farmer is so lacking in imagination that he cannot indulge himself even the simple fantasy of a change from his farm and its upkeep.

The pizza is cooked. Osiris slides it out and carries it into the kitchen. He cuts steaming wedges and dishes them out on the same two plates they always eat off. The oak cabinet in the kitchen is stocked with nice plates dating back four generations, yet Osiris uses only those two, washed immediately and set in the sink rack until the next meal. It's all in keeping with the man's religion of routine and his constant struggle, both heroic and ludicrous, to get the little things right in order to win control of his life.

As darkness blankets the windows, they sit down to eat in the dining room. "Serve the wine," growls the hungry and impatient Osiris. He hates eating off schedule, even if it is only five minutes later than usual. He sets his worn serviette in his lap and starts in without waiting for Stone to finish pouring. "And hurry up and eat while it's hot," he adds with a full mouth.

The simple thin-crusted pizza is drooling good, and simply the best Stone has ever tasted. "You could open up one of those roadside pizza trucks, Osiris."

It is the kind of light banter the farmer likes.

"*Ouf!* You won't catch me sweating like a cretin inside a burning truck!"

"Not a bad way to lose weight, though."

"Lose weight, *fada!*"

"Sure. You could wear a T-shirt all year long and show off your muscles to the babes. Handsome guy like you, spreading your sauce."

"You know you are an ass, you!" Osiris' lake-blue eyes are playful, his grin so wide that Stone can see the shadows of his back teeth, rather the gaps where teeth should have been.

Osiris is in a fine mood, and Stone is loath to spoil it. But he feels he must.

"I paid a visit to the Sabag enclave yesterday."

The tenuous light in the farmer's expression dies out. "Why? What are you doing messing around up there? Did I tell you to go messing around up there?" Nothing stresses him like a disruption in his routine. Sudden news snaps the delusion that there exists a chain of control.

"Not only does Sabag have your shotgun, it was the gun I heard fired at those young toughs last September. It was Sabag who scared them off, I'm sure of it."

"That's ridiculous. He hired them, for Christ's sake!"

"He hires, he fires. If it keeps you turning in circles, he's succeeded. The trespassers probably don't even know it is Sabag pulling the strings. No doubt he's paying off a middle guy with your truffle money."

"I don't understand any of it! I don't want to think about it!"

"You don't have much choice in the matter, Osiris. There's a little girl living in the cave up there."

"*Et alors?* What of it?"

"Something's fishy about her parentage."

"*Bof,*" he shrugs. "That child's origins concern neither me nor you nor any gossip," he grouses, paring the crust from a well-aged St. Nectaire cheese.

"So, you do know about her existence?"

"Of course I do. Everyone does."

Osiris' indifference stuns him. "Well, the situation could eventually spell trouble for you, if—"

"If nothing! I told you I wasn't interested!"

Stone is baffled. "If there's child abuse—"

"It is none of my business, and certainly none of yours!"

"That's the whole point. They are living on your property. If something bad happens, you are accountable."

"*They* are not my family!"

"Right, it is a shooting offense to steal fungi, but sodomy, incest, and child abuse are okay."

Osiris slams his fist, causing glasses, bottles and plates to rise an inch off the wooden table. "I defend no one, least of all the Sabags! But I do not act on rumors and that is all they are!"

"Sure they are rumors, but that's no excuse to stick your head in the soil."

Osiris' clear eyes go steel. "*Mon Dieu*, how you Americans enjoy sticking your noses in others' private affairs!"

"You seem to know a lot about America, for a guy whose idea of a big trip is going to Corsica."

"I know what I know! And for a watchman, as you call yourself, you should watch better how you talk to me!"

Stone stands and leaves the room. Osiris' booming voice catches up to him in the corridor, ordering him back to the table. Stone disobeys and continues walking to the Music Hall and sits on his mattress. He's upset with himself. He has over-reached. Why couldn't he have shut his trap? Why did he get involved! The plan was to blend in, vanish!

When he left the States nine months before, he was looking for a job that would allow him to sit back and observe. Like one of those UN peacekeepers. Taking no sides, keeping the world at bay, living the impersonal life, peeping out at beauty from inside a tank, from within his hard shell, from the distance of a rooftop shitter.

The thought of leaving sickens him, but what else can he do? He is no watcher. He's a militant, and no amount of personal hardship is going to change the fact. He refuses to join Osiris as a willing puppet in the Sabags' manipulative schemes, powerless to disprove the gold rumors, restricted from stopping the truffle trade, restrained from exposing the cave paintings, and resigned to accepting their child abuse.

Osiris shuffles into the middle of the room and glares at Stone, but unconvincingly. "I asked you to come back."

"No, you ordered me. And I am not your slave."

Stone looks up. Rage no longer rules the farmer's face. Fear is in his eyes. "Forget the whole thing, son."

"No, Osiris. The law of silence is your thing, not mine. I

won't equivocate about this. I can't. The gold thing, okay. But not the kid."

"I understand that, son, but we are not in American here. It is France. There is no black and white here. You must watch where you put your foot down."

"Look, do you or don't you want this vermin off your property?"

"*Bien sûr* I do!"

"Then get serious about fighting them. That means attacking them, not just waiting around and doing damage control."

Osiris, as incapable as his daughter of masking an emotion, goes white. A sense of dread, a primal superstition, turns him inside out. "It is not that easy."

"What are you so worried about?"

"*Qui sème le vent récolte la tempête*, that's what."

"Are you back on that hexing shit again?"

"You cannot understand! Not until you have lost a wife, a father, a mother, a son!"

"Nobody is cursed by any one person. No one has that power. For the simple reason that it takes a world and several lives and even lifetimes mixing to produce one such tragedy."

"How would you know? How would you know anything, at your age?"

"I know. Because . . ."

A knocking at the kitchen door interrupts him.

"*Et voila!* Now you have gone and done it! Don't answer it!"

"Don't be silly!" Stone gets up.

"I forbid you . . . ." The pallid Osiris trails him down the hallway, spinning words of doom. "Don't let her in or we're all sunk!"

"Crap, Osiris! Crap crap and more crap!"

"She must not touch you either!" he warns in the kitchen. "A touch or a hair, for that matter, and who knows what curse from her . . . ."

Heedless to the farmer's erratic warning, Stone opens the kitchen door and unlatches the shutter. Now is as good a time as any to loosen the spell she has on Osiris. Stone's staying on the farm depends on it.

The wind has died down, there is just the faintest rustling. A heavy figure stands in the shadows about 20 feet from the door, blending with the dark girth of the mulberry tree. She makes a shapeless stele transmogrified, squawking a tune he cannot begin to get his ears around. Osiris throws on the porch light, a yellow glare as harsh as a tossed jug of cold water.

"What are you doing here, La Suzon?"

She steps into the light, a large imposing woman of wild, gray-streaked, dark hair. "Some nerve demanding what *I* want, Sorbin. *You* called *me* down here."

"That would be the day. And stay where you are."

She halts her advance, but only for an instant, before huffing and coming to the door, then beyond it, poking a foot and her nose inside the kitchen. Stone gets a strong whiff of her, an acrid combination of garlic, body odor and booze.

"You sent your detective here snooping round my way, yes or shit?"

She flashes a glance at Stone. She starts to set a puffy dark-nailed hand on his, thick fingers that can kill, do kill, every day, chickens, guinea hens, rabbits, before diverting it at the last moment and placing her hand on the door frame. "You're the one? The shooter?"

"The watchman."

She takes his measure, then tilts her shoulder and chin into a spindled axis of flirtation, rather a telegraphed parody of it. Once upon a time, the bohemienne must have had an allure for gullible, hormone-heavy bonhommes such as Maurice, even a comeliness, now gone overwrought with the desire for property and a distaff's weight, an old country thickness and bitterness round the eyes, dark facial fuzz above her upper lip.

"So, tell La Suzon, *cheri,* what made you come up my way?"

"Your son."

"Are you gay? He's not."

"You would know his sexual leanings better than anyone, Madame."

She seems to respect the verbal blow. Her black stare settles into a wicked winking up curve of the left side of her swollen face. "The girl said you were handsome. For once, the brat was not lying."

"I'm surprised she got a look at all, she slammed the door so fast in my face."

He surveys La Suzon's expression, to spot where his lie has landed. His intention is less to cover for Sonia than to ascertain the extent of their punishment, if the little girl was imprudent enough to spill the beans. Stone is relieved to watch his lie bounce harmlessly out of her thoughts.

"Yes, the scamp is learning."

Suddenly, she reaches out and takes Stone's hand, making Osiris' hair stand up on his head.

"Let go of him!"

She cackles through her teeth. "Now, why the jitters, Osiris? I have no diseases."

She is terribly teasing, brazenly so, as she turns his hand, palm up and draws a caressing finger down his lifeline. "I see hair in this palm. Quit using your hand and come by my place for the real thing, *Amerloque*."

"Reality is a little too bitchy for me," he says, pulling away.

She laughs again and moves off, behind night's curtain.

"Quick," whines Osiris. "Come in and wash your hand."

"No, I think I'll just let the poison work in."

"What!"

"I'm kidding."

"It's not a kidding matter!"

Yes, La Suzon is no joke. On the contrary, she's one hell of an adversary. Stone reassesses his take on the situation. He has seen her malefic look before, in the most intelligent and street savvy criminals in Los Angeles. A look that says not only will I stop at nothing to get what I want, but I will also never tire of making trouble for you because trouble is what I do, like breathing, eating, defecating, talking. La Suzon is a woman gang boss. Osiris is no match for her.

IX

December starts with a violent wind and another argument with Osiris about enlisting his daughter's help against La Suzon.

"I don't want my daughter involved in this affair, understand!"

"Why? Don't you trust her?"

"Don't be a fool. Of course I trust her!"

"Then, what is it?"

Osiris refuses to reply, wearing the conflicting emotions of vexation and shame. Stone recalls his litany about children leaving home and never coming back.

"Do you think you can protect her better by leaving her out?"

"She's the one who wants to be out."

"Well, what's your idea of being *in*, Osiris? Living on the farm?"

"She'd be better off if she lived here."

So painful was the loss of his son, that the farmer has made a lifestyle of his fear of seeing it repeated with his daughter.

"Right. So, if you won't budge and she won't budge, what happens this spring when La Suzon comes around for a new lease?"

The farmer switches off the kitchen light and announces that he is going to bed. Stone flips it back on. "What are you going to do about the lease, Osiris?"

"Damn it, La Suzon will have her lease! Satisfied? As long as the cave stays hidden, I'll sign."

"That's what I call caving in."

"Call it what you will, I want no more trouble. That worthless parcel of land I gave them is not worth anybody getting hurt."

"And when you sign and they continue their blackmailing shenanigans anyway? Then what?"

"*Bonsoir.*" Osiris turns out the light again. This time Stone lets the dark prevail.

The wind sends the thermometer plummeting 30 degrees in 24 hours and is so powerful that it seems to bend the very white light it produces. For a straight week it disrupts the day's doings and the night's slumber with its vocal nuisance of whistling tiles, creaking boughs, howling faucets, battering shutters, and flying projectiles. Stone has never experienced anything like it. Osiris claims that a good Mistral will take the tail off a donkey. Maurice's metaphor is of the same vein, though cruder. "This bitch of a wind can blow the horns off a cuckold."

Biking against the Mistral is a shattering experience. Buffeted by 100 mile per hour gales, Stone struggles up the 10-degree grade into town, spokes bent, chain rattling, pedals scraping the pavement. Gales pound his ears, make his head ache, steal the oxygen from his lungs.

The village center is decorated for Christmas. Fifteen feet above the main road, an austere string of silver lights bobs like a drag-line in a swell. The wind tears to bits the pathetic Nativity scene in the square, blowing boards, straw, and the clay figurines across the square against the war memorial monument. Only an obdurate baby Jesus remains dangling over the crèche like a kite, held by an arm to an electric wire. Each gust sends the divine infant sailing away, only to return on the ebb. It gives the pastoral scene a sense of friction and futility.

Stone locks his bike and enters the post office. Everyone inside is talking of the wind, making more of it as it were, and in some cases displaying admirable linguistic agility in turning a non-subject into a conversation. None of the chatter he hears is negative. The wind is "a sort of vociferous but amusing boor of a relative". But it is also "healthy and therapeutic". The Mistral "clears the air of germs, lifts the gray ceiling and sweeps aside precipitation and pretension". Its intense light "brings familiarity, security and order to our perception of the world". A drunken philosopher from the *Bar des Remparts* claims that the Mistral "strips the veil off a virgin sun".

Getting to the counter demands patience. A lot of the customers are in the post office to do their banking. The French postal service offers checking accounts, and the majority of village people, including Osiris, does its banking in the same line as the letter senders. It being the holiday season, everybody is doing a bit of both today, and it takes Stone half an hour to reach the window.

He pushes his box through the revolving box slot. A glass wall separates him from the lone mail clerk, a nosy chatterbox who contributes considerably to the long lines.

"Bound for America!" she announces to the world, placing the package on the scales. "Christmas gift for Penelope?" she asks through the glass. In the post office, your private affairs quickly become public knowledge. "You did what I said, I hope. Chocolate truffles? Calissons? Nougats? Jellied fruits et dried fruits?"

"They're in the box."

"You are certain?"

"I packed it."

"You did not forget the oil cake?"

He pays and walks out. On the sidewalk he almost bumps heads with a teenage boy. Stone says sorry. But the kid has an attitude and pushes past him with studied cool. On the back of his white satin athletic jacket is the *NIKE* swoosh.

Stone tails *Nike* up the street and is not surprised to see him enter the *Bar des Remparts*. From a side window, Stone watches him step behind the counter and embrace the barman like a brother. Jean-Jacques hands an envelope to the kid, who exits and fights the wind back down the street to the post office. Stone follows him inside and takes a place in line behind him. The boy is a *beur*, a young North African born in France to immigrant parents. Wiry and tough, he has butted features, brown butter skin, a fashionably shaved head, and a layer of chips on his shoulder. Stone flicks off a couple of those chips with one hard tap.

The boy turns and betrays himself. His expression puffs and decomposes. He has made an error and is fully conscious of it, even as he backpedals, not in actual fact but in his regard, a retreat seeking shelter in a pretense, a decrying look that says: you may think you have seen me before but it's not true.

In actual fact, he ignores Stone, returning to a stiff forward focus.

"Not real smart to wear that coat in town."

No more pretending that Stone will just go away, *Nike* pivots 180 degrees and shows no sign of being daunted by Stone's size or age. "Man, do we know each other or something!"

"Sure we do."

The other customers stop their idle waiting to see what is going on. Their attention causes the kid to simmer and stress.

"Man, I don't know you, so quit breathing down my neck!"

"I'm watching the Sorbin farm, and you're one of the punks who intruded on his property last fall."

"Get lost, I've never seen you"—adding under his breath—"asshole American."

"No, but I saw you and your 'asshole American' coat . . . . Anyone know this person?"

The other customers, mostly old folk and young women, smell trouble and quickly seem to lose interest. Rather, they drop their curiosity out of self-interest.

"He's a Brouahoui," blabs the postal teller. "From La Roque. His sisters cross the river to houseclean, and his two brothers are always in trouble."

"Shut up, bitch."

"What did you call me, you . . ."

Stone knows the civil servant's political and personal views on Arabs, she being one of those gadabouts who tells you everything you never wanted to know and had no intention of asking. Stone shoves *Nike* out of line and out the door.

"Let go of me!"

"Who hired you, tough guy?"

"Go fuck yourself!"

"You keep talking to me like that and I'll march your ass down the hill to see Papa Brouahoui. Is that what you want?"

The kid settles down long enough for Stone to grab the letter out of his hand.

"You have no right!"

"No, and you had no right to trespass," he answers, keeping the boy at bay with a stiff-arm. "That makes us even."

The letter is addressed to Leon Sabag, poste restante 35 Lauris. Stone rips it open and reads the note inside aloud. *Sabag, I confirm I send some diggers to Sorbin farm on 23 December, ok? Jean-Jacques.*

A souped-up older Peugeot 205 with tinted windows, chrome muffler and blasting rap music, races up to the curb. Two toughs jump out and mount the post office steps.

"He stole J J's fucking letter!" *Nike* whines to his pals.

The two others are a little older than *Nike*, though neither of the new guys has reached a double decade of life. The stocky one in the leather jacket, Stone recognizes from the dig night, the one doing all the ordering. The other, a wiry, curly-haired punk in a trucker's zip-up sweater, could have been the third digger. Both wear double fisted rings; both are amateurs itching for trouble.

"What's your problem, *Amerloque?*" demands Leather.

"You guys are the ones with the problem. The barman sends nitwit here to mail a letter warning Sabag you're coming. So Sabag, who is paying the barman to pay you, is ready and waiting with his shotgun. Sabag's problem is that I'm breathing down his neck and shooting at clouds isn't going to do much this time. Maybe it's better if he hits one of you and pins the blame on me. You chumps following what I'm saying here?"

"This isn't your country, pale rider," barks Trucker. "Yankee go home, you get it."

Stone grins. "Fine, be chumps."

His challenge draws their scorn like puss. "We'll cut off your nuts, man," threatens *Nike*.

"You dumb fucks, don't you know you're in a bad film? You are dopes doing the dirty work for another dope being used by a bigger dope. There is no gold, so stay away from the Sorbin farm!"

"And I said I never heard of your farm!" spits *Nike*. "I wasn't there that night."

"Who said it happened at night?"

"Oh, man! Can't you ever shut your trap!" whines Leather to *Nike*.

Nike sinks so low in his error that he might have been slinking down the steps.

Stone can see it in their eyes, their perplexity, not just over the confounding details of the letter but also about how to place him. They can't figure him out. He has an authority over them, seems to come from the same milieu, and is way ahead of them in the bullying department.

Leather pauses too long before answering. "We got nothing to say to you."

The three pull back. Stone calls out:

"Tell Jean Jacques I said *bonjour*."

Trucker flips him the bird and they hop into their hot rod and wheel up the street.

WINTER

I

The longest night of the year is metal. Wind up, temperature plummeting, police blue heavens waxed and polished. The Grand Oak stands against the lighter firmament like a target-practice silhouette; the farmhouse, like a patch pasted on the horizon; the Luberon Mountains, like an irregularity scissored out of the glowing tapestry. Stone finishes scanning the perimeter and sits back down to bundle up in Osiris' woolen blanket. He pours himself another thermos-top of hot tea. Its steam and his seam of breath team and dissipate in the brittle air.

This watch marks his fourth straight night spent freezing outdoors, monitoring empty fields, miserable, alone, abandoned by all creatures. It is as if the whole world were hibernating and he, sole, were left above ground. As if Hades had been turned inside out and he had been stuck to the fringes of being, forever pestered by ghosts dropping like lint from the fabric of darkness.

But that's the way the Egyptian god wants it. Osiris' philosophy of life is: *The more things change, the more they stay the same.* The farmer expects the Brouhaoui brothers to return, even to accelerate their visits, and he wants Stone there when they do. He also means to punish Stone.

To Stone's surprise, Osiris attacked him over the letter incident. He accused the American of meddling. At first Stone thought he was kidding, but Osiris bristled at the suggestion. "Kidding? Do I look like I'm kidding? Because of you, every good-for-nothing in town is now sure there is gold!"

"You'll have to explain that one to me, Osiris."

"Sabag's stinginess is legendary. Those damn busybodies in town, they know Sabag would not spend money if there were no gold! You might as well have tacked up an open invitation to my lands!"

"Osiris, he *shot* at them. I didn't invent that. If he seriously believed in the gold, why would he shoot at the guys he hired to dig it up?"

"He's right, Osiris," said Maurice. "I was in the bar the other day. Folks are starting to think the gold story is hokum, that Sabag and Jean-Jacques made up the whole thing, map and all."

"Imbeciles, that's what they are!" grumped Osiris in bad faith.

"Stop taking people for idiots!" It was the first time that Stone had seen Maurice get angry.

"I take them for what they are! Sabag and Jean-Jacques would not know a Templar Knight from the temples in their heads."

Osiris was right on that score. Neither the weasel nor the skinhead could have devised such a hoax. "And La Suzon?"

"Her! That witch does not know how to write, much less write a map."

"What writing, Osiris? The map doesn't contain a word."

"The point," argued Maurice, "is that folks are dupable only to a point, Osiris, and maybe that point has come."

"*Foutaise*," said Osiris, bullshit. "The more things change, the more they stay the same. Those bastards are going to hit me again, harder, and I want *Roussel* in the west fields, waiting."

"All he's going to catch is a cold," griped Maurice.

"He'll catch what he catches!"

Stone doesn't hold a grudge, though he does consider it a sort of banishment. The fact is, his intention had always been to spend the nights leading up to Christmas in the fields. But the reason has nothing to do with discouraging gold hunters. His aim is to stop a poacher.

A month back, he paid a visit to Maurice, at the man's trailer home. The door was open and the filthy old geezer was reclining, reading on a bunk bed, essentially a rotted mattress full of holes stuffed with yellow newspaper. Stone stayed in the doorway, where the air was fresher. "Hope I'm not bothering you." The book in his blackened hands snapped shut, and the buggar bounced to a sitting position.

"Bother me!" Maurice sniggered, his shiftiness as obvious as his rotting teeth. "To be bothered, you have to be doing something, and everyone knows I'm the laziest son of a bitch that ever was born to these parts. Listen here, youngster, you know what makes time? Objects make time. Without them, we're timeless, that's what I say. And since I have no objects to speak of, I have no time to lose. In brief, my time is yours."

The dwelling had to be the foulest hole of a human habitation Stone had ever laid eyes on. Flattened discolored pizza cartons tiled the floor. Dishes fuzzy with mold overflowed a slime-blackened sink. Detritus covered the walls and windows. The tin house was enclosed in the gagging stench of rot and urine.

In contrast to the refuse, there were the old man's books. It was an impressive 40-year collection of mostly paperbacks, piles and piles of them, stacked above the filth like some pitifully noble statement about knowledge surmounting the deadening sloth of daily subsistence. The books also made a kind of barrier, keeping people at bay. Even had he wanted to, Stone would have had trouble entering the trailer, because of the wall of books.

"I was hoping you could give me some information about truffles."

"Truffles, you say? *Et beh*, that damn fungus has been the cause of more punched noses and snooty behavior than all the insults about one's mother and race and background combined."

"Just tell me how one goes about finding them."

"Why, to get a truffle, you need a tree. A sick or dying one. Usually it's oak, but it does not need to be. A sick hawthorn, birch, or elm tree will do. Don't need a dog or pig to sniff them out either. Just keep your eyes out for truffle flies."

"A fly?"

"Sure. A special one, a big flat brown one about the size of your fingernail—" holding out his unwashed thumb by comparison.

"Flies are like people, Maurice, they sleep at night."

"Well, what do you care about the night for?"

"That's when poachers poach, no?"

The peasant's eyes squint into a glare. "You didn't say anything about poaching, youngster. Are you changing your duties?"

"From my angle, it's all the same duty. When is the right season to start poaching truffles?"

"Soon as it gets cold. December's good. If you begin earlier, you dig up white truffles. Bitter, no taste. You must give a truffle time to turn black as this thumb. Right before Christmas is best, to catch the holiday market."

Catch the holiday market.

A snapping of branches carries across the frosty fields. Stone gets to a knee to locate the direction. The sound moves steadily down the ravine, a fact tending to eliminate an animal because the path is straight and resolute with a deliberate destination. He sees no light, but as the noise climbs the bank, he knows that any second now his hunch will pan out: that the Brouhaoui boys were only a diversion for the real business at hand, poaching.

Fifty yards from the Grand Oak, Sabag's skinny silhouette moves against the bright sky, a shovel handle growing out of his neck, a basket extending from his right arm. He is alone, moving like a man on borrowed legs, lumbering in rickety motions along the lip of the moonlit ravine. Stone grabs his foot-long fireman's flashlight. He also turns on a pocket tape recorder.

The clashing of a shovel against hard earth becomes louder. Just ahead, the weasel stoops, hacking furiously at the roots of a birch tree. Sabag is wearing a pancake cap, the kind Stone recalls men wearing at the dog track, and yellow suspenders on the outside of his coat, pulling up his britches in an unnatural way and giving him the puffy, disjointed look of a golfer from a ghetto. The fool did not even take the time to change his city shoes, those with the plastic shine.

Stone aims the flashlight and flips the switch. The perimeter goes white. Sabag is so startled he loses his grip on the shovel and drops it on his foot, which sets him dancing and cursing. The man scrambles away from the small ditch he's created. Then, it's as if he were out for a stroll. "Not warm out tonight, is it?"

"What are you digging for?"

"Well, you caught me redder than a tick. I guess I let this damn gold story go to my head."

"Looks to me like you're after roots."

"Roots? Ha!" Gripping his own gob, streaking more grime with his filthy fingers, Sabag makes a sickened snicker. "What a thought, roots!"

"No doubt you were planning on putting the gold in that little picnic basket of yours."

"True, one never knows what one can find out here. Rabbits, dormice. There's some who say the Romans ate dormice with almonds and treacle and swore by it."

"The dormice are in hibernation, Sabag. But some say if you dig in the right place, the gold is black."

"I would not know about that, monsieur."

"Stealing truffles is against the law, man, your mother must have taught you that."

"As you don't see any, I haven't broke no law."

Stone grabs him by the coat and is surprised at how light he is. He lifts him with one hand. "Allow me to repeat the question. What exactly were you digging for in that ditch?"

"Truffles! *Ca va*! They would only go to rot anyway. Sorbin does not care, shit! Otherwise, he'd be here himself. Now, you can't prove nothing, so let go of me!"

Stone shoves him back on the seat of his pants. "I can prove plenty."

He turns off the tape recorder in his pocket, rewinds and plays it back. *Truffles! Ca va! They'd only go to rot anyway* . . . . Click. Sabag, still seated, makes a squirming retreat with his elbows while making a pretense of a threat. "I would not play that for nobody if I was you."

"Are you threatening me?" Stone comes at him. The coward cowers. "Don't touch me!"

"I'd better not catch you ferreting around here again, or this recording goes to the police. Now, get the hell out of here."

Sabag skedaddles back into the wood, obviously unaware that private tape recordings are about as admissible in a court of law as a barking dog. But it's only a matter of time before his mother or some other edifies him. In the meantime, he won't be selling Sorbin truffles at the open-air market in Apt this Christmas.

II

Christmas morning, Dora gambols into the yard, followed by her master toting a pail of metal balls and an ornery attitude. "I want to play *pétanque*. Who's interested? You, the Amerloque, if you can't play the number one pastime in Provence, you don't belong here."

Stone has seen *pétanque* played in the village and knows that the game is as much an attitude as a sport. Boundless, refereeless, and with all the fairplay of a character assassination, the game consists of bashing each other by proxy with steel balls that could crush a skull. The crack of metal on metal is as overt an affront to the victim as a literal slap in the face. It is both horseshoes and hand-grenades, a working argument often reduced to millimeters measured with a stick, thumbnail or plane tree leaf. Disagreements become debates leading to fisticuffs and family curses over distances no greater than the width of a nose hair.

Beginner's luck, Stone bowls to within a quarter of an inch of the jack. But Maurice has a wickedly good shot. Feet together, knees bent, the old man flicks his wrist and sends two pounds of steel smashing Stone's ball into the fruit grove.

"I must admit, it gives me great pleasure to deprive youngster here of points," says Maurice to Osiris. "*Fucking Fanny*, as it were." Maurice is as malicious as he is precise. Either the game or the day is bringing out the old man's vicious side. By the end of the game, he has accomplished what he wanted, and Stone has zero points. Maurice leans back and hoots. "Go fuck Fanny in silence."

"Tell me, Maurice, is it my imagination or do you have something against me today?"

"Your watchman is getting testy, Osiris."

"All right, all right," intercedes Osiris. "He's American, he hasn't a clue what you are talking about." Osiris sets a fatherly hand on his shoulder. "Fucking Fanny means . . ."

"I know what the expression means." Stone looks at Maurice who continues to ignore him.

"Don't rightly recall where it comes from," carries on Osiris. "Maurice, you with all of your fool books, edify the boy."

Maurice puckers sourly. "The stationmaster of Eyguieres had a wife named Fanny."

"Eyguieres? You sure?" doubts Osiris.

"Of course, I'm sure! The station was made redundant after that."

"Lots of stations were made redundant. Lauris station is redundant."

"Lauris was not made redundant because the stationmaster was a cuckold, now was it? The men of Eyguieres liked to play boules, both *pétanque* and *à la longue* at the train station," continues Maurice, talking for Stone's benefit while addressing Osiris. "In the dirt beside the tracks, between arriving and departing trains. After time, it got back to the stationmaster that the real game was to come up empty. The `loser' was sneaking off to the station house and spending his penalty upstairs with the man's wife."

Osiris snickers. "You old fart, you probably knew Fanny yourself."

"Up yours," says Maurice with a rare burst of pique. "I read, and you could try it sometime yourself!" He picks up his pail of balls and storms from the yard.

Osiris laughs at the old hand's ill-humor. "Maurice does not care much for Christmas."

He is not the only one. Noel brings little peace and joy to Mathilde either. At the restaurant that afternoon, she is taciturn, humorless, shut-down. But her father, either heedless or inured to her behavior, barrels on anyway, raving about the cuisine while gulping down more and more wine.

"I have eaten here every 25th of December since my wife died. That makes what?" He turns to his daughter for help.

"Twelve years," she pouts.

"Twelve years already! *Putain*, it feels like 12 days."

"Watch your language, Papa. There are others eating here as well."

The owner, a pleasant woman in later life, clears their plates. "After 12 years, Osiris, you could take a chance and order something different than capon."

"I know what I like, so why change?" He passes his thick hands over his protuberant pot. "You just keep on castrating those cockerels, Alberte!" Christmas is undeniably his moment.

"Right then" says the woman, "and will it be the log cake as usual for dessert?"

Mathilde sounds the alarm. "No! Not another crumb for him!"

"Bring on the log cake!" roars Osiris, pouring down more red wine.

"Papa, you must watch what you eat and drink!"

"I don't care to watch, I want to eat and drink! It is Christmas, *oui* or *merde!*"

"You're not even tasting it. You're just stuffing your face."

"Oh quit pestering me!" Osiris pushes back his chair and wobbles to the toilet.

Stone himself is stuffed on a starter of foie gras and Sauterne wine, followed by a main course of lamb in prune sauce, dauphinois potatoes, fresh steamed string beans and a bottle of dark red Rasteau wine. As the waitress sets out the dessert plates, he snatches looks at Mathilde, seated to his right. In contrast to her weighty mood, her clothing chimes a light note of sexiness.

The ridge of a lace bra peaks above the décolleté of her dark sweater. Her legs are crossed under the table—he catches a glimpse around the draping table cloth of her left calf, a delicious shape filling a nylon and stiletto shoe. She has a dancer's port, long neck, shoulders back. In profile, her crenate breasts make meals in themselves. But he must stop treating her like a menu and get a grip.

"I was wondering if I could ask you a question about the farm."

She shakes her head in irritation. "Not if you expect an answer."

"Fair enough," he concedes, pursuing it anyway. "Actually, it's not really about the farm. It's about the Sabags, mother and son. You know they're blackmailing your father, don't you."

Her expression turns as dark as the wine. "Listen, if Papa is okay to be blackmailed into signing a lease, that's his business, not mine and not yours."

"But he wouldn't sign if it weren't for you."

She gives him a twisted look, tilting her head in an unattractive pose of disdain and cynicism. "Why are you pushing this."

"Believe it or not, he's concerned for you."

"I bet he is."

"You're his last remaining family, and he really believes that La Suzon can hex people."

"This is not about hex, it's about habit."

"Habit?"

"Papa's gotten used to the idea of having something to hide. If he's concerned about anything, it's seeing court-ordered bulldozers come in and excavate those cave paintings. That would put a wrinkle in his daily routine, wouldn't it?"

"That's pretty cynical."

She doesn't respond. Instead, she reaches for her father's suit jacket and starts fumbling around in one of the pockets. She pulls out his pack of cigarettes and lighter, making him wonder if she is confiscating them.

"I think he's afraid of more than bulldozers, Mathilde. He gave up on the farm because he thought La Suzon had something to do with your brother's death."

Her anger flares with the flame from the cigarette lighter. "He gave up on the farm all right, but it had nothing to do with my brother or La Suzon!"

"What was it then?"

She gets her cigarette lit before speaking. "Papa doesn't like being told what to do. That is, he doesn't like being in a position where someone can even suggest something. Since it's Christmas and one does not want to be *cynical*, let's call it pride. So, when farming got unionized and bureaucratic, Papa looked for excuses to get out. My brother died about the time the farming commissions in Brussels started telling farmers what, when and how much to plant and not plant. Rather than play the game and stay in business, Papa gave up. He's good at giving up on things. It's as simple as that. End of interrogation?" She rubs out the cigarette in her clean dessert plate and goes for a walk.

III

Winter in Provence—according to a host of opinions, from Osiris to Maurice, from the mail clerk and baker to the green grocer and village peacemaker—is not a season but a series of clumsy visits. A frosty gray uncle come knocking with a gold-digging new bride wearing a false spring; a perverse peddler selling sun one day and spewing icy chatter the next; a duplicitous witch coaxing an early end to nature's sleep; a dark hunter of tender buds and fragile subtended petals; a fugitive whose sweat turns to snow; a naked woman stretching bare white legs over an ice covered tarmac; a wild beast in dark leggings and head warmer digging for heat; a bleak sky seeking color; a fountain of sun at an all day barbecue.

The new year shines an imposter's smile, fresh, balmy, spring-like, as if winter had bypassed Provence all together. But the truth lies in little things, the absence of birds and insects, the absence of color on the plants.

The rose bushes on the side of the house have lost their last leaves. Osiris—working in a T-shirt—rakes them into a pile, which he claims he must burn. If not, worms will carry the infected leaves underground and the black-spot disease will appear on next spring's new shoots.

The farmer does not like the nice weather: "A January mild promises a winter of bile."

And one man's poison is another's meat. Stone enthusiastically takes to the open roads on his bicycle. It is Epiphany, and the weather could not be finer. Blue, balmy and no wind. A perfect moment to hit the Alpilles, as it's off-season, when tourist buses and cars are at a minimum.

He spins north, crossing the Durance into Mallemort, following the Canal de Provence through the shady village of Lamanon to the bustling bourg of Eyguieres, of "fucking Fanny" fame. Also, of gravedigger fame. "Once upon a time, there was this imbecile of a gravedigger," recounted Maurice. "First full-time gravedigger in France, I believe. At any rate, the fool took on airs and had no small consideration for himself. So, some villagers played a practical joke on him and sent him an official-looking letter stamped with the Order of Merit of Agriculture, though no such thing existed, announcing that he was to be awarded a medal, called *The Leek*, for his devotion to getting people back to the land! The idiot bought it lock, stock and barrel and eventually drove himself crazy waiting for the medal to arrive." As Stone watched Maurice and Osiris chuckle over the story, it dawned on him that there was something mirthful about Osiris' irascibility and something nasty behind Maurice's bonhomie.

Eyguieres marks the eastern gateway to a vast sun-baked, wind-swept plain of Olive orchards, stretching to the Alpilles, a ragged ridgeback of mountains rising 1500 feet and stretching 25 kilometers. The French writer Daudet called this thorny crown of conical peaks, "pretty trinkets on a shelf". The shelf is littered with the gutted ruins of medieval forts and crushed lookout towers.

The road winds steeply through a valley of red and white clay, the stuff that gave its name to bauxite and, ultimately, aluminum. At the top of the pass, ranging the highest ridge, rests the silicate bones of Les Baux de Provence, an austerely beautiful ruin, a tragic cataclysmic smashup of a castle destroyed not all at once but in petty increments throughout the Middle Ages. A catapult and battering ram still remain from the ultimate battle. The castle walls offer a sheer-drop panorama of southwestern Provence, of the fertile, olive and cypress-lined plains of Mouries, Maussane, Paradou, Arles, and on to the sea, to the Camargue, that endless marshland of wild white horses and pink flamingos.

The descent from Les Baux is fast and breezy. He presses the pedal, creating a dynamic that no longer needs him, wherein he becomes a bit player of his own making, listening to the hum of his wheels. A wheel, a circle, a cycle, a world turning, time passing. The power of movement, the ability to forget. The faster spin his wheels, the less the need to worry. He drops past the Roman ruins of The Antiquities and Glanum. The ancient world. Cold stone. Timeless. Gone. Continuing to St. Remy, then starting up the backside of the Alpilles, direction home.

A sight awaits him in the yard that jams his heart against his throat. Osiris lies slumped across his rock. Stone drops the bike and rushes over. He is semi-conscious and has difficulty opening his eyes. His face, drained of color, twitches furiously. His bluish lips tremble, but no words come. Jesus, the man is having a stroke.

"Osiris, I need to get you inside and call for help."

The idea of Stone's calling anyone jars Osiris out of his stupor. "I'm . . ." He struggles to say it. "I'm all right. It's nothing." He sits up, then tries to stand but only staggers. Stone grips him by the forearm, helps him to sit. Fear pours into Osiris' eyes, followed by a false bravado.

"It will pass. I'm just a little short-winded, that's all."

"Let me get you a drink."

"No. Go take your shower."

"Forget the shower. I'll call a doctor."

"Damn it, don't talk to me about any doctor! Go!"

He knows that Osiris is tired, worn out by the farm, fatigued by an enslaving devotion to order, and that each new year must bear a certain sense of futility. But right now the man needs to see a doctor. All Stone's arguments, however, bounce off the farmer like the distilled percussion of car music off a pedestrian, so Stone gives up and goes indoors. The phone is ringing.

"*Bonjour,* it's me." Mathilde's voice is huskier than usual, and a little defensive.

"You couldn't have picked a better time. Your dad has had some kind of attack."

"Did you call for help?"

"He refuses to see anyone."

"You must not listen to what he wants!" She starts coughing. The fit carries on for an embarrassing moment. "Look, this is not your problem. I'll take care of it. Don't worry. Do nothing until I get there." The phone clicks, leaving her final cough lingering on the line.

IV

If Osiris is surprised to see his daughter and the village doctor walk into the kitchen, he doesn't show it. Deadpan, he takes his elbows off the table, scratches his chin, and pushes up. "All right, come the both of you into the living room."

As Stone looks on from the hallway, Doctor Guillot, a thin, splotchy-cheek man of indeterminate age and lousy health himself, checks Osiris' chest, tests his blood pressure, taps on his back, sounds his throat and ears, and prescribes drugs to fortify his immuno-defenses. "It was a warning, Osiris; if you don't cut down on . . ."

"Sure sure, my smoking."

"Well, get some rest. That goes for you too, Mathilde." True, Mathilde isn't much to look at today, either. Her hair is oily and uncombed and the bags under her eyes are like makeup mistakes. "Your daughter has a bout of bronchitis."

"How would I know? She communicates nothing to me."

"I am my father's daughter," she bites back, grabbing the prescription and leaving the room.

On the way out she bumps into Stone. For an instant she stops, they exchange a glance, then she is gone.

By the time Stone finishes showering and dressing, she's back. The kitchen door bangs open, and her furious footfalls beat down the hall into the living room. "What are you doing, sitting in the dark?" she grills her father. Osiris stays mum. Stone walks in and flips on the light. She tosses the paper pharmacy bag in her father's lap. "Take your medicine this time."

"*Bof!* A waste of time, his prescriptions!"

This infuriates Mathilde. "Fine! You seem to know better than anyone! Croak, if that's what you want!"

"If I croak, I croak. We all go sooner or later."

She pshaws, all spit and spark, and exits with a hand-washing gesture and several dry coughs.

"Oo la la!" he hollers after her.

"Give her a break, Osiris. She obviously got out of a sick bed to come down here."

"A temper case is what she is."

"Oh, because you are not?"

Stone expects an argument, but none arrives. Drained by fatigue, the farmer curls up in the palm of his hands.

"You know the doctor's right about your smoking."

"Of course he's right. Plenty of people are right. What does it matter to be right? Being right gets one nowhere in this world."

"Why are you so bloody stubborn, man?"

"I am what I am. That's how I'm made."

Stone hasn't much to say in response. He knows what it feels like to want to abandon one's life, even the feeling of having a good reason to do so. But, he cannot know the sensation of being old and empty. Of subsisting beyond despair. Of going through the motions. Of reaching a point when the cycles cease to turn, when the seasons no longer rejuvenate, when the five senses no longer sense the miracle of nature's fresh return. How reason with a man incapable of producing new blood, a man allergic to the present and future?

By finding an appropriate medicine from the past. "Why don't you tell me about your childhood, Osiris."

"*Bof.*" His favorite expression of contempt.

Stone goes to the Music Hall and returns with the framed photograph of Marcel Sorbin. "Talk about him then. Tell me what was it like being the son of Marcel Sorbin?"

Osiris waves him off, refusing to look at the picture, as if all his shame were to be found there, boxed into a page-sized frame, contained within the critical regard of his own father. "You damn American, Why must you always try so hard? Can't you let things be?"

Stone won't be dissuaded. He holds out the picture until the farmer takes it. As he looks at the picture, a flame of respect flares in Osiris' resplendent regard. Stone pulls up an armchair. "I'll bet he was a hell of a guy."

Osiris' silence lasts a lifetime. Then, finally, he mumbles: "He was a god."

"Is that how folks around here saw your father? A great man?"

"Folks! Who the hell knows what folks see or think! Who cares? It's how I saw him!" Osiris, perhaps sensing he has let his emotions stray too far, becomes more circumspect. "My father was feared and respected. He had few friends or enemies, kept interactions on a professional level. From a social standpoint, he and my mother stayed to themselves."

"You said he was a good farmer."

"The best, *pardi*! He knew his work. And I'll tell you something else. He liked farming, and that makes all the difference because, the truth is, most farmers hate what they do and hate people because of it and would stew their own children if it would change things around."

"When did he take over here?"

"After the war. Fourteen-eighteen, I'm talking about. He was only 20 years old, but emotionally scarred by the horrors he lived through in the Verdun trenches for a year. Maman said it was fortunate that my grandfather's phlebitis forced him to turn over the running of the farm to Papa. The responsibility made my father turn his attention anyway from his nightmares."

"I can image the farm itself being good medicine," offers Stone.

"The healing went both ways. You see, Elysian Farm was"— Osiris advances his callused right hand and makes a gesture of mediocrity—"only a so-so operation before Papa took charge. And, the moment was propitious. The world was normal back then, when a farmer could work his fields and not be told by some distant bastard body of bureaucrats *not to farm!*"

"And what was he like as a father? Was he as hard as he looks in this photograph?"

"Harder!" Osiris' expression lightens. "No. With me, it was different. I was his only child. He went easy on me. No doubt, too easy."

Twelve frustrating years of trying to have a child. His mother had lost hope and wanted to adopt, but his father was too proud to allow it. A child of his own, or nothing. Marcel thought he could will a child into being, as he willed the crops to rise in the spring. And he was right. Osiris, named for the God of Renewal, was a late blossom of luck on an otherwise dry branch. He was born between the two world wars, coddled, pampered and spoiled.

"That is, not like kids are spoiled today, with gadgets and plastic food. I was the center of my parents' life. I got all of their attention. They made me feel like a little king. I was their renaissance, and they expected me to be a throwback to my great grandfather Osiris who got the farm going in the 19th century." Osiris' voice tapers off into some distant swamp of self-reproach. "Elysian Farm!" he huffs, visibly pained. "Good God, now there's an apt name! Time stood still here. When the second war broke out, I might as well have been on another planet. I never heard cannon fire, never saw anyone shot, never even laid eyes on an enemy soldier. While the rest of Europe was exploding under bombs, I was playing army in the fields and woods."

"You were lucky."

"I was *sheltered*. The closest I came to a real life experience was the day I got kidnapped."

"Kidnapped?"

"I was waiting outside the primary school for my father to come get me. Next thing I know, I'm being pushed into a barn. My kidnappers were older kids. Their intention was to hold me for ransom and then send the money to the French Resistance. Everyone knew that my father was rich but wasn't supporting the cause."

"He was a collaborator, your father?"

"No, he was not a collaborator! Don't be so Manichean. He was like a lot of Provençaux during the war. He did not trust anyone, not the Resistance, not Vichy, no one. He had fought his war and just wanted to be left alone."

"So what happened, I mean with your hostage takers?"

Osiris' apple cheeks puff with amusement. "No one wanted to be the messenger! They were scared of my father. Who wouldn't be! They even asked me to deliver my own ultimatum. In the end, *they* were begging *me* not to tell my father anything about the kidnapping. My father had a good hoot over that one."

"You told him?"

"*Pardi*. I did not want to catch the strap for being late! My mother convinced him to meet with some Resistance people and settle the problem. I suspect she gave them some money."

His mirth dies out, and his mood slips into dark regret. "I was even more sheltered after that. My father did such a good job of cutting me off from real life that when he died, I knew nothing about anything except farming, and even that knowledge was theoretical. Papa wasn't one to delegate, and neither am I, I confess."

"That was his fault, not yours."

"Who talks of fault? It was a question of competence. I was older than my own father when I took over. But I did not have his acumen, his savvy, his know how. I was navigating without a compass and quickly I was in over my head. I had no control over anything. And that led me into making a mistake I'll regret to my grave."

Stone waits. The explanation is so long in coming that he fears Osiris will not be able to get it out. But now that he has started his story, Osiris battles to tell it:

"I was one hundred times worse than those boys who kidnapped me. My son, you see, didn't want to be a farmer. So, I resorted to blackmail. I swore that he would never get a cent out of me if he did not agree to manage the farm. When he refused, I said . . . things. I called him . . . gutless. I accused him of being the assassin of his ancestors. What kind of father says such things to his son? What kind of a man am I?"

"Just a man."

Osiris lifts his eyes, begins talking to the ceiling, father to son. "I'm sorry! I was a cretin. Forgive me my rages, my meddling in your life!" Osiris' head falls into his own open hands clamping his face like a vise.

"Osiris, it doesn't do any good." But the man is in communion with the spirit, and Stone can save his breath.

"I forced you, I disgusted you with farming. If only I had gone easy! Then, you would be running the farm, giving me grandchildren to play with. Instead, I drove you away. *I* drove you into that car. *I* drove you to your . . . My god, how could I! How dare I!" Tears drip down his wrists and make dark spots in his lap.

Stone leaves for the kitchen. He makes a pot of coffee and carries the tray back to the living room where Osiris is still staring into space, his body listing like a doomed ship. Stone sets down the tray and pours him a cup.

"Get me a cigarette, would you?"

Stone fetches the pack of Gauloise on the kitchen buffet,

and the man's blue lighter. Osiris shakes one out, straightens himself and, with renewed dignity, lights up. "Give me a moment and I will start dinner."

"No, I'll make dinner. Osiris, where does your daughter fit into all of this?"

Wearily, he releases smoke through his nostrils, and his expression goes cloudy. "Mathilde? What are you talking about?"

"Why is she so resentful of you and the farm?"

"I have no idea what her problems are. She's a woman."

Stone won't be drawn into that debate. "Osiris, not having kids of my own, I can't begin to appreciate what a difficult balancing act it must be, I mean, you know, giving each kid equal time. Is it possible that you, I don't know, you neglected her somehow?"

"Don't be ridiculous." A bit of ash threatens to tumble from the end of his cigarette. Osiris shrugs off the insinuation, in the process dropping ash between his shoes. "My daughter never lacked attention."

"But she did come second to Jean Horace, no?"

"Mathilde, second?" Osiris looks at him as if he were cockamamie. "Does my daughter strike you as second best?"

"You tell me."

"I did not play favorites."

"Oh come on, Osiris! To this day, your bedroom is full of pictures of Jean Horace, but I'll be damn if I can find a single photo of Mathilde anywhere in the house."

"Of course you can't! Because she took them all!"

Stone is stunned. "Pardon?"

"You heard me. She cleaned me out. After her divorce, she stormed in here and took every last picture I had of her. Stole the lot. It was the last time she put a foot in here, until today."

"But why, Osiris? Why did she do that?"

"How the hell should I know? Go ask her."

"She's a tough nut to crack."

Osiris throws up his arms in petty triumph. "*Et voilà!* So forget it."

V

The Twelfth-Night cake season spans the month of January. Colorful *Gâteaux des Rois* come in two competing styles, the Provencal milk-bread brioche shaped like a Magi crown topped with jewel-like candied fruit, and the gilded, creamy, Parisian turnover. Stone doesn't know which one will make Osiris happy, so he buys both. In fact, neither does the trick of snapping Osiris out of the doldrums.

"You should have saved your money. I could not give a damn about either. I'm not hungry, and I'm not thirsty, so quit pestering me."

Stone, playing the temptation and recalcitrance game, sets the cakes and a pot of tea on a foldout table between the farmer and his fire, then feigns an interest in stoking the flames. After a while, Osiris sneaks a few bites of the Provencal pastry. "There, so that you won't have wasted your money. Now, take the rest to Maurice or to the trash bin."

Maurice prefers the flat and flaky Parisian version with its frangipani filling. He and Stone sit outside in the frigid weather, on concrete bricks upwind of the smelly trailer. They hold their paper plates and plastic cutlery on their knees. Maurice feels compelled to explain his choice.

"Do not get me wrong. It is not that I prefer the Parisian," he splutters, his breath visible in the chill air, his words vanishing a foot in front of his nose. "I'm a Provençal, proud and true. But it's the chewy stuff on top, you see. It is too tough for my broken teeth and lousy gums."

"I promise not to tell."

"Actually, what I like best is the wine."

Stone gets the hint and pours the old man another full goblet of sparkling wine, his third in as many minutes.

"Maurice, how can we get Osiris out of this funk of his?"

"Aw, forget it!" he jabbers, ejecting bits of cake. "Every new year he gets depressed. Goes with the season. Hang-dog in winter, sprightly in spring. He will snap out of it."

"I'm not so sure."

"You're young. What would you know of depression?"

Stone grunts and looks around. Wispy ribbons of cloud lint the colorless sky. Under a stewed sun, the hard-packed hillsides are a dull copper and verdigris. In the distance, a part of the farmhouse, shuttered and gray, stands between leafless branches.

"He talks to his dead son more and more. Worse, he continues to ignore his one living relative. He hasn't met his daughter in town all month."

The old bum bows before "this unfortunate yet unavoidable fatality", and tosses down the rest of his drink. He does not wait to be served again, but tops his own goblet, saying: "It's temporary, it will pass, as everything does, eventually."

"His condition doesn't have to be a destiny, Maurice. He thinks it does, but it doesn't. This *more-things-change-more-they-stay-the same* idea, everyone around here accepts it like the Gospel. But nothing stays the same. Not even nature. The seasons come and go but are never the same. If they were, there would be no magic."

"You just think that way because you're young and full of sass."

"No, I think that way because I've changed."

"Well, good for you," he teases, rightly setting Stone back in his place.

Stone grins and reaches for the bottle. "Level with me, Maurice. What's up with Osiris and Mathilde?" He gives Maurice's goblet another dose while verifying that the man is not preparing to jump down his throat. "Why is their relationship so sour?" To Stone's relief, Maurice takes the question in stride.

"Just father-daughter nonsense, that's all."

"I'd call it a rift."

Maurice does not take the bait, so Stone finds another approach.

"I guess you've known Mathilde Sorbin all her life."

The statement elicits a hoot from the peasant. "I guess you could say that! I've been here longer than she has."

"What was she like as a child?"

"A right hellion, she was. Kept everyone running sunup to sundown. That child's batteries never wore down. Osiris called her a *boulegon*—that's Provencal for someone who cannot sit still an instant. Her favorite pastime was getting into things that did not belong to her. Keys, jewelry, pens, books, clothing, wallets. Folks found their lost items stuffed away in the damnedest places. Inside old boots, under furniture, in teacups. Drove her *maman* crazy."

"You mean she was a kleptomaniac?"

"Don't be so literal, youngster. We're talking about a child here. She was mischievous, that's all. She just wanted to possess what belonged to them others of her family, maybe to feel more a part of the goings-on."

"Insecurity, maybe?"

"I'm no psychologist. Maybe it was insecurity. Maybe simple curiosity. Maybe both. I do know that she liked to see how things were put together. She ended up breaking enough objects to suit 30 childhoods! But I'll give her this; she could take apart any tool in Osiris' garage before she was five. Never seen anything like it. By the time she started school, she could also put it back together. Not that she was much interested in re-assembling anything. Brother, the fights they used to have, her and Osiris! One could hear the clacking across the valley!" he whistles, snapping his wrist. "Osiris didn't care for having his affairs messed with, and his daughter had a chip on her shoulder the size of the Luberon. She would not back down for anyone. Still won't."

"You say she liked to get into his tools. Did she also like to help farm, back then?"

"*Pardi!* She loved it. Loved to ride on the tractor and drive it and pick the crops and fill the baskets and panniers."

"Hard to believe, today."

"Like you said, youngster, people change."

"Well, speaking of change, when did it happen, I mean Mathilde going from loving the farm to hating it."

The old man's squint turns critical. "How do you want me to know that?"

"For example, was it before or after architecture school?"

"She got sullen long before she left for Paris."

"But after her brother died, I take it."

"I suppose so."

"Did it ever cross Osiris' mind that Mathilde was maybe the natural choice to succeed him?"

"He had his son."

"I mean after his accident."

"By then it was too late."

"Why too late?"

"That disaster changed the whole deck of cards for everyone, youngster. Nothing was the same after that boy's death. What are you driving at, anyway?"

"I'm trying to understand how she could go from loving to hating the farm. Her options were pretty much the same before and after the accident. I mean, if she was already playing second fiddle to her brother while he was alive."

Through his cataracts and stupor, Maurice scrutinizes him as he might a peculiar hunk of earwax. "Who said she was second fiddle before his accident?"

"It's so obvious, it pokes your eyes out."

"Then get yourself some bifocals, youngster. Osiris had his favorite all right. But it was not the boy."

Stone catches his own mouth agape and closes it.

The geezer nods his half-besotted whiskered head. "Like I said, she had him wrapped around her little finger. She was sharp as a tack, and Osiris was nuts about her. Daughters can be a sweet poison for some fathers," he philosophizes, looking achy with nostalgia. "Sure the girl drove him crazy, but I tell you he could not get enough of her company. Osiris could stare at that little girl like he might a chimney fire. Sat on that stone of his and watched her for hours, mesmerized by her and her little make-believe world. Aw, put yourself in his shoes. Matty Sorbin was born with the knowing."

"What do you mean, the knowing?"

"Knowing how to pull men along by their nostrils. Young as four-years-old, why, folks remarked on Mathilde's talent in that regard. In the way she moved and the way she had of looking a man up and down. And her being cute as any button, and her soft little ramp of a nose and long curls nobody could get a comb through and all that light coming out of her face and the fact she was a perfect imp. I tell you, that child could get away with murder! And it didn't help at all that folks couldn't stop fawning over her and her *maman* all the time going shush lest you ruin her head with such talk. And, let me tell you, her *maman* was right! Her head got ruined. Osiris was the principle cause. I remember one time he started scolding her like there was no tomorrow. But his eyes were shut tight as zippers. And I said to him, 'Osiris, how can you scold your daughter with your eyes closed?' And he says to me, 'Maurice, I look at her, she looks back with those big biscuit eyes, and I end up hugging the kid. I can't do anything else. I feel her little heart pounding against mine, and I swear, I'm not holding her, she's holding me—in the palm of her little hand!'"

Stone catches Maurice's shifty gaze, clouded now with booze. Can he take the old man seriously? The relationship that Maurice describes resembles nothing that he had assumed to be the foundation of Osiris and Mathilde's mutual antagonism. It's like digging for gold and finding cave paintings instead.

As if sensing Stone's doubts, Maurice taps his veined temple and boasts: "I still have it all up here. Stocked and catalogued." He tosses back the rest of his goblet and sinks his gums into a wedge of cake. He clamps down on something hard and spits a little ceramic Magi king into his hand. "Bingo! Got the subject. That makes me king."

Woozily, Maurice picks up the gilded paper crown sold with every cake and bestows it crookedly on his own, knotted head. "Bring on the gold, frankincense and myrrh!"

"If what you say is true, why isn't she here today, seeing to the farm?"

To Stone's disappointment, Maurice is not yet *that* drunk. He rolls his heavily lined face into a tight pucker and shrugs his shoulders through his ears. "Little children, little problems; big children, big problems. It's no one else's concern."

Stone feels his anger starting to rise. "Your boss' health ought to be something of a concern to you."

Maurice ignores the comment. With a grunt and wobble, he pushes himself off the brick; he possesses an amazing jauntiness for an 80-year-old drunkard. "My bones are chilling, it's time for me to go lie down beside my dog to get warm."

"Maurice."

"Youngster, she was everyone's favorite and everyone was wrapped around her finger, me included, and that's why Osiris and all the rest of us have always felt some guilt vis-à-vis the boy, because he was often forgotten and neglected in all the excitement over the girl. But I'll tell you something that I got no business saying but which I'll say anyway because I like you and because I'm sauced. It's like these here *gâteaux des Rois*. The cake you eat isn't always the one you prefer. Osiris never gave Mathilde the reins around here because he never trusted her."

"Why wouldn't he trust her?"

"I told you why. Because she's always been good at taking things apart, with no interest in putting them back together again, that's why."

VI

High in the leafless apple tree pruning, he spots the little girl and the pig walking together in the west field. They look painted against the frozen landscape. He snips another branch, gives another glance at the field, but the girl and swine have disappeared. The earth seems to have swallowed them whole.

Stone doesn't give it another thought, until the girl's voice, distant, ghostly, climbs the tree like a chill. He looks down, expecting to see her standing at the base of the trunk. There is no sign of the girl.

He scrutinizes the orchard and beyond, without sighting her. He can still hear her talking as if she were inside the tree. He can hear the pig, too, its raucous snorts, muted and tubular, drifting up like thought borne over a breeze.

Stone climbs down the ladder and sets his pruning shears against the trunk. The sleeping boughs are balled with the frozen brown rot of forgotten fruit. A fine February frost whitens the orchard. The soil is packed and crunches under boot. The air is as brittle as praline.

The mystery intensifies at the frozen brook that separates the apple and pear orchards, where the babble is loudest. He cracks the thin ice and sets an ear to the spring. By the sound of it, the child is locked in verbal conflict with some underworld god, an innocent Persephone pleading with her kidnapping uncle to see her mother again and thus end nature's misery and wrath.

Sonia, he calls into the spring, Sonia! The dialogue stops. He feels a cold breath on the back of his neck. He whips around, and a yell escapes him. Staring at him is another child, the boy who used to be Peter Terrell, bald, eyebrowless, his lips blue, his eyes sallow. His guts are hanging out, shot out. Stone makes a move, but the image dissolves. He drops to his knees and buries his head in his arms.

He stands and berates himself. He was a fool to think that he was on the way to being cured. The farm is not impermeable to what haunts him. Nothing can protect him. Just a lot of delusion, that's what! Set up like a sap by his own pride. And here he is criticizing Osiris for his overbearing pride!

Later in the morning, the girl is kneeling in a weak pool of sunlight in a meadow, chattering away while raking a pink doll's comb across the sitting pig's fat-furrowed head. Neither is fazed by the sharp retort of gunfire from somewhere in the hills. "Sonia, this lesson stinks. Look at it! That's not the way to make a gee, you nasty little pest! Get up and do it again! You, Benoit, stop bothering her. What hair! What writing habits and indiscipline. Elody has a Barbie, she's so lucky. Erwan peed through his pants and made a puddle." She drapes an arm over the animal as she might a very large girlfriend. "That's better, *très bien*, Sonia. You see that you can do it."

The girl cannot be still, but needs to speak as another child might need to play, to color, to breathe, to escape the crushing silence. Suddenly, her voice goes from schoolmarmish to menacing. "That's three hundred batons, Betty, 30 million centimes lost!" She clips plastic earrings onto the pig's ears. "I say break his neck. Careful where you step. We will make that fucking foreigner pay. They are not cartoon pictures, Betty. They go, we all go. Hurt him, I say. It's the only way to make the *Amerloque* go home. Let them prove it's us who hurt him."

Stone calls out her name. Girl and pig look around as one. The animal clambers to its hooves and commences an earth-bashing tantrum. Stone stays where he is, regretting having left the clippers beside the tree. The girl steadies her animal and tosses him a quick hard look before dropping her regard. "What do *you* want?"

"To say hello. I haven't seen you in a while."

"You stay where you are!"

"All right. But can you come here for a minute?"

She makes her companion sit and, peeved, insecure and not sure what to make of him, starts to approach. But she stops a yard from him and gives him the cold shoulder.

"Don't you remember me?" he asks.

She ties her hands behind her back and sways with indecision.

"I'm the guy you demolished at Lion King cards."

"I remember," she grumbles, her attention placed on the ground in front of her. "I'm not a baby."

He smiles and takes a step towards her. She takes one back. He insists and bends and kisses her forehead. She smells unwashed. She ventures a peek at him.

"What's the matter, frog got your tongue? Give it back or I'll steal your nose!"

"You can't steal my nose."

"And why not?"

"Then I got nothing to blow."

"Hm, never thought of that. And what if I stole an ear?"

She cups her ears tightly.

"In that case I think I'd better settle for your . . . belly button!"

He grabs and tickles her, and her wild, birdlike glee hits all corners of the property. The cheap coat on her back is losing its stitching and cannot possibly protect her from the chill and underneath she wears a raw T-shirt, too small at that, exposing her little belly. He sets her down, and she goes back to being mad.

"I don't want to talk to you no more."

"What did I do?"

"Only killed Father Christmas, that's all!"

"I did what?"

"You took our truffle money and I didn't get a Barbie for Christmas."

"Sonia, Father Christmas is alive and well, and as a matter of fact he left a surprise for you."

"For me?"

"That's right. Can you come back here this afternoon?"

"Oh *oui*!"

"But first, I want you to tell me your secret. Were you in the tunnel this morning? You know, the tunnel that runs under the orchard?"

She nods.

"Can you show it to me?"

She shakes her curls. "I can't never."

"Says who?"

She purses her lips shut.

"No problem, Sonia. You shall still have your surprise."

Her dull demeanor cracks a shimmer.

VII

The day is duck-cold out, as Osiris would say. Stone's riding legs are not what they were only a few weeks ago. Stiff. Achy. Powerless. The drop in temperature has little to do with it. This bike ride is his first in almost a month. Osiris has been so tired and depressed of late, that Stone hasn't had the heart to leave him alone.

He peddles down the highway, 15 kilometers of flat, smooth country track separating Cadenet and Pertuis. Under normal circumstances it is the sort of road he avoids. Not because it isn't scenic. On the contrary, the D973 is a pretty strip running under spanning plane trees, with lush properties and farms on both sides of the road. But the D973 is murderous, a long narrow track of blind curves where every driver is convinced of his own racing superiority and immortality, and oblivious to solid white lines and bikers. Still, it is the shortest line between two places. Stone wants to get to the store and back before Osiris has a chance to miss him.

The mega store in Pertuis sells everything from toys to turnips. The kid rack offers five different kinds of Barbie doll: blondes and brunettes, Barbies in bathing suits, Barbies in a ball gowns, princess Barbies, disco Barbies and even spark-producing Barbies. All with the trademark plastic smile, pointed bosom and flawless legs. He thinks of Penelope, of her plastic, and of the myths about dolls and real women broken daily.

On the ride back, he is so concerned about cars that he takes the dark form paralleling him along the right shoulder, for a dog. He smells it before he sees it, a raw pungency that only a large swine can produce. The boar scampers off the bank and cuts across his path, a shaggy hog some 300 pounds and bigger than him and his bike put together. Stone brakes, tries to swerve, but collides with its coarse rump.

A second boar pops up on the same shoulder. At that instant, an eight-wheel truck rounds the bend and bears down on them. The first boar falters, unable to get its hooves going on the slick road. The second makes a late charge for the opposite bank. The truck driver brakes too hard, throwing his vehicle into a skid, crossing the median, heading for Stone. The lead boar digs in, sacrificing itself so that its progeny might live, and meets the engine head on. The hellish squealing collision of flesh, bone and metal lifts the truck's hood, explodes its radiator in a geyser of steamy vapor, and propels the boar back at Stone, who leaps out of the way.

The truck jacks and screeches to a stop diagonally in the road. Traffic on both sides slows and finally coagulates.

Stone sets down Barbie and bike, and the truck driver leaps out of his cabin and comes running over to where the animal lies on its side, heaving, bleeding from its nostrils. Its left fang is broken. As the habitual impatient beeping starts, the boar makes a shuddering last grunt and dies. The second animal turns and runs, joining a clan of 8 or 9 other boars heading across farmland towards the river. The trucker finishes inspecting the dead beast and offers to split the carcass 50-50 if Stone will help him hoist it into his truck bed. "A shame to let it go to rot."

Sunset is a drop of blood in a glass of gray milk darkening. Stone pulls into the farm, leaves his bike in the barn, and hurries to the west field. He is relieved to find Sonia still waiting for him, by the tree, shivering in her thin clothing and hugging the pig as much for warmth as affection. When she sees what he has for her, she throws herself into his arms. He tells her to hurry home and get warm. Halfway across the field she calls back: "The tunnel's over there—" pointing north into the lip of trees rimming the old vineyard—"where there are some rocks to move. Monsieur, watch out because they don't like you. They said they are going to do something bad to you."

Back at the barn, he locks his bike properly against the old wagon. When he comes back out, night has fallen. It has been a close call, getting back to the farm without a light.

A strong, gamy smell of stewing meat invests the kitchen. Osiris is standing at the stove, stirring a simmering saucepan. He jumps all over Stone. "Do you see the hour! Where have you been!"

"I went shopping in Pertuis."

"Pertuis!"

"Look, I'm sorry. I didn't mean to make you worry. I got

held up." Good sense tells him to shut up about the boar and the doll.

"All right, the important thing is that you are back. Go clean up for dinner."

"What are we having?"

"Pig's feet."

In the bathroom, Stone grabs a bar of Marseille soap and starts scrubbing his hands and arms. So, he's a target. How will they attack him? He's no easy set-up, has no regular schedules, doesn't frequent any particular place in the village. He uses all three bakeries in town, on the rare occasions when Osiris doesn't get the bread himself.

About the only thing he does on a regular basis is bike. But even this indulgence doesn't give an attacker much around which to organize an ambush. He has no set riding hour, can take off at a whim, early or late morning, during lunch, mid-afternoon, even early evening. He rarely follows the same itinerary or, for that matter, sets out in the same direction. It's not that he has been overly cautious, just that the area is so rich in roads that any one of the four cardinal points offers a great ride.

To get to him, La Suzon and Sabag will probably need to lure him into a trap. As he rinses his face, he imagines a *Godfather*-type scenario. They nab Osiris, telephone Stone, tell him to come quickly to town because Osiris has had an attack. They're waiting for him at Fucking Fanny's railway crossing. He's trapped. Guys toting 30's-style Tommy guns leap out of vintage Renaults and gun him to pieces. Goodnight, Sonny Stone.

Blindly, he grabs a towel, presses his eyes dry, opens them, and jumps. Osiris is standing behind him, framed in the bathroom mirror.

"Jesus, Osiris, you scared me! How long have you been standing there? What is it?" Osiris' bloodless face packs a shot of fright and rage. "What is that stink you have brought into my house?"

"Stink?"

"I can smell it, the stench of death. I may have bad ears but my nose still works. Why is blood on your sleeve? Did you have an accident? Tell me, damn you!"

"Okay, settle down. I told you I got held up."

Stone tells his story, trying to put a light spin on it. "The crazy truck driver wanted to carve it up right there!" But he sees that Osiris is anything but amused.

"Things happen for a reason, don't you see?"

"What are you talking about, Osiris?"

"You know perfectly well what I'm talking about! I warned you not to let La Suzon touch you. She's put a hex on you. That boar was meant to kill you."

"Oh, for Pete's sake, Osiris, the boar was just there. The truck was just there. I was just there. Am I dead?"

"Tomorrow I take them the new lease!"

"Osiris . . . ."

"No! You won't stop me! I will not have another death on my conscience!" His face reddens, his chest grips, his breathing grows dense. Stone sees the adult boar's last breath shorn like a ribbon and ballooning away from its cold carcass.

"Osiris!" He latches out and catches the man before he can fall.

"Take me to a chair."

"You must try to calm down, man." Stone helps him back to the kitchen and seats him. He brings him a glass of water.

"It's too much," he moans. "All of it is too much for one man."

"All right, Osiris, all right," Stone gasps, fright having stolen his wind. "Whatever you want. Just take it easy."

VIII

Dawn breaks across the hills. The dew point rises, whitening the roadsides and fields. First light is colder than the darkness that preceded it, and Stone sinks his chin farther into the collar of his riding jacket.

He rolls into the village as the bells are striking. The bakery's wall clock confirms the hour, seven. He orders two croissants and *pains aux chocolats*. Mathilde Sorbin's residence is around the corner, castle wall, left. He enters a narrow medieval street like a rift separating the towering walls, more a cavity than a passageway, as if hollowed out of one giant block of granite, a damp root through a dark tooth. *Rue Esquiche Coude*. Scratch Elbow Street.

The heavy oak door that bears her name is hundreds of years old. In contrast, its timer light and intercom system still have their purchase stickers. He gets the blood flowing into his numb fingertips long enough to be able to press the doorbell.

Seven o'clock on a Sunday morning is a tad early to be waking her up to talk about a subject that will send her shooting through her roof tiles. Does he really want to be doing this? And for whom is he doing it? Mathilde doesn't care about the farm. Osiris is prepared to do anything to avoid confronting the Sabags. So, that leaves just one person who cares—himself. But why? Why should he care? Why is he so determined to dig himself further into this imbroglio?

Her static sleepy reply: "*Oui*, who's there?"

"Mathilde, it's me, Russell Stone."

The door unlatches. He pushes it open and leaves the street to enter a garden courtyard. The area is still dark enough for the motion-sensors to work, and floodlights pop on. A charming stage springs to view, of stone walkways, a horse chestnut tree minus its leaves, a denuded arbor of climbing roses, a sober stone fountain, and vine-covered walls. Across the court, in an open doorway, she is waiting, gripping her night robe tight to her neck. He leans his bike against the fountain.

"Come in quickly. It's not warm," she calls.

Yawning, she lets him into the hall. Her hair is an electric mess. Pillow marks are still stamped into her left cheek. "Would you like some coffee?"

"I could do with a little coffee, yes."

The kitchen is off the hallway. She opens the shutters, which give onto her courtyard. Untied, her robe comes apart. Underneath, she is wearing button-up pajamas. He can smell her warmth. He pulls up a chair. "I should have called."

"No, thank goodness, that would have been worse!"

"Yes, I see what you mean. I'm sorry I woke you, but this couldn't wait."

She says nothing. As the coffee percolates, she prepares the cups and saucers. "Have you eaten? I don't have much. Maybe some *biscottes* and jam."

"I brought you some things." He unzips his knapsack and removes the bakery bag.

She pours the coffee and they sit in the kitchen, chewing, sipping, and watching the courtyard turn to day. His nerve and the right timing converge finally.

"Last night, your father had another malaise." He studies her expression. Curiously, there is not much of one. "That is, I set it off. I went to get a gift for the Sabag child and, well, I know you don't want to hear this."

"Go on."

He recounts the story of the tunnel, the girl's confirmation of its existence, her warning to him, and the incident with the boar. "Now your father is sure I'm next on the hex list."

She stops fingering the fine flakes of pastry on the table into a mini heap and shakes her head. "I can't blame him. You really had no business doing that."

"I agree. I got carried away. But, well, I do feel sorry for the child."

She is conciliatory. "Look, as concerns Papa, don't worry about it. He is always troubled over something. If he has nothing to worry about, he invents it."

"That's not all. He intends to sign a new lease to the Sabags, effective today." He waits for her to say something, but she doesn't. She lifts her mug, sips, shrugs. "I doubt it, but if he does, *c'est comme ça*, and there's nothing anyone can do about it."

"You might be able to." She sits back and chooses to ignore

the suggestion, so he gives it another go. "You can stop him, Mathilde. If you don't, well, after the new lease, the sky's the limit. In 10 years' time, La Suzon will probably be living in your family home."

She stares at him, seemingly without anger, or even much criticism, for that matter.

"Tell me, Russell. What brought you to France?"

The question takes him off guard. "Why do you ask?"

"Well, you must know that you're a mystery to everyone, Papa included. He says you never talk about your life. Not even the simplest pleasure or pain"—she pauses, before lowering the boom. "On the other hand, you are bound and determined to stick your nose in other people's affairs."

The comment stabs him. Her beauty itself is a kind of dagger.

He gives her a long hard look. He knows his anger shows. "I guess I'm a right-and-wrong kind of guy."

"Come on, you woke me out of a sound sleep, so the least you can do is give me a better answer than that."

"Give me a better question to answer."

"All right. Why do you care so much about what my father does? Why are you investing so much of your time and feelings in a stranger's life?"

"I don't consider your father a stranger anymore."

"What, he's your friend now?"

"Is that so strange?"

"Papa is the friend of nobody. He's a loner, an only child become a lonely man, a recluse. He has never had a friend and would not know what friendship was if it fell off a tree and hit him on the head."

"It doesn't matter. He's a dignified person who deserves better."

Angrily, she pushes back her chair and goes to the window and stands there a moment, facing out. He can see that she's trembling; her back expands with heavy inhalation.

"Are you all right?"

She turns and glares at him. "Look, talk to me about pride, ego, naiveté, rage, monomania, even will and hope, but not about dignity, okay! Speak to me of catfights, and people fights in the dead of summer, and of bloodsucking mosquitoes. Speak of jealousy, for example, or blind stupidity or simple obtuseness. Speak of a refusal to listen or see, or a willingness to deny the most commonsensical messages of one's own nature. But don't deliver any bullshit myths to me about dignity. Everywhere you point and say, look, there it is, I will show you something else stumping for dignity. I will show you crookedness, self-aggrandizement, ego, stubborn pride, frustration, even a death wish. Papa is not about dignity. It's not him."

He nods. "Are you done?"

"Of course I'm not done. Not until you tell me why you are doing the things you do."

"Okay, this is my deal. I'll tell you everything you want to know about me if, and only IF, you answer *my* questions about *you*."

She sits back down, reaches for the coffee pot and refills his cup and her own. "Fine. Start your questions, Monsieur Le Watchman."

"Let's start by your not calling me that anymore."

"Why? I thought that's what you did, the way you described yourself the first day we met. I'm not a detective, I'm a *watchman*."

"You're talented at putting people on the defensive, aren't you?"

"Sorry. Personal defect. This little siren goes off in my head when I hear hypocrisy."

"Right. Your father is a slave to habit, and your thing is hypocrisy sirens. Charming."

"I thought you had some questions." She gives him that black unyielding look of hers, provoking him, and, yes, he feels provoked, feels like squashing her face into the croissants. Instead, he picks up his paper napkin and wipes his mouth.

"Tell me who your father was going to give the farm to."

An unwanted smile almost breaks loose, but she reins it in. "The farm was to have been mine."

"After Jean Horace's accident?"

"No, before. Papa and I spoke about it often and we both agreed it was the best decision."

"But your father told me that he tried to blackmail your brother into running the farm."

She crosses her arms and settles her nerves. "That's the way he wants to remember it. He has to believe he was responsible for my brother's accident. To give it some sense. If it makes sense, he can control it. Then, he can flog himself every moment of his existence."

"You're hard on him."

"I'm hard on *him*, am I? Suppose for a moment that I'm telling you the truth. How hard, then, has he been on *me!*" Her hands grip the table as if to keep from flying off into pain. Her eyes twitch. "The day after we buried my brother, Papa was already at work, creating his myths. The farm had never been meant for me, oh no! A farm, run by a girl? Never! *You misunderstood,* cherie, *the farm was Jean Horace's operation for the taking! Alas,* ma cherie, *now, it is for nobody!*" She takes a deep breath, lets it out slowly; he can see her tongue, and is suddenly aware of his own, as if it could of its own accord have imaginings, longings for what his eyes have seen.

"I didn't want to upset him further. I convinced myself that he was delirious with grief; no parent should have to bury his child. Eventually he would come round to seeing what was the right thing to do for the farm."

"But he didn't."

She shakes her head. "As time passed, he just got more settled into his myth. He fashioned a fiction into a reality and turned my brother into something he never was. There had never been any question of Jean's sticking around to run the farm."

"Jean Horace didn't want it?"

"Papa did not want him to have it! It would have killed him to say so, but he knew that Jean was too much like him, wasn't cut out for it, didn't have the toughness or feel for farming. My brother knew the score. But things have never been clear and open in the Sorbin household. No one talks, no one opens his heart. Everything must be kept buried until it rots. But nothing on the farm stays buried. The land just pushes it back up to the surface. When Jean died, Papa couldn't handle all that truth being pushed back up. It was easier to make up stories than to face the truth."

Her lower lip tucks, she looks askance, tears welling. When the overflow starts down her cheeks, she seeks solace in the direction of the kitchen cabinets.

"Mathilde?"

She whips around. "You asked me why I don't care about the farm. Well, this is your answer. My farm was condemned when my brother died. It was given posthumously to my brother. Elysian Farm, Mr. Involvement, is for the dead." She grabs a paper napkin from a rack on the counter and blows her nose. Calmer, she glances at him, now a little abashed, her eyes sparkling. "It was a terrible disillusionment."

She sits back down and, having nothing else to do with her hands, goes back to brushing crumbs off the table top. He takes both of her hands in his and presses her into looking at him squarely. He can smell her morning breath and a fragrance, probably from her hair, from the shampoo she uses.

"What if he didn't do it out of guilt, Mathilde? What if he changed the facts to protect you? What if he was afraid in the same way I saw him afraid last night."

She pulls her hands free and explodes: "It doesn't matter why he did it! He did it, that's all!"

"You're right. But you're so busy being right that you can't get beyond this thing." His sincerity gives her pause, and there is a moment of calm. "Do it for yourself, Mathilde. Try to see things from his point of view? He lives in a pit of anguish and anxiety."

She shakes her head. "Look, I appreciate your thoughts, Russell. But you don't know him like I do. He's self-destructive."

"And what do you call what you're doing? Living alone, being miserable, trapped in the past. At least your father had a family and a life."

She gets up from the table and takes their cups to the sink. "I'm going to have my shower now."

"Mathilde, he placed an ad in the newspaper, asking for a watchman. If that's not a call for help, what is? Help him, and help yourself in the bargain."

She finishes rinsing the dishes but does not turn back around. She leans against the counter, locked in a struggle with her pride. After a moment, she pushes off the sink and faces him. He knows the victor by the quieter look on her face. "I will come by this morning. I'll do it for you, Russell, not for me, because I know where this is going. I will be shut out again, and when that happens, no one, not you or him, will get me to do this again."

IX

Her turquoise Renault Clio swings into the yard, its quiet engine drowned out by the crack of gunfire from the woods and the water running from the hose. Rubber-booted Osiris is spraying off the patio, oblivious to his daughter's arrival until she calls out to him. Stone, cracking dead branches into a workable size for the fireplace, drops his gloves and goes for a walk.

He returns an hour later. Her car has gone. Maurice is just leaving the house, wagging his right hand furiously, causing the wrist to snap crackle and pop. "What a scene! If I was you, I'd give the old man a minute to cool down."

Osiris stands alone in the kitchen, sautéing chopped vegetables into a hot skillet and looking petulant. The odor of contention is as pungent as the onions.

"Smells good, even from 2 kilometers away," says Stone, unzipping his coat.

The farmer grunts but adds nothing.

"When did Mathilde leave?"

The response lags. "Not long after she got here."

"What happened?"

Osiris throws down the spatula. "You know how to step in shit with both feet, don't you!"

"Don't expect an apology."

Osiris mumbles a swear word and picks up a knife and goes after the sticks of celery. He knives the bits from the chopping board into the pan, mixing it with the onions, and sprinkles in more salt and pepper. Stone starts to walk away, but Osiris halts him. "I told you once, I'll tell you again, stop sticking your nose into what doesn't concern you."

"What did you tell her, Osiris, that's all I want to know?"

The farmer is wiping his gnarled fingers on an apron as old as him, maybe older.

"What do you think I told her? I told her no! I will sign the lease today. Or tomorrow, as today is Sunday, a day of rest."

The two men stare at each other until the food starts to burn. Osiris returns to his culinary duties. Stone goes to the Music Hall to pack.

A moment later, Osiris comes to fetch him for lunch. "What are you doing?"

"Exactly what it looks like." Stone tosses his sack into a corner and lifts the mattress back onto its bed frame. "I'm taking my nose somewhere else. I'm leaving." When next he catches the farmer's eyes, he sees bewilderment fast becoming fear. Stone sits on the bed, sighs and rubs the back of his neck. "Tell me, Osiris, when you were a kid, did you read comic books?"

"Eh?"

"Your daughter said that I never talk about myself. So, before I leave, I'm going to share something of me with you. As a boy, I collected comic books, the superhero variety, you know, Superman, Hulk, Spiderman. But my favorite wasn't strong in a physical sense. He was a Humpty Dumpty looking creature from another planet, whose particular power was clairvoyance. He knew how each story was going to turn out, but he had taken an oath of non-interference, so he was condemned to watch people go clueless to their doom. His name was The Watcher.

"Me too, I was a watcher. I watched my mother and father sink into sickness and despair. I watched them fight with each other and poison each other a spoonful a day. Even a kid like me could see that they were heading for a dismal end. But I couldn't do anything about it except watch. I saw my father killed in a car crash when I was 6. The next year I watched my mother die in a hospital bed, strapped to more tubes and wires than she had hair on her head. I weighed ten pounds more than she did.

"Nine months ago, when I came to France, I was back to being a watcher again, content to keep the world at bay, to live the impersonal life, to smash stone to bits with a sledgehammer. It felt good and secure being a non-person. When I saw your ad in the paper, I thought, perfect. The very job to finish my disappearing act.

"Then, a funny thing happened on my way to oblivion, Osiris. I became involved with this farm. I accepted the challenge of protecting it. And I grew fond of you, your daughter, Maurice and his dog. Life seeped back into this old stone heart. I couldn't have stopped it if I'd wanted to.

"The problem is, ever since I got here, everything is about what I can't do. I can't interfere with the gold rumors, can't talk about the cave paintings, can't discuss Sabag's child abuse, can't dissuade La Suzon, and can't solicit your daughter's help."

"No one asked you to do any of that!"

"Of course you didn't! But do you think you can protect something by letting it deteriorate, Osiris? That's not protection. That's just incarceration. You have turned a paradise into a prison. I know plenty about prisons. I've been living in one for the last two years. One is enough for me. So, I'm off, *mon ami. Bonne chance.*"

Stone gets up and hoists his bag. Osiris, his fists clenched at his side, is trembling with rage.

"Well, perfect! Go on, then! I have never been able to count on anybody but myself anyway!"

"Mathilde's visit today was an attempt to disprove that, but I suppose you set her straight, didn't you?"

Outside, Stone spots Maurice and Dora on a ridge beyond the garage. He calls out and joins them, to say goodbye. Maurice listens quietly to what happened and chews on Stone's decision to leave as he would a blade of grass, turning it over in his teeth and sucking the sense from it. "Let me talk to the fool and change his mind on this lease business. Then, you can come back and not need to swallow your own pride. What do you say?"

"That's nice of you, Maurice, but, as far as I'm concerned, it's not a question of pride. Maybe you were right all along, and change is just an illusion of youth."

Stone's sadness runs deep and he does not have the courage to stay another instant. He hands Maurice the book he borrowed and goes about his way.

Osiris is looking on from the patio, arms crossed, steeled in a coat of pride. Stone signals farewell, but the farmer chooses to ignore the gesture. So, he wheels bike and bag out of the yard, hops on at the stone bridge and pedals for the main road.

On the way through town, he stops by Mathilde's place to say *au revoir*.

"Well, two visits in one day," she bites from her entryway. She looks collegial in a 50's style dress light and airy with matching belt, and so unlike her heavy workweek black. She has tied her hair in a ponytail. "If it's more noble interfering that you peddle, I'm not in the market."

He stops at the first step. "I wanted to say goodbye."

"Goodbye?" She looks down at him, not so much examining as digging, trying to excavate some truth about him. Her eyes, full of noble defiance, soften a bit. Ashamed of her own acid perhaps, she steps away from confrontation. "In that case, at least come in for a moment."

He follows her down the hall, away from the kitchen, into a grand living area. "Can I offer you something?"

"Thanks but I can't stay long."

"If it's adieu, at least have a drink before you go."

"If you insist."

"I won't be but a moment."

She leaves him, and he steps to the picture window with its panoramic view of the Durance Valley. Her living room is a designer's dream, terraced into three ½ levels, each connected by stone steps. The interior walls are of the same stone, sandblasted and treated against humidity. In fact, she has managed to create an outside décor *inside*. The south wall is almost all glass, with minimalist, garden-style furniture: low glass tables, sleek steel and leather chairs, a few well-placed pedestal lamps, some Grecian jars, a few modernist sculptures, and lots of plants. Replicas of Kandinsky and Andy Warhol hang on one wall. He thinks he understands the statement she is making: this is not my father's farmhouse, but its antithesis. The layout and furniture are meant to flow, to create the illusion of lightness, of freedom, across space.

Sorry, Mathilde, but your house does what it should not. It deflects space to the advantage of time; it defines what it shares with the ancestral home: stones. You just can't escape the family bedrock.

Mathilde returns, carrying a clinking tray of bottles, glasses and bowls of olives and salty snacks. "Unlike Papa, I eat very late on a Sunday, if at all. Care for an aperitif? Or maybe you have eaten already."

"We had it out before the mushrooms hit the fire. Just give me what you're having."

From a mildewed bottle she pours walnut wine, a liquid so black that no light comes through it. Her eyes can be like that, but not today, not now.

"Vintage Osiris Sorbin 1998," he comments. "I recognize the product."

"Yes, Papa's good at turning dead fruit into nectar."

She takes her glass and sits back in an armchair, tucking her skirt between her knees. He turns away and pretends to discover the décor.

"This is some place you have here."

"It's been in my mother's family since, well, I don't know, forever. Probably the crusades."

"Not like this, it hasn't."

She nods to the obvious. "No, it was a real dump when I bought it. Unfit even for the rats. The roof was caving in. The pipes were old as Methuselah and rusted through. There were no windows, just a lot of cold dark chambers. When I moved back from Paris with my husband, I had it gutted."

"You did a great job with the walls."

"The walls were already here," she sighs, taking the comment as something hurtful.

"I meant that you found a terrific balance between light and weight."

"If I had been able to, I'd have let in a lot more light."

"No, I think it's fine the way you have it."

"If you say so," she answers, tempering her criticism.

"Your husband must have been pleased with the result."

"He left long before it was finished. Bernard had trouble adapting to provincial life. He was a Parisian intellectual."

"I know, an architect, like you."

She stares at him.

"Your father told me. You met at a school of design. Which one of you designed this place?"

"I did."

"Do you miss it, architecture?"

"Occasionally."

"Why did you stop?"

"Earlier times, other passions," she says dryly.

"So what's your new passion, village paperwork?"

Her face blushes with pique, and her glass hits the glass tabletop rather hard, breaking the fecund silence.

He apologizes immediately. "That was tactless. I'd better be off."

She accompanies him to the door.

"I enjoyed meeting you, Mathilde."

"No, you didn't, but who can blame you. I'm not very likeable." She unlatches the bolt. "Sorry things did not work out between you and my father." She holds open the door. "You know he didn't mean it, don't you? He's probably sitting in the dark turning himself inside out right now. He regrets a lot, my Papa."

"I know it, but does that make a difference? When I stay, I stay 100%. Otherwise, I leave 100%."

To her credit, she says only: "Nobody could expect you to stay."

"Mathilde, you're a great architect."

Before he reaches the gate, she again calls to him. "You have to come back. You still owe me your story."

He laughs. "You didn't miss much."

"A bargain is a bargain."

Stone rolls through the high-walled streets out of town and gains speed on the downside of the ramparts. A winter fog hangs over the river and environs and obliterates the valley to the hills. Their summits float on a whitened sea.

Halfway down the incline, where the road is steepest, he spots the Peugeot, a baseball cap on wheels, waiting in ambush. It's a perfect setup, and too late to avoid. The vehicle pulls off the sidewalk, engine gunning, shooting for him. He swings right, throws out a protective foot. Since they don't want to kill him, the car veers at the last moment, sideswiping him and propelling him still gripping the bike between his legs against the wall. The same foot that saved him from the car takes the wall. He careens back across the road and plummets bike and all over the guardrail and down into the ravine.

He comes to a stop fifty feet down the bank, lying on top of his knapsack. He is too shocked to move, and prefers to ignore for a few moments longer the nasty truth about his bodily injuries. The din of passing traffic rises from the valley floor. A dog barks somewhere in the village. He tries to raise his head, but feels queasy and sets it back down. After a moment, he gives it another go. The embankment disappears into the ocean of mist and he has the impression of hovering over the valley. His head spins. He is ready to be sick and vomits across a broom plant. A few feet away, his broken bike lies among the barren bushes like the physical manifestation of a personal violation. Its rims make mangled silhouettes against the dull afternoon light.

He is lucky to be alive. His head is untouched, and his back feels fine. He manages to stand, but the foot, his right one, which took the blunt force of a car and granite wall, no longer obeys. He sits back down and pulls down his sock. No swelling, no discoloring yet. He gets up and gives it another go, with the same negative result. The ankle is useless.

Half an hour later, he hobbles out of the ravine, using the bike now as a crutch. As battered as his machine, he mounts the guardrail and starts a slow hop back to Mathilde's house.

X

Stone's ankle balloons on the way to Pertuis hospital, a delay reaction that has the merit of pre-empting Mathilde's insistence on his going to the police. Instead, she drives him to the curb of the emergency unit, helps him inside and sees him through consultation, x-rays, and a plaster cast. The lady surgeon says that the ligaments on both sides of his ankle are torn and there is muscle damage. Such injuries, she stresses, are *très* long to heal.

"How long is *très* long?"

"Six months maybe."

Stone decides three weeks will suffice.

Treatment, medicine and crutches go on Mathilde's health care number. The crutches are more like canes. His weight is on his forearms, not his armpits, and they take some getting used to. He stops often for breathers, caning himself down the dull deserted Sunday hospital corridors.

Night has settled over the city. The car's cabin light pops on as she opens his side and helps him in. "While you were getting your cast on, I called Papa, to tell him what had happened. He wants you to return to the farm, at least until you are on your feet."

She closes the door, rounds the car and gets in. He watches her legs part under the steering wheel, that twin-lever movement that raises a man's temperature faster than fever. She starts the engine, goes to shift, but he sets a hand on hers. "Please. Not just yet."

He holds nothing back in the look that he gives her. She turns off the motor and leans towards him. Their lips meet above the gearbox. He takes her head in his hands. She closes her eyes, as if romance could not but be experienced blind. Her lips stay sealed at his touch, but only for an instant, before her mouth opens with abandon. He loses himself in a kiss for the first time in his life, and when he finally becomes conscious of the exercise itself, of the texture and taste of her lips and tongue, he knows too that the right kiss is an absolute like a gene, carrying in it the first and last of its kind.

Because he cannot move, or perhaps because she would do it anyway, she climbs upon him, straddling him and the gearshift and his knee knocking up her dress and his hands doing the rest and when she at last comes up for air, it is to laugh. "Let's leave before we are arrested."

They make great disorder in her bedroom, pants and nylons, shirt and that collegial dress now bunched with their underclothing, the bedspread and sheets. He lies between her branched thighs, her contractions making quick work of his impatient seed. Her hot blood infuses him, drives him. They sweat and twist, wetting deep into the mattress. Her earthen hair sticks fever-like to her damp skull. In his hands her heavy white breasts repose like valley-trapped cloud. "Don't close your eyes this time," he says, "I can't get enough of looking at them. You are so very beautiful."

She scoffs. "Rubbish. My nose is crooked; my hips too wide. I have Papa's ears."

"I agree about the ears."

She drops her head over the edge of the mattress, to experience his thrusts while staring at the ceiling. She seems either incapable of or unwilling to achieve internal fulfillment from his sex alone, but instead takes to falling back on her own devices and uses her hand on herself. There is something sadly logical in the exclusionary act. She admits as much. "It's been so long. Anyway, I have never trusted anybody but myself."

"You sound like your father. Try trusting me."

"I wouldn't know how."

"Try."

They lie sticky and entangled, but he is far from finished. "You're horribly sex starved," she teases.

"Only the first pop was about me. The last three have been about you."

"By tomorrow, your silly talk ends up in the washer with the sheets."

"Please, this time, do not use your hand."

She smiles feebly. "You ask a lot."

Mathilde keeps reaching out of habit, and he keeps taking away her hand. At long last his patience results in a rhythm that touches her and starts to bring her on. Her panting grows, the time between them shortens, and he can see it in her eyes, that she is approaching the mark. Her breath escapes all at once in a heaving joy originating in the very core of her. She screams and breaks out crying and laughing and desperately seeking a Kleenex off the dresser.

They eat dinner naked at 3 in the morning and go at it again on the bathroom rug. "Oh, God!" she screams, "you are going to kill me! I won't be able to walk!"

"Good, that'll make two of us. We can *not* walk together."

He crutches to the toilet bowl and sprinkles urine from a crusty and sore unit. His forearms ache, his legs hurt, his whole body is abused. But he has never felt better in his life. He flushes, pops a pain pill, and drags the bedspread into the bathroom and covers her where she sleeps beside the tub.

When he wakes, she is gone. The bathroom is as dark as a cave, but the square of daylight in the hall tells him that the hour advances towards late-morning. Damn pain pills knocked him out longer than he wanted to. He can't locate his crutches, so he hops down the hall to the kitchen. The pungency of over-cooked coffee. Her daisy bathrobe is folded over a chair. She has set out a cup and saucer. There's a terse note stood up against the sugar bowl. *Gone to work. Call me when you are ready at 0490858501. I'll drive you back to the farm.*

Mathilde is waiting in her car when he gets down to the

street. Her *bonjour* is edgy, her regard furtive, and her kiss clipped. "How is your ankle?" Her concern also is perfunctory.

"Swollen and painful. I took some more pain-killers. Ah, is something wrong with you?"

"With me? What would be wrong?" she asks, jaw tightening, an air of complexity swirling about her. He can tell that she's putting distance between herself and the events of last night. She's probably traveled miles since early light.

She drives in silence, turns up the way, crosses the stone bridge and kills the engine next to Osiris' clunker. The sun is hitting the west face of the house, turning its stonework pink. The ivy climbing alongside the kitchen wall is full and lush. Having lost the farmhouse forever, Stone sees it again for the first time, and it has never been more beautiful to his eyes.

He senses that Mathilde is up to something. The top three clasps of her cardigan are unbuttoned, and the love mark he left on her neck makes a scarlet insignia that her father will not fail to see. As she gets out of her car, he can but speculate about her intentions for going into the house. "Are you sure you want to come in?"

"What are you talking about? I grew up here, remember?"

Osiris is not in the kitchen. Except for the creaking hot-water pipes, the place is quiet. She fills the kettle, crouches in front of the cabinet, pulls out three teacups and, disgusted, takes them to the sink for cleaning. "Last time anyone dusted anything around here was probably me."

Stone launches a pique: "I've never seen sex have such a positive effect on someone."

She throws back a grenade of a look. But before she can actually say anything, Osiris' stiff gait carries down the hall. The farmer waddles into the kitchen, still pulling up his britches. "Oh!" he says, startled. "*Bonjour*, my dear," continuing numbly to Stone, "you're here, finally." He glances at his cast.

Mathilde hoists herself onto the kitchen counter and starts spooning tea grains from a tin, packing them into a strainer, much of the old man in her gestures and the tone she uses to say—"it took us a night to get here," looking up only the time to catch his reaction, before pouring hot water. She isn't wearing pantyhose. Her skirt stops at mid-thigh. Stone can see the V of her panties, therefore so can her father. She crosses her calves, dangles her bare legs over the dishwasher, bobbing them like those of a feckless school girl, provoking her father, throwing in his face her night of love-making.

Osiris, befuddled, finishes fastening his britches. He follows that with a backhanded comment about her having found her *old spot*. She makes a sharp retort: *the more things change, the more they stay the same*. Stone has no reason to feel guilty but does. Osiris flashes him a look. "And you! Maybe now you will understand." Though to what the man refers—the accident or his daughter's impertinence—Stone can only guess.

She answers for him. "Just what is he supposed to understand?"

"He did this to himself, that's what."

"Sure, you hire the fellow to protect your farm, but stay purposefully vague about what that means."

"I was clear! No gold hunters on my land. How much clearer could I be? It was never part of the job to stick his nose in their truffling, to make tape recordings, to buy information from that offspring of theirs with dolls and such. He reaped what his interference sowed, is how I look at it."

Furious, Mathilde pushes herself off the counter. This is déjà vu for Stone. He is back in the village square last autumn, being used as a pretext for their having at each other's throats. The difference is that this time it's meaner.

"You did this!" she yells at her father. "It's all your doing! You got him run over! Because first you let them run all over you! You've always let everyone and everything run you over!"

"And everything you do, child, you do to get back at me!"

They stand glaring at each other, and for a moment Stone wonders if she won't haul off and whack him or else the other way around. Combat does not happen because neither one is given to violence, not the physical sort anyway.

Osiris goes redder than a radish. "You don't think I know what you are up to here!"

"Go on," she challenges. "Tell me and Russell. What am I up to?"

"You are here to cut me down. You have always looked down on me!"

"Bullshit, Papa. Pure invention, like your hexes. You make up excuses to cover your weaknesses and failings."

"You can lecture me about failings, you! And your divorce? Your architect diploma going moldy in some chest? Your revulsion for the farm? Your coming in here waving your ass in the air?"

"At last! Finally we are talking about something other than onions, conserves and hexes!"

"Your failures are of your own doing."

"Of course, they are, as are yours! But how convenient it is to brush them aside and blame Russell here for getting himself run over."

"Bah! What do you want me to say to that gibberish!"

"Tell Russell the real reason he was hired!" Her black eyes smoke with resentment. "Tell him who he is protecting the farm against. Tell him who you are afraid of."

"Who!"

"Me! You've been afraid of me since Jean Horace died!"

"*Foutaise!*" Osiris goes livid, his jowls tremble. "And you have the nerve to lecture me about inventions! I never blamed you!"

"No, you were too busy blaming yourself to understand what you were doing to me. I'm talking of trust, not blame, Papa. Someone had to be accountable for the farm's failure, with Jean dead and gone, and it wasn't going to be you."

Osiris throws up his hands and storms out of the kitchen, with his daughter in close pursuit to the doorway. "Go on, run away!" She is shaking, her hands are knotted, as if stopping her fingers from tearing at the air she breathes. "Running away, it's what you do best!"

Stone tries to calm her down, but she pushes him away. "Don't," she warns him.

"Fine," he says, nettled. "But let me tell you something. You used me here today, Mathilde. You used me like you accused him of using you. And I don't like that."

"Oh grow up a little."

"That's funny, coming from a woman who's still trying to get her daddy's attention."

"Look, you got your piece of ass last night, so get off my case."

"If that's all you think it was to me, you really are screwed up."

His comment stings her, and she rushes out. He listens to her car start and roar from the yard. Languishing, he bends over the kitchen sink and makes one, audible moan.

XI

Stone finds Osiris knuckled on the edge of a chair by the chimney, too tired and miserable to bother getting comfortable. He's holding his head in his hands like a sack of trash. Stone crutches to one of the three comfortable armchairs in the room and sets himself into it. Osiris looks up.

"Does it pain you, the leg?"

"It's tolerable. They put it in a half cast. When the swelling goes down, I'll need to get a full one."

Osiris nods and reaches for a piece of wood from the wreck of a wicker basket beside the fireplace. Without actually getting up, he throws the log in the fire and stokes it with an iron.

"Anyway, thanks for letting me stay."

"Biking is for fools, you can't say I didn't tell you that." The seasons have etched angst lines in Osiris' face, converging in tight critical spirals.

"So, did you take them their new lease this morning?"

The answer is much shorter than the time it takes him to expel it. "No." That leads to a pregnant pause, after which Osiris speaks into the fire: "Not after what they did to you."

Stone looks affectionately at the farmer. "I appreciate that, Osiris."

"Bah," he says. "Save your thanks. What does a person have to do to live his last years in peace, free from all these squabbles?"

Stone wishes he knew. But he is off the hook as concerns an answer, because just then someone knocks at the kitchen door. Osiris goes out grousing a guess as to who it is. A moment later he leads Maurice to the fireplace with a critical chime, "*Eh beh*, the rumors didn't take long to reach your ears."

Maurice chuckles while raking his whiskers and giving Stone's cast a hard look. "True, I never needed no mobile phone to get news. Words are like insects, you listen close, you can hear them buzzing."

"And gossip is grime looking for a place to settle," concludes Osiris, taking up his chair again.

Maurice sighs. "Look what they did to you, youngster. What's this world coming to, anyway? Using a car. *Putain*, just let them show their faces again!"

"Stop flapping, you! You wouldn't be able to see their faces if they bit you."

"I never was much of a fighter, true, and I may be old, but I can be dangerous." Maurice looks from Stone to Osiris and waxes reflective. "Time was when you could leave your door wide open without a care," he says, drawing up a chair. "Remember that year of the Great Cold? When your father and I collected all those truffles? Must have been 14 bushels worth. We were peddling at the village marketplace. It was so damn cold, icicles were hanging off the plane tree branches. The village fountain was one big ice sculpture. It got to the point where the two of us were stamping our feet so hard that the tops of our heads were becoming loose. So, we left the goods in the middle of the square. Stuck up a sign telling anybody who was interested to serve themselves and come pay us in *Bar des Remparts* where we were having cups of hot cocoa and trying to get warmed up."

Osiris isn't listening, so Maurice turns emphatically back to Stone, his ancient peasant's demeanor a pachyderm of comic rimples. "We did not lose one fucking fungus!" He slaps the back of one hand into the palm of the other. "Folks came and paid. *Putain*, people were honest then. You think you could do that today? Why, nowadays folks steal your wares out from under your nose!"

"Especially if the nose is tipsy," harps Osiris.

"Run him down on the road! The horror! Everything has gone to the dogs, I say! That is why I have decided to vote Far Right."

"You never voted in your damn life, so I doubt you are about to rectify that practice."

"You see what they did to his leg, Osiris! Why, if that doesn't get me voting, nothing will."

"My bet is nothing will."

Maurice haws. "Well, maybe you're right at that. Only thing makes me angrier than what happened to our American friend, is paying taxes. And I'm afraid if I vote, some damn bureaucrat's going to catch up to me."

"What are you worried about, you fool. You don't own anything! And even if you did, and even if the tax collectors demanded 50 years in arrears of taxes, why, you can cash-in that mountain of bottles you live above. Granted, first you'd have to pour out the piss that's in them. You have enough fucking bottles to cover the debt of fucking Russia."

Maurice laughs. Stone laughs. Then, finally, after three months, something resembling a smile stretches the putty of Osiris' cheeks. Maurice declares, "Well, would you get a load of that! It's about time you lost that snagglepuss! So, what's the plan of action here? You aren't going to sign them a lease, are you?"

Osiris shakes his head.

Maurice hollers, "That's the spirit! Though"—softening his stance—"La Suzon will come back with a vengeance."

"Let her come! Last night, they went too far and now they will get nothing!"

"Right you are!" cheers Maurice. "So, I hope we are all

prepared and on our guard. I sure am, I will stab them with a dibble!" Energetically, he claps Stone on the back and says in heavily accented English, "So long and goodbye."

Osiris starts to mount the stairs but stops on the second step. "Oh, before I forget, last night your girlfriend called."

"Penelope?" he asks feebly.

"*Eh beh*, until last night I did not know you had another!" Vindictiveness is oozing out of Osiris.

"You didn't say I had an accident, I hope."

"You are getting like my daughter, you take me for a fool."

"No, Osiris, I don't and neither does she."

"I told her you were out on the property, hunting prowlers. Vague enough for you?"

"Thank you."

"Don't bother thanking me. She will know about your condition soon enough."

"What do you mean?"

"She is coming to France. She told me she has her ticket."

XII

There is a calendar spring, and the one Osiris calls a rogue spring. The false one comes too early and feints, lunges, and pulls back like some kind of modern military operation. Hot and fecund, it raises the sap, pops the buds, colors the hillsides, meadows and orchards, and fills the air with premature perfume, only to jilt its maiden.

"It betrays the land," says Osiris, digging into his proverbs. "Sin in January, penitence in March; an untimely flourish knows a wicked frost; borrow an early bud, expect boughs barren and fields of mud. A false spring is no good a thing. You will see, *Roussel*. Winter has not spoken its final word."

"I believe you," says Russell, enjoying a beer with Osiris on this balmy late winter afternoon under the porch. "But let me ask you this. How can a season be false?"

"Well, look around you," he cries impatiently. "The damn cherry trees are blooming."

"Thank you, I have eyes. I'm talking about nature being wrong. I don't think of weather being wrong."

"Why, of course nature can be wrong. It's like anything else. What do you think! Do you see an order to this heat in winter? No! There is an order to things, and this is disorder."

"Sure," agrees Stone, pleased to be having a philosophical conversation with such a literal-minded man. "The question is, why only four seasons? Depending on the climate, why not five or seven, or just three?"

Osiris regards him narrowly. "*Ridicule*! Did they teach you nothing about nature in the city? Winter to spring to summer to autumn. Things grow, prosper, wither and die. That's the order of things."

"Yes, but . . ."

"But nothing. That's the way it works. Nature is order."

"But you just said it could be wrong."

"That's right, and when it is wrong, it is false!"

Stone laughs out of frustration. "And is there order in the seasons of a person's life?"

"*Absolument*! We are born, raised, have kids, and break our pipes."

"That's the general plan, yes. But in the meantime, we do all of that at once sometimes, and sometimes out of order. Like nature."

"I dare you to tell me of someone who died, then had kids," he hoots, his dialectic triumph rising with his index finger above his balding head. There is a twinkle in his eye.

"Not literally. But we die a little sometimes and are reborn into something new."

Osiris swipes at the air. "Bah, you talk to say nothing!"

Stone bursts out laughing.

And Osiris, he thinks. With his attention to order. How ordered, how logical is he, really? Is there not a world of contradiction between what he says and what he does? Between his threat to sign the lease and his actual refusal to do so? Or, between his apparent inability to confront the bar man, and then his sudden decision to stop his truck out front of the *Bar Des Remparts* and go inside for a showdown?

Osiris had just driven Stone to Pertuis hospital to have a full cast put on his leg. On the way back through Lauris, he angrily tossed the remainder of his cigarette and downshifted in front of the bar. "We shall see about this!"

Osiris strode to the counter and minced no words with the bartender. "So, from two-timing to terrorism, that's a big jump for a blockhead!"

Jean-Jacques continued laconically wiping down his counter. The skinhead barely looked up to give Osiris the time of day. "I don't know what you're talking about, Sorbin." He raised a snooty, ring-punctured eye at Stone leaning over his canes in the doorway. "But it looks to me like somebody finally got what he deserved." Stone did not react, choosing to ride this one out in silence. This was Osiris' moment. Stone knew another time would come for him. "Tell your *Amerloque* it's illegal to steal people's letters."

"No, I'm here to tell *you* something. What you did, even a gutter rat would not do. You are going to pay for it."

"Oh, I'm shaking," sneered the bar man. "What are you going to do, throw rotten apples at me."

"Don't under-estimate me," he said, as much for those others in the bar, hiding in their drinks and cards. Though some among them probably did side with Osiris, they needed to protect their interests. There was no other bar in the village. "I'll close you down."

"*C'est ça*, old man. I'll be doing business here long after you've croaked and are planted and forgotten with the last of your race. Now beat it and take that crippled degenerate Yankee with you."

Back inside the truck, Stone wore his contentment like the sparkle off a badge. Osiris, who could see him in the rearview mirror, feigned irritation. "What are you so happy about? Me and my ancestors just got stepped into the ground and forgotten."

"That's not what I saw," said Stone, leaning over the seat. "I saw a guy standing up to a bully."

Osiris brayed, ordered him to stop talking to say nothing, but there was nonetheless a lingering satisfaction brightening his mustaches.

"So, can you really make trouble for that bastard, or were you playing to the gallery?"

"Playing to the gallery."

Stone laughed and dropped back into the truck bed.

That was last week. Now, as the two of them, separated by a generation and a world of thinking, wax philosophical about nature, only Osiris is sure that the pining goddess of nature is busy preparing to put her house in order.

The following week will prove him right. Three feet of snow will land in 5 hours. The buds will freeze and burn, and Provence will lie under a blanket of snow until the official calendar date of spring.

SPRING

I

Repeated passings have slaked to mush the footpath leading from the kitchen. Stone limps across the yard to the idling truck, which now has a passenger seat, fitted and bolted that morning. Osiris sits behind the wheel in his Sunday best, pate oiled, mustaches clipped, enjoying a cigarette. Stone climbs in. The cloud of smoke and cologne is dense.

"You are not prudent, *Roussel,* to abandon your crutches so soon. Do you want to end up like me, hobbling just to take a piss?" He chucks the butt. "And between you and me, you have the face of Lent today."

Stone isn't sure what a face of Lent means, but he assumes he looks bad. "I'll be fine."

"Are you not happy to see this girl?"

"Of course I am."

"You have a funny way of showing it."

"Oh just drive!"

They arrive early at the airport, but her flight is late. They wait a further three quarters of an hour before a tall blonde on a steep escalator makes a much-regarded descent into the tobaccoey terminal. Penelope is young and trim, with straight hair that makes sunlight across her level shoulders.

She throws herself into his arms, gives him a long kiss and works parts of herself against parts of him. "Ehhm," she smiles lasciviously, "is that a pogo stick I'm feeling, or are you hopping to see me?"

"You're a turn-on, what can I say?"

On the way out of baggage claim he hides his stiffness of ankle and ardor behind the luggage trolley.

Osiris is waiting in the airport-parking zone, holding open the passenger door for her. He offers her flowers, calissons and a warm welcome: *"Bienvenue en Provence, Penny-Lowp!"*

"Merci, merci, Mr. Sorbin. How nice! I . . . ." Her French starts to falter, so she turns to Russell. "Tell him that I really should have rented a car. *You* should have rented a car for us."

Russell translates and Osiris swipes it away.

"Nonsense! It is my pleasure, and *Roussel* all he knows how to do is pedal." The farmer makes circles against his temples with his hands.

"Oh oui!" She agrees blithely, and slides in. Stone crawls in back with her bags and melting manhood.

Back at the farm, the luggage goes to Mathilde's bedroom. Osiris toiled three days to prepare the room, which had not been touched in 15 years. Stone thought it unnecessary. "My friend is pretty rugged. It's simpler to throw another mattress on the Music Hall floor."

His offer incensed Osiris and met with a stern rebuke. "Are you out of your mind! No guest of mine sleeps on the floor! This is not the wild west here!"

"I sleep on the floor."

"You are not a guest," he answered with complete seriousness. *"Penny-Lowp* will have a proper room. Now hush up and let me think."

It is not just the man's Gallic gallantry at work. Stone sees a certain deliberation in Osiris' opening his daughter's chamber to a stranger. The unhappy man is paying himself the fantasy of a full family. The act might even be some sort of revenge against Mathilde, but he doubts it. The farmer is cantankerous, not scornful.

"This is so *charmant!*" Penny says, her French starting to kick in. The bedroom shutters are open and sunlight spills across the terra cotta floor, quaintly uneven. Once upon a time a Sorbin ancestor had taken an entire tree trunk and treated it and run it from stonewall to stonewall serving as the master beam 20 feet over their heads. There are new sheets and pillows and a maroon and yellow bedspread the colors of Provence. "My goodness, *c'est ça, la* Provence! Just look at it."

Osiris, taking full advantage of the moment he had worked so hard to achieve, shows her the towels and facecloths and is very deliberate in his explanation about how to latch and unlatch the shutters and windows which he suggests she not leave open all day. "Otherwise, all night you will have the bugs."

"Six days here will be too short." She holds up six fingers and says: "*Pas assez.*"

"Then, you must stay longer."

After tea and pastries, Osiris tells Stone to show her around the property. "Take a pair of my boots from the barn. And be careful of your ankle!"

"Did he say something about your ankle?" she asks on their way out. He avoids the issue with a shrug, as if he too were perplexed by Osiris' comment.

They cross the old vineyard, which is muddy from the storm. Remnants of snow lie clumped under the dead vines; the mid-afternoon sun dazzles off the dark sod. The sky is bluer now than it was an hour ago, and a gentle breeze from the east fingers strands of Penny's golden hair. An armada of white clouds amasses in the west. She says, "I see why you like this place so much."

She takes her camera and fires off in all directions, at meadows like poured green liquid, with dashes of dandelions and white butterflies that only a week before were poisonous caterpillars. "Awesome," is her adjective of predilection. The farm's faded glory and beauty is awesome. "It's like strolling through a Van Gogh painting, don't you think? Awesome, totally."

They pass through the lavender fields and she snuggles against him and kisses his hand and makes a quip about busy bees, but he steps wrong on the ankle and winces.

"There *is* something wrong with that foot!"

"Just a little stiffness."

"Yeah, I can see your little *stiffness.*"

The walk takes them by Maurice's beehives. She asks to meet the old hand. They continue on to the trailer, but no one is home except old Dora lying chained under the chassis alongside the piss bottles.

Maurice appears half an hour later, crossing the western fields, trying to anyway, making slow progress stumbling over the humped grass. He is a walking bag of bones in hobo rags patched everywhere a patch will fit, even patches on patches, his torn cap visored low to the afternoon sun. He's drunk. Singing and sputtering and long since oblivious to the public mockery he makes of himself.

"Mademoiselle," he blathers at Penelope, "take this boy home to America and make him a child. There's nothing good as children in this world and all the rest is hokum!"

Penelope couldn't agree more and nudges an elbow into Stone's rib.

On the way back to the house, Stone can barely walk. With his good foot he kicks a log to scare away any skulking scorpions or millipedes, then sits.

"A little stiffness, aye?"

"I twisted it."

"Lemme look."

"It's all right."

"Let me look!"

She removes his shoe and sock and uncovers the misshapen joint. "This is twisted? And I'm your uncle. This is not even an ankle anymore. It's mutton. How the hell did you do this?"

"Someone ran me off the road."

"You mean the weasel and his mother, don't you?"

He nods. Her tight jaw line draws her ears closer to each other. She throws up her hands in disbelief and paces back and forth in front of the log, swearing and questioning his good sense if not sanity.

"I can't believe you, Russ! How could you get yourself into this!"

He anticipated her reaction and finds little comfort in seeing he was right.

"So, what happens next? They leave you in pieces?"

"No, they don't leave me in pieces."

She brays exasperatedly, tugs up her skirt and plants her fanny beside his on the log. "What needs to happen before you come to your senses?"

"I'm still a professional, Penny. I can take care of myself."

"But do you need this? At home you can do something *else*."

"What *else*?"

He waits, expecting nothing and earning as much.

"Teaching or training or, Jesus, I don't know"—flummoxed—"something different, for fuck's sake! Anything beats this!"

"You mean *this* that only an hour ago was like walking through a painting?"

"Oh screw you. You know what I mean. The situation here stinks. Be for real, would you. This aint you. This is some fantasy you're hiding in."

"I've taken a stand, and that's no fantasy. I'm starting to live again."

"Are you? You look miserable."

"That's a step forward from what I was the last time you saw me."

She screams because it's what she does when she's cross and doesn't know what to think or how to reason with a big lug who doesn't have the brains to come home when he's in danger and someone loves him and wants to care for him *at home*. The echo of her voice traverses the fields and scares birds out of the poplar trees. She takes a deep breath and releases air slowly. She grabs his arm, rubs his muscles. "You're not a cop here."

"You know that's the last thing I want to be."

"Sitting in a field with a gun, trailing punks, provoking poachers, what do you call it? Knitting?" He says nothing. She takes his hands. "Russ, you have to forget and move on."

"Forgetting is not moving on."

"Neither is running away."

He shakes his head and stands. "Let's drop it for now. It's

your first afternoon here, for crying out loud. Come on, I want to show you something spectacular."

He leads her to higher ground where they can see smoke billowing above the dark farmhouse. "The weather conditions are perfect. There's just enough wind and humidity. Watch this."

A moment later, the western horizon ignites. The underbellies of clouds burst into flame in a steel-blue stratosphere. She snuggles her face under his coat collar and kisses his neck. "Watch, Penny, it will last only a second." The heavenly fever peaks, wanes and dies. The troposphere fades and darkens into twilight. "Show's over. Let's go back."

She places a hand high up his thigh. "Nope, the fireworks are just starting."

It's dark when they get back to the house. Osiris is in the parlor, hunkered before the chimney, feeding the fire. The sweet smell of burning acacia. A tray of appetizer's and alcohol are set on the table. Penny, a foot taller than the farmer, throws an arm over his shoulder and says that if he ever plans on remarrying, she's available.

The three of them have a drink by the fire. Penny goes down well with Osiris, as evinced by his will to converse and his body language. The farmer sits on the edge of his chair, hip twisted towards her, outstretched hand guiding his speech like a laser, and gives her quite a bit of personal history including a few details of which Stone was unaware—Osiris had been a one-term mayor of Lauris, the youngest in over a century. He tells her about his son's death, too, though he skims over it, with none of the distress that Stone had been privy to.

They dine on fresh steamed broccoli, flat beans and roasted mutton. She wipes her lips and bows to Osiris. "I can't remember eating so well. *Mes compliments au chef.*"

"The chef is not I. *Roussel* prepared everything beforehand, I just warmed it up."

She haws. "*Roussel* can cook?"

Stone downplays it. "Let's say it was a joint effort. Besides, the only thing extraordinary about this meal is the third plate.

It's probably the first time another plate has been used in this house since Charlemagne."

Osiris serves strawberries from the open market, placed next to individual finger bowls to wash them in. The farmer likes to clean a berry thoroughly by dipping it three times and shaking it dry by its stem. "Bah," he says, "not so good. The first of the season are rarely edible." He tosses the stem and pumps Penelope for personal details about her old beau. "You know, *Roussel* here, he says very little about why he came to France, except to escape comic books or some such thing I did not understand."

She has a glance at Stone, who shakes his head. Penelope answers, "I suppose he is sowing his royal oats. How do you say that? Wait, I used to know. *Jeter sa gourme royale* or something like that."

"Oui!" laughs Osiris.

"Quite normal on a farm, no?"

"But you must not let him."

"Shit, I encourage him!" She winks and whispers, "Sometimes you have to humor children."

Osiris gets a kick out that one. "What a girl!" He's as animated as Stone has seen him. "You know, you speak good French. Good French, indeed."

She'll have nothing of it. "*C'est la merde*. It stinks," adding, "I studied a year in Paris, but there's little left."

"Bloody hell do all Americans speak French!"

"Not on your life," she says. "We can't even speak our own language worth a shit."

After his habitual thyme nightcap, Osiris leaves the two of them on the living room sofa. But before climbing to his room, he imparts a regret: "Seeing you two, like that, together, I cannot help but think how things might have been here at Elysian Farm. A son, a daughter. A brother, a sister." He turns and mounts the steps.

Penelope doesn't lose a beat. "I don't want to be your sister."

She takes his face in her hands, a tender clamp, the ring he gave her cool behind his left ear. She gives him a peck on the mouth. "Do you want me or not?" He says nothing, makes no move.

"Ha!" she laughs. "Your passivity is the better part of cowardice. Though, knowing you as I do, it's probably the opposite. You're too much the fucking gentleman, eh?" She unzips his trousers. "Will he come down?"

"Not as long as your hand stays there."

"I meant Osiris, fool."

"I know what you meant."

She frees his bloated knob and brings him on with slow deliberate strokes of tongue and thumb, making fast work of him. "An encouraging sign, Mr. Stone," she says, setting him upright like a bowling pin. Doffing hose and panties she sits on top of him and rides. Unshowered since the previous day, she emits a stale but not unpleasant odor of whatever perfume got sprinkled in Los Angeles and carried to Lauris like olden day olfactory scents transported from the Orient. "This," she swoons, "is a pilgrimage of pleasure in Provence."

Penelope is a workout artist, sooner miss a meal than a gym session, and it shows. Her body fat is down to nothing, ribs stretched, breasts erect. She's an athlete whom he's never considered a sex machine but rather a success machine, perfect and positive Penelope going after and getting what she wants. He watches her sway above him, face buried in hair like spun gold spilling over her breasts, shoulders and boyish arms, a towering woman, not beautiful but certainly comely, on a self-serving ride. Though, he is one to talk about self-serving rides.

She yelps, excusing herself to greater and greater heights of personal pleasure, screaming to her heart's content. Stone says, "Don't worry, he's deaf."

"That's what I'm worried about."

"I told you, he won't be back down."

Stone wonders at the strangeness of it, that is, his choices, or lack thereof. Falling in love with the farmer's daughter, a woman so deeply buried in personal problems that she can't be blasted free, and turning away from Penelope, this loom spinner whose only real issue in life is having her way without making it look too easy. Penny's only problem is that of staying motivated. But that is probably why she loves him, because he makes her work for it. He's a warrior voyager never likely to come home. But she is no fool. She won't self-destruct in the name of love. Penny's not the waiting type.

"That, *mon ami*, was *delicieux*," she sighs sinking down, spent, flushed, forehead peppered with sweat. Catching her breath. "Must admit, sex has always been our thing. We're a great fit."

"And how are you fitting with the new guy?"

She stiffens with guilt and gets off him. "What new guy?" But his snort of disapproval calls her bluff. She pays him the weak smile of the good loser. "Okay, there is someone."

"From work? Someone I know?"

"Not in-house, no."

"So, when's the marriage?"

The question addles her. "How did you know!"

"Did you think taking the ring off would remove the mark on your finger?"

She bows to his sagacity. "The observer. Always the observer. You know they still talk about you at the bureau. Scoot over!" She shoves his legs in and leans back against him. "This summer. The marriage is on for June. That is unless you come home beforehand, you bastard."

"So, I take it this visit is a sort of adieu?"

"Russ"—she turns fully facing him, tucking a leg under her bare bottom—"if you asked me to wait . . . ."

He pulls her into a tight embrace, which he holds for some time and gets on top of her and works between her legs and makes love to her. And the whole time he can't stop envisaging Mathilde.

Long after the sweat of their bodies has dried and all that remains of the chimney fire is its glowing cinders, he gets off her. She lies asleep, jet-lagged, mouth open, breathing easily. But she was always a light sleeper and her blue eyes open and she stares at him a moment. "Russ, I'm still waiting for your answer."

"It's been a long day for you, Pen. Go upstairs and get some sleep."

"Aren't you coming with me?"

He shakes his head. "I'm a night worker, remember?"

II

Penelope does not rise until the sun is high, the grass dry. She flip-flops into the kitchen wearing the same dime store thongs he remembers from LA, and a silk bathrobe worth a month's salary. Her hair is still damp and honey-dark from a shower and brushed long down her back.

"Osiris has some collection of soap in the cabinet there! Yo, is that coffee I smell, laddy?"

"Sure is, ma'm."

"You're a god!"

"Something to eat?"

"Are you kidding, I could eat *you,* I'm so famished."

She draws a chair away from the table and sits and stretches yoga-like to her knees, back arched and rounded, making long luxuriating sighs of content. "A vacation. A fucking vacation. Here, with you." The sun streams through the door panes and washes the floor tiles. "What silence! No backfiring cars, no whining aircraft, no farting lawn mowers, no semi-automatic weaponry. How does an LA boy like you manage to sleep?"

"Takes some getting used to. A couple of months, in fact."

He pours her a cup of coffee and sits down. She asks after Osiris.

"Putzing around, being a farmer. Planting chives and fennel, I think."

"What a sweet avuncular guy."

"Can be. He's had a tough winter. Seems you've brought him a bit of springtime."

"He's very attached to you, that's obvious."

"Pen, I want to ask you something."

"Anything but sex."

"What became of that paint sample I sent you?"

"Took you long enough to get around to *that*. So happens, yeah, I came up with something."

"And?"

"Is that homemade Osiris jam I see on the counter there?"

He gets up and opens the jar and hands it to her.

"Hmm! Apricot! My favorite."

He cuts more bread and sticks them in the toaster. While waiting for the pop, he hovers over her shoulder, expecting an answer but getting none.

"Relax, would you. I swear it's like sharing space with a vulture. Put your butt into a chair and let's get cozy."

While she butters and jellies some toast, she says: "Okay, Colombo, I did indeed run down your sample, but . . ." She takes a handful of her own hair and swats his nose with it.

"But?"

"But you being a dirty rotten bastard, you're going to have to wait." She takes a sip of coffee.

He crosses his arms and leans back, smiling. But she's firm. "Nope, you must work for this one, bro."

"What do I have to do?"

"Spend the next five days with me, giving me your total and undivided attention."

"You'd get that anyway."

Her bright brow and coy expression shine beside her coffee mug. "I don't know if I'd get it anyway, but one thing's for sure, you're gonna get it piece by piece—and I'm talking metaphors galore. You're gonna have to fuck the info out of me, Russ."

"Sowing *your* royal oats, are you?"

"You won't regret it."

Suddenly, her expression darkens. Daylight is cut in the kitchen door. Stone, his back to the door, twists round to see what took the sun. La Suzon's scowling person fills the entry, disfigured by the door's individual panes. "Damn, what does she want?"

Penelope hums. "Is this the stormy petrel?"

"You guessed it."

The woman, her face a swollen, grim tale of hate and pain, her hair flying off in all directions, has crossed field and woods dressed in a man's brown overcoat, some kind of night robe, and slippers, transporting a scrolled paper which she shakes in his face the moment he opens the door.

"He won't get away with this! Where is he?"

"He?"

"You know who I'm talking about. That limp dick with the melting gonads, that's who! I've had it up to my tuff with him. Osiris has no idea who he's fucking with."

"He knows."

"This is your doing, isn't it, this non-pursuance of my fucking lease!"

He takes a hard look at her. "Lady, I've got to tell you, if this were my doing, I'd have you up before a judge already. Your days on the farm are over. Take the offer and run."

"We'll see who runs, you dried up faggot of a used condom, you degenerate, you nosey *Amerloque* faggot."

"You're repeating yourself."

"Oh you think you are so clever, don't you? I'll tell you how clever you are—zero, zippo, zilch! Me and mine didn't have anything to do with starting those gold rumors. But we sure know how to stop them and let everyone know what's really in that cave."

La Suzon tries to stare him down but sees it won't work. Instead, she throws a look inside, at Penelope. "Hey, Blondie, you tell Osiris, tell him he has until next week to reconsider this fucking eviction notice or the shit hits the fan about those paintings!"

When she sees that Penelope is not intimidated either, La Suzon turns and strides off. Penny looks at him and makes a comic grimace. "Now that's a woman who speaks her mind!"

III

They cycle along a quiet rural road that rises and dips through the farmed foothills, from one sand-colored village to another on the high southern flank of the Luberon. Today, the mountains move closer to them, inviting them in some way, under a ceiling the color of herbal tea. Penelope is fast, and Stone has trouble keeping up. A painful sensation of needles in his ankle stops him from standing out of the saddle.

They cross few cars, pass an occasional tractor keeping noisy pace up the deserted country route. They come to a particularly steep hill, where the road seems laid on its head, giving a gradient of 15%. Penny decides to show her stuff and charges ahead, knees pumping, back pressing, ponytail bobbing.

At the summit, he finds her pulled over to the shoulder, straddling the horizontal bar of her rental bike, hands gripping the handlebar, breathing deeply. "Good job," he shouts over. But she neither answers nor even looks at him. He rolls up to her. Her face is drained of color.

"That'll teach you to leave me in the dust," he teases. But mockery becomes alarm, when he notices that she is trembling. "Penny?"

"Bee," she whispers, like a cashier in a holdup. A hairy black bumblebee the size of a walnut is ascending her brake cable.

"Hold still. I'll flick it off."

"No! My allergy . . . ."

"I know."

"If it stings me, I'm dead."

He sets down his bike and with surgical calm reaches for the bug.

"Russ, what are you going to do? What are you going to do?"

He bats the bee, which buzzes off heading south over the fields and high pastures, in the direction of Sainte Victoire Mountain high in the sky 35 miles distant. She loosens her white-knuckle grip on the bike, which lands sideways between her legs. She steps over the machine, covers her face, and starts sobbing. He brings her into his arms.

"It's all right now." He holds her until the tension drains. She dries her eyes with the backs of her bike gloves. "Whew, that was close, I almost went home to my wedding in a box." Her face brightens. "What a cliché ending that would be, no?"

"No."

"It landed on my hand and I almost fell and it jumped on my arm and . . . I've never seen a bee that size, it might as well have been a tarantula, you know. For me it's a rattlesnake, Russ. No different."

"It's gone now, kid."

"Fucking nature!" she laughs through a wet-eyed look of abashment.

"Yeah, yeah, some people will find any excuse for pooping out on stiff hills."

She swats him. "Pooping out, my ass. I was kicking your butt!"

"Yeah, you were."

The atmosphere is rather hazy. A lusty perfume of overturned earth floats in the air. Forty yards on, a buck tractor combs a field, its big hind wheels coaxing smaller front ones through the ooze. Across the road is a hillock and a copse of pine trees which she judges an ideal spot for him to earn another piece of the puzzle.

They walk their bikes up the hill out of the sight of the road and the nearest farm and lay them on the grass and continue farther into the wood to a glade. They strip out of their bottoms and lie together and indulge in shuddering pleasure, pressing bodies into the land and feeling all that land come pressing back through the shoulder blades and buttocks.

It is their eighth "sexcapade" as she likes to call her urgings on hill and dale. There have been, over the past four days, the more citified callings as well, in the dark corners of palaces and abbeys, behind ruins, and even the toilet of a 4-star restaurant.

She brushes off his back and he does likewise for her.

"So what's my payback today?" he asks.

"You're such a whore. Do you need to be paid for this?"

"You better believe it. I don't come cheap."

"All right, here's your clue. There must be two ways to get into the cave. The hole through the roof is simply too small."

"Too small for what."

"Ah!" she warns him with a finger, "that'll cost you another go."

He shakes his head. "I'm out of change for now. So, to summarize: Osiris has nothing to fear from La Suzon, the weasel or the barman; none of them can hurt him with the paintings; the little girl holds the key to the mystery; and there must be two ingresses to the cave because the field entrance is too small for something."

"You've got it."

"And you're going to get it, if you can't do better than that. Come on, Penny, you're pissing me off."

"Good."

An hour later, they roll into Peypin, a pastoral one-block village with a small square, a fountain, aged black-clad widows, and a rosy café. "Come on, let's get a drink."

They settle into plastic terrace chairs. The waiter, a younger guy bent on flirting with Penny, brings their bottles and comments that it's a nice day for a bike ride. The weather has been "accommodating". Sure has, she says back. "Sun gaining every day in confidence." You can say that again. "The wind's lost its bite." And how! A fucking fine day indeed!

Once they're alone again, Stone asks her for a favor. "Don't tell Osiris about the bee incident, okay? He'll just go to pieces. He thinks La Suzon can send animals after people."

"To tell you the truth, that bee looked an awful lot like her. Same fuzzy face and stinger."

"Serious. He has built up the gumption to fight the Sabags, so I can't risk a relapse."

Penelope launches a look of disapproval. "You know, Stone, La Suzon was right about one thing. This is your doing. Osiris didn't sign their lease because you pushed him into not doing it."

"Sure I did. So what?"

"Well, maybe you're wrong to be stirring things up that might not need stirring?"

"I'm not stirring anything. The whole mess existed before me."

"That's right. These people had their arrangements before you arrived and they'll have them long after you're gone."

"Penny, I'm just trying to help. The farm's not working, Osiris is not working, his relationship with his daughter is not working."

"None of it is your business, Russ. You're not here to get anything working. You came here to watch."

"No, I was hired to stop people doing certain things."

"Fine, but that doesn't include convincing Osiris of what sort of relationship he should have with his neighbors, who he leases his land to, how he should be with his daughter, etc."

He tosses down his drink and throws some coins on the table. "You, me, we were trained to get to the bottom of things, trained not to accept things at face value, yes, or no?"

"Listen to you. Did Osiris ever ask you to get to the bottom of anything? This is France and they have their own ways of doing things."

"Let's go." He grabs his bike, but is unable to stop it there. "Before I came along, Osiris didn't have a choice. The bad guys weren't giving him that right. The bad guys have no problem stirring things up."

"This is not about bad guys and good guys, Russ. It's about people making their own choices. Osiris has a choice, Russ, he always has. I think you've done enough. It's just the simple advice of a friend. Let the players choose on their own now. Go back to being an observer."

Biking back down the hill, she begs him not to be angry.

"I'm not angry, I'm just, I don't know. You really think I've over-stepped?"

"Yeah, a little."

"Great, I'm becoming my old self again, sticking my nose . . . ."

"No, stop. Don't beat up yourself. That's who you are. And

I'm not saying you've done wrong, only that you don't want to push too much."

"It's tough to know when to stop."

"Nobody's perfect. It's all a question of re-adjusting. You're great at that, sweetheart. It's your strength. All right, why don't I help you get on with what you were hired to do."

He throws on squeaking brakes, and her momentum carries her another 30 yards. She checks for cars and circles back.

"Let's have it," he says.

"Find me the little girl's tunnel, Tonto. It's where the real villain in this story got into the cave."

IV

A rose-colored dawn breaks over the eastern property. He locates the tunnel entrance dug into a headland and hidden under an ensemble of scrub oak and hawthorn trees. "Okay," he says, scaring two jackrabbits which bound off through the wet prairie grass. "There it is. What now?"

"In we go."

"All right, you're the boss. Keep an eye out for vipers."

"Super! Bees, vipers."

"I can do this alone."

"That's the problem: you can't."

One behind the other they descend sideways and crouched into the tunnel. The passage is slick and the resinous walls crumble in their hands. They keep their balance by clinging to roots dangling like haywire around their heads. The ceiling peels and drops chunks of soil full of pill bugs on their heads. The air is starch with the raw musk of undiluted inner earth.

Depth comes quickly. The tunnel widens slightly. Holding lamps like pirates or banshee hunters, they come to ankle-deep dredge. Stone has Osiris' compass to guide them.

"Now I know why those silly gold rumors caught on so strongly. When you grow up living above things like this."

"Subterranean passages and caves thrill us all, Russ," she says, keeping a firm grip on his arm. "It's not just the reward of buried treasure. There's the primal fear side, too. Every labyrinth has its Minotaur, every hell its devil."

"Did I tell you that a couple of months ago, some archaeologists were digging in that hole in town and unearthed a pair of 800 year old Templar skeletons? Both over 6 feet, one a woman, a queen they think, taller than the men she ruled. Sort of like you."

"At the moment I can easily imagine how they died. We won't suffocate down here, will we, like in a mine shaft, you know, poisoned before we know what hit us?"

"It's not a shaft, Pen, it's a stitch. If you're right and the stitch runs to the cave, the air should be free flowing."

"*Should be* is little comfort to me. There may have been a cave-in."

"If it helps, try reminding yourself that a 7-year-old girl without a light and a trusty pig do this all the time"

"I see the reason for the pig. We should have brought a parakeet with us."

Stone grins. He targets the ceiling with his lamplight. "There's more head room up ahead. By the compass, I'd say we have gone beyond the orchard."

The tunnel flattens out where it meets the underground stream, and expands into a taller corridor with an arched ceiling and a clay and cobblestone strip built along the stream bank. "This is getting sophisticated," she says. "Looks Roman."

He lowers the beam to scrutinize the path ahead. A pair of cat-sized field rats scurries for cover. Stone kneels and hunts for prints. "Hm. Kidsize tennis shoes. And these must be pig hooves. We're on the right trail."

Penelope borrows the lamp and has a look for herself. "But no adult tracks."

"That's because the last adults to pass this way were wearing swords and leg plates."

Penelope, imitating the French, shakes her index finger in

lieu of her head. *"Jamais de la vie.* The last adult down here, Watson, was wearing brand-name footwear and wanted to hide his tracks. My guess is he or she trudged in the brook."

"What's the point of hiding your tracks down here?"

"To bury the evidence."

"What evidence, Penny?"

"Take me to the cave and I'll show you."

They continue in silence for a long stretch, moving under the west fields. "The cave must be a minute ahead," he calls out. But instead of the cave, the passage suddenly dead-ends into an obstacle of river stones and mud. "Shit," curses Stone, "you were right. A cave-in."

"Not so fast," she says, giving the dead-end a closer inspection. "Yes, look, it's a sham. See where the spring flowing under it follows a westerly direction? This wall bulges in the opposite direction. Fucking dike was built from the outside in."

"Meaning?"

"Meaning the last people down here wanted to make it look like the only way in and out of the cave was through that dinky hole you first climbed down. If you don't believe me, then start digging this out. I'll show you."

It takes them three quarters of an hour to break through. But she is right again. On the other side of the dam is the cave. They move into the sanctuary, towards the shard of natural light falling through the roof of the cave. He gives the north wall a blast of lamplight, and they are transported 20 thousand years into a field of galloping marauding extinction.

"Incredible!" marvels Penelope. "Absolutely awesome. If I had a hat, I'd take it off. They got the whole collection. Cave bears, woolly rhinoceroses, mammoths, even the hyena. I am overwhelmed." At that, she picks up a stone and starts rubbing out the hyena.

"What are you doing!"

"Relax, Max." She pestles the flakes into her palm and tells him to shine his light up close. "Colored earths and auroch fat, that's what Cro-Magnon artists used to paint"—she licks a finger and tastes—"and not cow and veal fat. No cows in the stone age, Mr. Stone." His shock gets her laughing. "Yes, *Roussel*, you've been had. These are fakes."

"Fakes!"

"Forgeries would be a better term. My paint tests proved they were fakes but I couldn't get over how good they were. I was sure they must be copied from an already existing find. So, I did some hunting of my own, in the public library. The solution was here." She fingers a cave bear. "It's a dangerous animal. In earlier caves, say, Lascaux, for example, the figures are non-threatening. To paint your fears is to express a higher form of social consciousness. This is a jump in time. Meaning that these were copied from a newer cave. It took some time to find it, because French archaeologists have been discovering a cave a year for the past 60 years. Then, bingo. I found a Paleolithic cave in the Ardeche. Quasi perfect copy. I'll show you the pictures. There's no mistaking the forgery."

Stone bows to the facts. "So, Osiris' great woolly mammoths are as phony as his gold story."

"It's a great hoax. And not something you could pull off by squeezing in and out of that rat hole in the roof. They needed space, and that's where the tunnel fits into it."

"Why do you keep saying that? A can and paint brush aren't much to shove down the hole."

"Russ, dear, these paintings simulated Cro Magnon techniques to perfection. The problem is that Cro Magnon didn't use a brush. He blew it on the wall with his spit, which takes ages not to mention ending up poisoning yourself. Our forgers needed to work fast, so they used a machine. I found traces of turpentine."

"Damn."

"You got yourself a real talented crook on your hands, Russ. And it aint the Sabags and it aint Pierced Ears the Bar Man. So that leaves who?"

Stone is confused and conflicted. Penelope voices what he is loath to consider.

"Come on! You know as well as I do. This is a labor of love, or rather hate. And it took an illustrator of immense talent. Who else went to a top school of architecture? Who else can draw well enough to design her own home? Who else would even go to the trouble and expense? Who else loves or hates this place enough to want to do this?"

"Penny, it's the Sabags who're benefiting from this, no one else."

"That's just your angle on it, and I think it's the wrong one. Come on, Russ, it's as clear as the painting on the wall. She did this to get revenge on her father."

Stone nods. The chances are good that Penelope has connected the right dots.

"Russ," she says kindly, "you fell for the wrong babe."

V

The morning air is charged with fragrant electricity. Under the flowering acacia tree Osiris and Penelope are squeezed onto his sitting rock, Osiris leaning into a cigarette, Penny leaning into him, giving him the news. She has her arm draped over his oppressed shoulders, ready-made Yankee flippancy trying to break through generations of Gallic gruff.

Stone, the only one standing, studies the downbeat farmer. Yes, Osiris has come through the winter, as Maurice predicted. But to call it intact would be a misnomer. The farmer sits more crookedly than ever. His ears are redder and flakier. His fingers tremble. His face bears the grooves of his emotional struggles, not least of which is this latest one, learning that his daughter may be behind the cave hoax.

Look at him! Some God of renewal he is! God of aging, decay and decrepitude, is more like it!

Stone is shocked to hear such negative feelings for Osiris pass through his head. Is this Mathilde talking? Or do these remarks stem from his own family, his own childhood? His parents spat out such scathing judgments of each other's faults and weaknesses. They habituated him, their only son, to those kinds of condemnations, kicking him down the path of righteous control, judging and condemning those who don't walk a straight line, disparaging the spotty, the weak, the human, leading him to stare down the barrel of a gun. Deciding who lives, who dies.

"I'm a police investigator, Osiris," Penelope pronounces. "My specialty is scientific research, for the Los Angeles Police Department."

Stone looks away, to the lower fields. There is a flourish of gray-blue cabbage. The carrots and zucchini are doing fine. There is a fervor in the air like the heat of a birth. And the scent of rosemary and thyme. Even the Grand Oak, the oldest living thing and biggest split personality on the property, is growing new leaves.

"It wasn't my intention to cause a fuss. And you can't blame Russell, either, for sending me pictures and a sample. It's better to know, isn't it?"

"But my own daughter?"

"Russ, are you all right?"

They are both staring at him.

"Yeah, fine. I . . . tuned out a moment. Osiris, there's no proof yet," he says, earning an accusing look from Penelope. "For now, it's only speculation about Mathilde."

"All we know," Penny adds sharply, "is that someone with the means and know-how went to great lengths to . . . Russell, what's the word for blackmail?" She makes him translate, then repeat it, drilling it into his brain. "Right, *chantage*. Whoever is doing this *chantage*, they need a motive at least as big as that effort, do you understand?"

And if she is guilty? What right does Stone have to judge her? How dare he judge her father, who has spent his whole life trying to make things right and decent as he understands them to be? How dare he judge his own parents, or anyone else for that matter, when he himself is guilty of the worst act known to man?

"Osiris?" Stone does not know exactly what he wants to say, so he merely sets a hand on the farmer's shoulder. Osiris suddenly reaches up and takes Stone's hand, grips it hard, more a brotherly than fatherly gesture. For Stone, it is a gesture that will stay with him and comfort him for as long as he lives.

"It makes no sense, *Roussel.*"

"Can you think of another credible suspect?" asks Penelope.

He throws up his hands. "I don't know! I don't know anything, me! Of course she resents me! Everyone knows it. You heard her. She thinks I hired you to protect the farm from her! But I cannot believe she would hire people to sneak on my land—her land—and do this. Is she in cahoots with the Sabags, too?"

"Not necessarily," answers Penny. "But it doesn't matter, if the result is the same."

"This is all too complicated for me!" Osiris lets go of Stone's hand and sinks over his knees.

"Osiris, I should have asked you this long ago. Who told you first about the existence of those paintings?"

"Mathilde!"

Penny flashes Stone an I-told-you-so smirk.

Stone continues: "Under what circumstances?"

"After those damn gold rumors started, she went behind my back and hired some geologists to discover yes or no if there was a Templar Knight tunnel running under our land. They stumbled on that rabbit hole there behind the Grand Oak and that's how we learned of the paintings."

"Look, Osiris, what counts is that the riffraff no longer has any hold on you. You can tell La Suzon where to get off, at least."

Osiris raises his face and stares him in the eye. "And what do I tell my own daughter?"

VI

Osiris, mopish and languishing on his stone, hands over the keys to his truck. "I do not have the courage to go anywhere today, *Roussel.* You take Peny Lowp to the airport. Take your time. Do not hurry to get back."

Penny gives the farmer a goodbye embrace, both embarrassing

and delighting him—who knows when someone last hugged Osiris. "*Bonne chance*, Ozzie. I know you will resurrect this wonderful place of yours again."

"Ouf!" he says. "I do not have the energy for resurrecting anything."

"I will send you some vitamins, and Russell will teach you *le* yoga."

The ride to the coast passes in heavy silence. At the airport, she refuses his company. "I'd rather wait alone. Just go."

"Pen, these last couple of years . . . ."

Tears start into her eyes. "It was my choice. I have no regrets."

"You got the raw end of it."

She puts on a brave face. "Especially these last few days, but it isn't anything that a little cream can't cure."

"When is the wedding again?"

"Damn you, Stone! You have until June the 21st. After that, don't bother looking me up. You see how good I am at pretenses." She kisses him on the lips and pushes the trolley down the concourse. She does not look back.

The return trip is sad and long and even the horrible racket of the motor cannot stop him dwelling on his travails and mistakes, past and present. His failed relationships. The catastrophe bringing him to France. His handling of the farm problems. Mathilde's deception. *Alleged* deception. As probable as it seems, something about the accusation does not add up.

Driving through the village, he pulls over and parks near the town hall. He expects the worst, and is treated to worse than expected. Mathilde, seated behind her desk, is infernally welcoming. She has that disarming glow in her face again.

"Funny, I was just going to call you, Russell. Would you and your friend like to come to my house for dinner tonight?"

"She's gone, Mathilde. I've just taken her to the airport."

"Oh? That was a short trip. I'm sorry I missed her. Maybe the next time."

"There won't be a next time, not in France anyway." The chill in his voice freezes her.

"Sorry to hear that."

"Are you?"

He pushes aside furniture and the invisible obstacles of bureaucratic power to reach her chair, placing a hand on the armrest and giving it a quick violent swivel and pulling her out of it. "What is your game, Mathilde?"

"Let go of me!"

She pulls free and steps back. "Before this gets any crazier, I was going to apologize to you."

"I'll bet you were."

"It's the truth. The night after the hospital, your attention was . . . so giving, so warm that it overwhelmed me. I didn't know what to think, how to take it, how even to talk about it. We French, or maybe it's just we Sorbins, we are not so direct."

"Right, so you spat on me instead."

"That is how you took it, not how I meant it. When I'm lost, I withdraw. It's a . . . mechanism, a . . . reflex. I swear, not a day has passed since then that I have not regretted what I did. I didn't intend to be mean, Russell. In my heart, I *appreciated . . . .*"

"Appreciated? I wasn't dispensing advice, Mathilde. You know what I think? I think this is just another way to get me off your real game."

"What are you talking about?"

"Fakes, that's all they are. The cave is a scam, the paintings are fakes, and you are the number one suspect."

"And you barge in here thinking I had something to do with that? Take your fucking suspicions and get the hell out!"

"I'm not finished."

"I am." She picks up the phone. "Leave or I'll call someone."

"Who are you going to call, Mathilde? The geologists you hired to paint the cave?"

She sets back the receiver. "What did I ever do to you, Russell? Did I ever treat you with disrespect?"

"No, you just stopped treating me all together."

"And that's what this is all about? A stupid fit of jealousy?"

"Just doing my job, Madame. I was hired to watch the property."

"You sound stupid. Pig-headed. You remind me of a breed of cop."

"I am a cop. Was."

She stares at him a moment. Consternation and its opposite, recognition, draw vertical skin lines above the bridge of her nose. Her black eyes thicken like drying paint. "It figures, that you would be a *poulet*. Well, unless you have a warrant, go cluck somewhere else."

He starts for the door, stops, and calls an end to the bluff.

"In fact, I know you're not guilty, of those paintings at any rate." She does not look up, but he knows she's still listening, the way she tries hard to pretend otherwise. "Your independence, your house, your meetings with your father in the village square, your moods, your secrets, your loathing of the farm, even the way you make love, none of it matches the hoax. With you, everything has to be original, even to your own detriment. You don't follow anyone's lead. You're incapable of copying anyone or anything. You're stubborn, but you're no cheat."

"Go."

"What's less original about you is that you hide from the consequences of your acts. You practice a willful disregard for the influence you have on other people. You drive them towards their destinies, thinking that, just because you're not directly at fault, you are innocent. You pushed your husband into this architectural dead-end and pretended you had nothing to do with his getting chewed up. And, you put me on a collision course with those delinquents who ran me over."

"You are crazy! You sound like my father!"

"Your father? Ha! I thought you were going to say your brother. I can only imagine the collision course you put him on."

"I said get out! Get out!"

She storms over and throws her door wide open for him, but she is the first to go through it, sprinkling tears down the hall.

VII

One weekend in May, he catches sight of her descending the street by the left sidewalk. Stone slows his bike and tries to prepare something to say. But what is worth saying, other than those simple words fighting to break free in his heart? His pride won't allow him to give her that satisfaction. At the last moment he grips the brake levers and coasts unseen behind her until she disappears into the green grocer's.

A few day's vacillation later, pride be damned, he goes to the town hall to see her. But the receptionist tells him that Mathilde has left on vacation, "a nice long cruise," she adds with more emphasis than necessary, making him wonder if she had been cued to inflict pain.

Stone asks Osiris if he knows where she went. "Ha, you ask me that ! Mathilde goes away and I am not in the picture until she gets back and tells me where she went. She never leaves for long. A week here, a week there. She likes May. Weather, and of course all the religious holidays."

At the end of the month, she returns from a trip to Corsica. Because of Osiris' bad hearing and loud voice, Stone is put in the picture. Their telephone discussion takes up where it left off, hacking away at each other over the usual subjects, Osiris' smoking and drinking and imprudence with regard to his medicine, and her moods and standoffishness. They do not discuss Stone or the cave.

When Osiris hangs up, he surprises Stone with a question. "Do you think she is guilty, my daughter?"

"Of what ?"

"The cave hoax, of course."

"No. I don't think she did it. And you?"

Osiris makes a feeble puckering. "It makes no difference one way or another, does it." His daughter's guilt or innocence is now immaterial to Osiris. His tired blood cells and nerves have already memorized the effect of a presumed guilt. The damage has been done. In Osiris' psychosomatic world, effect is 9/10ths of the law. "So, who do you think painted those pictures, *Roussel?*"

"Someone who had everything to gain if we thought it was Mathilde."

"And what now?"

"We wait for him to come to us."

*   *   *

The fine weather allows him to increases his distances on the bike. The sun browns his face, paints an agricultural tan on his arms and legs, dries him out as they say, thins him, lengthens and tightens his muscles. The heat is a balm temporary soothing his emotional wounds as well. When he is riding, he thinks less of Mathilde.

But below the sun, an acute reminder rises off the horizon. Wherever he may be riding, south to the Sainte Baume, east to Europe's Grand Canyon of Verdon, north along the Luberon, or west into the Alpilles, it is impossible to escape the eye of the Giant of Provence. Mont Ventoux towers behind the haze like the remnant of an incantation, pyramidal and mystical. From a distance, its lunar peak of white sandstone looks vaporous. The mountain challenges his reason about the unreasonable, the superstitious, the stewed and diced and conjured spells of the witch's cauldron. The giant is a reminder to him that hexing exists, and that the real sorceress in the affair injected him with a sweet poison and now possesses him to the marrow with her feel, smell and the recollections of her person. This, no amount of sun or wind can exorcise.

The Sabags have until the first of June to clear out. But with only a day to go, Stone sees no evidence of a move. La Suzon spends the afternoon sunning herself in her underwear, splayed in all her bovine horror on a blanket spread among the chickens and frazzled tulips. Sabag crawls from a chair in the shade and pisses on a rosemary bush. The girl comes out of their troglodyte hovel, looking for the pig, calling: "Betty! Betty!" Sabag shoos her back inside, some would say for wickedness, while others, Maurice among them, argue that the weasel is not like that. "If he touched the girl in that way, I'd kill him myself, sure as Abraham slew Isaac."

"Abraham did not slay Isaac," points out Osiris.

"Well, he should have. Today there would be no problems betwixt Jews and Arabs, now would there?"

"They will not be gone by tomorrow, Osiris," informs Stone. "It is the law's turn to do its job."

Osiris says to hell with the law. "I know how to get them off my property."

He goes inside and telephones a man he knows up the road, with a backhoe for hire. "Bring a division of bulldozers if you have to," he says into the receiver. "But I want it over and done with by tonight."

The plowing is finished before sundown. Osiris' rash, last-minute decision has turned the west field into a battlefield of trenches, craters and dunes. The Roman tunnel and cistern, the cave and its magnificent fraud, lie pulverized under the setting sun. As they stare down at the mess, Stone gets the feeling that Osiris is having second thoughts, by the distance he sees in the man's regard, as if he were following time like a lifeline back into the past. But if Osiris thinks that he has made a mistake, he's too proud to admit it. "What is done is done, and that should take care of the matter."

Stone has no illusions about the matter being taken care of. On the contrary, the excavation will probably flush out a last attack, which is not necessarily a bad thing in itself. The bad will be in the consequences, in who gets hurt. Who will they send? The bartender? Leather, Nike and co.? Nastier thugs? And what weapons will they bring? These are the questions going through his mind as he keeps watch beside the Grand Oak, cradling the musket and feeling quite inadequate for the challenge. The night air is soft, with a ¾ moon and millions of constellations burning the heavens. The limpid sky seems to accentuate the darkness on the ground, a curtain of obscurity 10 feet thick. In the distance, a dog howls, maybe Dora. A nightingale whistles, and he remembers Osiris' maxim that the bird's strong song in May assures a happy harvest day. Harvest day. The day has been nothing short of a harvest hell.

Above the fresh mounds of earth, a small silhouette moves to the top, profiled against the bright night. Sonia? He sees that she is not alone. On the highest mound, where the cave used to be, awaits a thin figure of the beanpole variety, phantom only in its gesture, since there is no gesture, only an inert patience. Sabag? What are the two of them up to?

Stone winds around the craters, bent to the level of the dirt piles. When he reaches the area, they've gone. Instead, there is only the unearthed cave, the soil's pungent perfume wiping out every other smell. The pit stares up at him, its refractory eye the ultimate proof of innocence in a butchered landscape. But that accusing eye is not the only one watching him. He hears a grunt. For an instant, he almost imagines that the sound is coming out of the hole. A second snort sounds from behind him, veiled by shadows. He, the tracker, has been tracked. And, it is too late to do anything about it.

"Heeya !" he cries. He has no chance to repeat the warning.

The pig charges through the wall of darkness. He doesn't have the time to aim the musket, only to use it like a shield to block the animal. The animal rams him against a pile of loose earth. It lowers a shoulder and noses him towards the crater. The damn beast knows what it is doing! Stone raps its snout with the gun stock and clambers to his feet. The riled pig recovers, snorts louder and stomps the earth, kicking dirt everywhere. So, what's it going to be, Stone? Let it break you in half and roll you into the hole, where oblivion waits? Or save your miserable hide?

The pig charges again. Stone lifts the barrel and fires low, to wound rather than to kill. The pig veers, whines, scampers off course and runs by him. Then, it disappears from sight, vanishing like a bad dream. For a moment he wonders if he touched it at all. Until he hears the brute thump of dead weight.

He walks to the edge of the crater and looks down. The hole mocks him with its unfathomable murk. He can see nothing and he hears even less. A sudden wisp of air gets under his buttons and pushes out his shirt. His fingers tremble on the rifle handle. Enraged to have been pushed to fire and destroy again, Stone turns from the pit and screams at a mute Milky Way: "You fucking imbecile, Sabag! Your own daughter's pet! With twice your intelligence! Come over here, you bastard!"

But it is not Sabag who steps out of hiding. It is Maurice. And the girl is there behind him, screaming Betty, Betty, Betty, where is my Betty!

VIII

The next morning Osiris throws open the kitchen shutter on the person of Maurice. "Damn it, man, you gave me a start!" The old hand is waiting in the yard, hands pocketed, chagrined, mop-haired, wearing an oil spill for overalls and work boots like kin rodents that have survived all weathers and substances. "Have you been here all night, you fool?"

"No, I haven't been here all night."

Osiris and Stone go out to meet him and get his side of the story. Maurice's explanation sounds more like an ignition than a rendering of the facts. "Something was driving the dog crazy! So, I came out to see what. The girl was there, crying her fool head off. She said she did not want to leave the property. I came out of my caravan to comfort the child. And that's when youngster got himself steamrollered by her pig."

The yard is awash in early morning shadows. Stone can see Maurice's tracks in the dew, uneven footprints backing crookedly away from where the old man stands gesticulating.

Osiris says, "All right, pipe down and let me think."

But he doesn't have long to think. La Suzon and Sabag come into the yard, the son small and lanky and the mother making two of him. Gravely, she approaches Osiris, throwing a fist to either side of her girth. "Me and him are here to collect the pig."

Osiris cocks his chin. "And just how were you planning on hauling it?"

"I don't know that yet. Show us where it is and me and him

will think of something afterwards." She glances at her son, then at Stone, says nothing, and throws a nasty look at Maurice. "I see you are still looking your Sunday best."

Maurice spits in the dirt. "You have room to talk."

She turns back to Osiris. "You confirm it is dead, don't you?"

"It's dead," answers Stone. "But it wasn't the shot that killed it. It was the drop."

"We will see about that." But then, to Stone's surprise, La Suzon sounds conciliatory. "Anyway, it was a dangerous beast. I'd have eaten it long ago if it wasn't for the girl."

"Or junior's truffle trade," snipes Maurice, with a sideward glance at his reputed progeny. Sabag neither answers nor looks at his supposed father. Apparently, the two of them will always need two separate worlds to inhabit.

"Shut up, Maurice," orders Osiris, matching La Suzon's placating mood. "This is not the time. Your pig is down the hole," he tells them, "and you'll need help getting it out and back to your place."

"I'm open to accepting some help," says La Suzon.

Her reasonableness throws Stone. Has he been as wrong about her as about everything else on this farm? Is she simply not as tenacious as he thought? Or is she being pushed into this new stance, and, if so, by whom?

"I have an idea," says Osiris. It's the first time that Stone has heard the farmer make a decision based on sound judgment rather than fear or irritation.

Osiris throws open his barn. The five of them clear the clutter off the horse-drawn buckboard. "Might as well use it for something," says the farmer, hitching the wagon to his father's old Japanese tractor. "Climb in, all of you."

Across emerald and yellow pastures, Osiris motors the contraption, with Stone, La Suzon, Sabag and Maurice bouncing in the buck bed, breathing tractor exhaust. They hook up with the gamboling Dora where the excavation site begins, and she tags after the wagon on its winding path around the piles of earth to the exposed cave. There, the flies swarm like raised dust, attracted to the smell of congealing blood. Dora steers wide of the hole and yaps.

Maurice talks to his dog as he would a person. "Two hundred kilos of stiff pork, and you are still too scared to approach it, eh?"

"Your dog won't go near anything except you," says La Suzon.

Osiris snickers. And a brief flush of amusement crosses the woman's face.

Stone locks a chain around the tow hitch. Sabag, using the same chain, lowers himself down, leashes it around the pig's girth, and then climbs back up. "Broke its neck, just like he said," he declares, brushing off his shoes. "Must have happened in the fall."

"And where else do you think it would have happened?" scoffs his mother.

Stone calls to Osiris, "you can start towing now."

The beast, packed with the mortar of rigamortis, slides out of the pit, eyes and tongue bulging, the girl's plastic earrings still clipped to the tips of its ears. The ball of lead passed through the right front leg, badly gashed. Worse damage was done in the fall to the animal's rear quarter—its left hind leg snapped in two. Stone and Sabag do most of the lugging, lifting and loading. The others climb aboard. But the weight is too much. The tractor cannot tow its cargo. "Everyone who is not dead had better walk," advises Osiris.

Stone, Maurice and the Sabags get out and parade behind the trailer.

"I'm 80," says Maurice, "but I'll be damned if this isn't the first time I participated in a funeral procession for a pig."

"Then the pig didn't die in vane. The procession fits you," says La Suzon.

Osiris hauls it to the extremity of the Sabags' weedy lot and stops beside raw metal gates that aren't even attached to their pillars. "No, keep on going," shouts La Suzon. "Bring it in the yard and leave it where the girl's been digging since sunrise. She deserves her funeral at least."

"You inviting us in?" wonders Maurice.

"I asked him. You're too filthy even for my lot."

"You don't say," mumbles Maurice. "Maybe you should just remember that it isn't your lot anymore." He gives her a pointed look, which silences her.

The girl steps outside, her miserable face muddy with grief. She breaks for the wagon, leaps in and throws herself screaming on the pig. La Suzon reaches in and raps her head and the girl stops. It seems to be the woman's habitual reaction and one she suddenly regrets performing in front of strangers. Maurice glares at her. "Touch that child again, you cow, and . . . !"

But the girl's screaming at him stops Maurice from finishing his threat. "It's all your fault!" She jumps back out, bounds to Maurice, gives him a kick which mostly misses its target, and bolts like a jackrabbit into the fields.

Maurice's rictus is yellow and shamed. "What's got into her?"

Stone spends the morning looking for her. He finds her in the blue tea meadows, picking umbels and talking to herself. He calls to her. She looks around, stares vacantly in his direction, and goes back to talking to herself.

"Can I come over, Sonia?"

She shrugs.

He sits down beside her. She glances at him, a clear-eyed, grimy-cheek expression of childhood incomprehension. "Do you think Betty will come back?"

"No, honey. When things die, it's forever."

"Is forever more than a year?"

"Yes, Sonia. I'm afraid so."

"It isn't your fault, I don't blame you. Mama and Papa said bad things about you in front of Betty. I told Betty that you gave us a Barbie and you are nice and she must be nice to you. But Betty didn't obey me. She was naughty."

Stone pulls up his knees and looks away, to the hills and beyond, before his attention returns to a spot no farther than the grass around his shoes. He picks a shoot.

"Tell me what you and Betty were doing in the west field last night"

"Pappy wanted us there."

"Maurice?"

She nods. "I hate him. All he does is drink. He smells like a goat. He lies all the time. It was all Pappy's fault!"

"What was his fault?"

"Pappy wants to scare Osiris so we can stay. That's what he said. He said if me and Betty want to stay, we have to help scare Osiris. Now, my Betty is in heaven. All because of that stupid cave and those funny animals he painted!"

Stone looks at her. She sighs, oblivious to the importance of what she has just revealed. The girl stares at the clouds, those fluffy nimbi that children equate with heaven. She has an infatuated way of regarding clouds and the daylight that pours through them.

IX

Stone bangs twice on Maurice's trailer. "Open up, you old buggar, and explain this 10-month boule game of yours, bowling for a jack that never was and fucking Fanny because of it!"

He does not knock a third time. He picks the lock and enters.

The odor is unbearable. The metal contraption isn't insulated, and the hot sun raises the reek of baking mold, piss, frowziness, and old dog. Wearing his T-shirt over his nose as a bandit wears a mask, Stone gets down to business.

Maurice is clever, probably too clever to keep clues around, but Stone is counting on the old man's vanity, if it can be called that—his inability to throw away books. He rifles through piles and piles of them, discarding paperbacks. His hunt is for pictorials. Penny said that the paintings were copied from an actual cave.

The book lies within a stack that is itself buried among other stacks. It is a bound collection of scientific articles and color photographs of Stone Age cave paintings, checked out of the Aix library, stolen rather, seven years ago. The Elysian Farm fraud is set out on pages 12 to 17, detailed under the title *Chauvet Grotto, Ardeche.*

Stone chains his bike to a lamppost in front of the *Bar des Remparts.* He steps inside and the laughter stops, the sound of it anyway, while the dopey rictus on the patrons' faces takes longer to settle. The barkeeper swaggers from behind his counter and leans back on the rail, waiting.

Stone lets the book in his hands do his talking. Five pounds of stiff weight pounds the wobbly card table, rattling Maurice's many empty liquor glasses and jolting him from his afternoon stupor.

Maurice considers the book with a bloodshot smirk, grunts, and slowly sits up. "Jean-Jacques, bring youngster here a Little Yellow."

"Hold the drink!" orders Stone, without taking his eyes off Maurice. "You're dirty, *mon vieux*."

Jean-Jacques reacts first. "You don't come in here insulting my customers, foreigner." He makes a menacing approach to a chair at the same table and plants his thick ringed hands on its backrest.

"Tut tut!" shushes Maurice, waving off his excitable ally. "None of that *High Noon* nonsense now. Life's too short for fisticuffs."

"But not too short for trying to drive Osiris to an early grave."

"Be serious! I have nothing against Osiris personal-wise. He's a lousy farmer who lacks backbone, but that's his problem and one he has to live with and not my affair."

"I don't know how much backbone it takes to use a little girl to do your dirty work. Whatever you say about Osiris, at least he's honest. You, you're a wiggling little night crawler, something fit on the end of a hook. Just like Sabag. Nobody needs a gene test to determine Sabag's paternity."

Maurice doesn't like getting compared to Sabag; his glare narrows into a squint of rage. "Youngster, you are talking out of your ass. You don't know anything about me, so you can shut up about Sabag!"

The man tries to swallow but has trouble doing it, and roars for another drink. The barman transforms into a servant, hurrying to the bar and returning with a bottle of Pastis and a jug of water. Maurice grabs the bottle, serves himself a concoction that's ¾ liquor and ¼ water, the water being, he once said, for color not taste. He downs the drink in one, and recomposes himself.

"Listen closely, youngster. That farm owes me more than I owe it. Osiris wouldn't have lasted a day without me. Not that he would ever admit it—so much for his honesty, eh! But I don't hold him any grudges because, lily-livered as he is, it's like you say, he's always dealt straight with me. Which is better than I can say for that mother of his."

"His mother? What's any of this have to do with his mother?"

"Everything. After Marcel died, I kept the operation running, me and no one else. I was a one-man regency, me, dealing with a bitch queen and a ball-less prince. Marie Devos didn't like having someone like me giving orders, me, a simple low-class working stiff. Her problem was that she couldn't fire me because she knew as well as the nose on her face that Osiris couldn't handle the affair. So, even as she worked me, she tried to ruin me slowly, bad-mouthing me behind my back to Osiris and her highfalutin sycophants among the ranks of artisans and merchants and such other townie folks."

"You're still here as far as I can see."

"Because I outlived her, youngster, I outlived her! If you think I'm wormy, I am nothing compared to Marie Devos. She pushed that fool Osiris to be mayor and he knew a pickle when he tasted one, knew 350 acres weren't grounds for a candidacy if you have no fire for those things. But she got him elected, all right. That is, she got *herself* elected. *She* was mayor, not him. He was just the de facto dolt. I felt sorry for old' Osiris, I did. She drove him crazy and he drove his wife crazy until she got sick and died. She used him. She was leasing and sub-letting her own property from Osiris, collecting Brussels stipends for it and keeping the farm equipment for herself, selling it off a bit at a time and stashing a mountain of loot, cuckolding her own son in the bargain."

"As you're fond of saying, old man, that was their business, not yours."

"You still aren't getting the point, youngster. There *is* a treasure on the farm. I saw her take her earnings and subsidies and hide them in the tunnel."

"The tunnel that was dug up?"

"There aren't two of them. She stashed her entire savings there and carried the secret of its whereabouts to her grave."

"So, all of your bullshit was about treasure after all."

"If I told you no, you wouldn't believe, would you?"

"No."

"Well, there you go then. Anyway, the fool has now gone and bulldozed the tunnel."

"That's what you were doing in the field last night, looking for treasue?"

Maurice doesn't deny it. "Whatever money there was in the tunnel is gone for good now. His own damn legacy."

"A real pity for you and the human pin cushion there."

"Like I said, the money didn't interest me."

"So, why did you do those cave paintings?"

"Me?" He makes an insincere gape, exposing the few, urine-colored teeth left in his head. "Why, youngster, you surprise me, thinking an old fart like myself capable of managing something like that. And the book there doesn't prove anything."

The barman rises, having heard enough. "Let me take him out."

Maurice holds up a liver-spotted hand. With the same hand, he seizes a small whisky glass filled with toothpicks and holds the glass out to Stone.

"Go on, youngster, go on and remove it."

"Remove what?"

"Why, the bad toothpick. You, who claims to be such a good watcher and judge of character. Go on and show me the bad toothpick. Some are short and some are long and some are starting to splinter, but I want you to show me the *bad* one. See, people are like these sticks here. Good and bad aren't part of the equation. Good and bad have nothing to do with how they fit between your teeth."

Stone accepts the glass, holds it out and pours the contents onto the floor. "Go ask Sonia if she has any trouble identifying the bad toothpick."

"Pour out my toothpicks, will you!" yells Jean-Jacques. The barman grabs him by the shoulder. But Stone maneuvers so that the man's hand is above the other shoulder, then above no shoulder at all because Stone is behind him and the barman has nothing between him and the sitting drunkard. Stone yanks the man's arm up and starts strangling him with his own limb. He jams him against the table, forces his cheek into the sticky film of previous drinker's messes.

"Just desserts, was it?" Stone, trying to control himself from really hurting Jean-Jacques, raises his voice. "Come on, let's have it, J.J. Tell everybody in here who ran me off the road last winter." The barman resists, so Stone chokes him harder. "Say it, before a bone snaps and you're suddenly a paraplegic. Say it!" The fight starts to leave Jean-Jacques. "Say who ran me over so that everyone in here understands who's a victim and who is the snake in the grass. Say it!"

"I did," he croaks.

Stone releases him and leaves him gagging and spitting on the table. Winded himself, he delivers a warning to the barman. "If I catch you or your punks anywhere near me again, I will come back here and pull those earrings out of your head with tweezers. And you, the ringleader," he says to Maurice, "when you sober up, come talk to Osiris. I'm sure he'd like to know your theory about toothpicks."

X

The first week in June, a toasted wind from the Sahara brings yellow rain depositing a fine mustard dust on the area. Rills of pale gunk run down the country roads. The farmhouse windows are opaque with sand, and Osiris' truck looks like it has done a desert rally. A nasty gale whips out of the west and sweeps the area for another few days, before a hard, clean rain washes everything clean. The temperature rises into the mid-90's.

Osiris, who hates great heat, rails against the Provencal spring. "It doesn't have the right to be called a season!"

But it is not the weather that has Osiris turning in circles. The real stick in his craw is Maurice and his deceit. He knows he must do something about the ingrate, but an infection of excuses tetanizes him. Each *this or that* engenders a *that or this*. A criminal complaint? "Difficult to make a charge sick." Harassment? "Bah, he caused me no more torment than my own daughter." Throw him off the property? "*Bon sens*, he's 80 years old, where will he go!" Go tell him what one thinks of him? "I'll be damn if I go to him! *He* must come to *me* first!"

And so it goes. Stone realizes that Osiris is, essentially, a coward. He is afraid to act. True to his big-bark, little-bite personality, he seeks to retreat and forget. The farmer has made an art of what Stone tried and failed to do when he came to France. Retreat and forget.

The difference is that Osiris knows how to live and let live, a quality that is foreign to Stone. Its verbs and syntax escape the former cop. How possibly understand the fact that, after everything Maurice did to him, Osiris is still more concerned with Maurice's health than his stealth? "Go have a look in his trailer, *Roussel*. The fool could croak in this heat and no one would be the wiser."

"Let him croak, Osiris."

"No. No one deserves to die alone in a caravan."

If Stone's reaction is to label Osiris a wimp, the judgment ignores a greater truth: the farmer simply does not want Maurice to leave. Like the aggrieved party in a longstanding feuding couple, Osiris prefers living in contention than undertaking a divorce. He can no more imagine the farm without the rogue than a trip to California with Stone.

One night, between sips of thyme liqueur, Osiris turns the corner on his rationalizations and accepts that which Stone cannot: the immutable absurdity of the facts. "You have to admit, *Roussel*, it was a hell of a hoax. Only that old fox could have pulled it off, no? Ah, the more things change, the more they stay the same, no? To tell you the truth, I don't blame him for trying. Maurice's life has been no apple tart."

Stone, incapable of chuckling away the crime, refuses to give Osiris the vindication he seeks. "I still don't think he deserves a pardon."

"Come on, there are worse things, no?" asks Osiris, inadvertently and very effectively putting Stone in his place.

"Yes, Osiris, much worse. And much better, too." Though he would never dare say it, Stone is thinking that there is also a steep price to pay for ignoble compromise.

Over the coming days, it would appear that Osiris is paying it. He wastes away the beautiful days, smoking on his rock, filling crossword puzzles, running away, as it were, from responsibility, from the failures of his life, which will no more leave him in peace than the white rain of acacia petals landing on his baldpate and shoulders. He stops doing the small tasks that are crucial for the season: treating the lilies against vermilion beetles, watering the lettuce grains, tending to the seedling beet leaves sprouting like whiskers from the rich soil, or clipping the peonies, his mother's favorite. The task of filling the vase above the chimney with flowers falls to Stone.

Maurice continues to wait him out, while the Sabags still squat the northern property and flaunt the fact, stealing the farm's electricity, siphoning off spring water, hauling in more salvage from the junkyard, and throwing barbecue parties.

"Let them alone, *Roussel.* They can stay. I don't care anymore." The ruby blazonry that only a few weeks ago was back in Osiris' cheeks, has faded like the red poppies of Provence.

"So, Maurice has won. You've given in to his treachery?"

"There are no winners and losers. Only this wretched existence. You know, I envy them."

"Who?"

"Why, the Sabags."

"And why on earth would you envy them, Osiris?"

"Because they have each other while I have no one."

"Lest I'm mistaken, you still have a daughter."

Osiris shrugs. "*Roussel*, I'm tired. I'm 68 years old. I shall be the only Sorbin to die without an heir."

The man feels let down by everyone. There's Maurice of course, but also the mother that sold him out and buried his legacy, the father that cocooned him, the son who got himself killed, the divorced daughter who resents him, the town folks who turned a blind eye to Maurice's schemes, and finally the watchman who trespassed the bounds of his duty.

Stone has no illusions; he, too, is on Osiris' shitlist. He has lost the privileged status of being from the outside. He is no longer innocent and uncontaminated by events. Osiris now looks at Stone as a depressed person stares into a mirror. In Osiris' eyes, Stone's quality is no longer raw integrity, but that of treated glass, reflecting Osiris' failings back at him, bringing the farmer face to face with his own disappointment with life. For Osiris, who had his paradise and lost it, Stone's promise of light is nothing more than glare on the cheap.

Osiris is hard to be around all day, so Stone escapes on the bike. The roads have become a sort of savage garden. Wild flowers overflow the edge of the tarmac. Cardinal thistles, purple sage, raspberry-colored moss, the buttery broom that sweetens the air, and poppies so sun-bleached that their petals are transparent as the wings of insects.

Occasionally while riding, he crosses paths with Maurice, bumbling along the shoulder of the road, drunk and heedless to bikes and cars, a walking effigy of himself, too frail to scare crows out of a field. Stone yells at him to show some guts and come apologize to Osiris. The burped and blathered response is indecipherable. Maurice changes direction and cuts up into the woods.

But a balmy evening in June, the traitor comes calling. Osiris and Stone are sipping beers on the lighted patio, when the old man's crusty roar shoots out of the dark. "Ho, there!" His salutation bounces off the quiet countryside like the cry of a night hawk. He steps into the light, a truck-purchased pizza carton under his arm. "I got me a pizza here if anyone's interested," he says jauntily, as if the recent events don't add up to the cooked dough of his peace-offering.

A sigh of relief escapes Osiris, who can now ignore Maurice with something akin to peace of mind and ruffled pride. Osiris gets up and says to Stone, "If you're done, give me your bottle and I'll take it to the barn."

Osiris waddles bent and stiff-jointed up the dark path, ignoring Maurice who maladroitly heads after him. Stone can hear Maurice's pleading voice trailing behind miserably. "Say, Osiris, did you treat your apple and pear buds for bugs?" There's a rapid, sputtering panic to Maurice's voice. "Another week and it'll be too late. And the cherries? Most I've seen in many a season. Osiris, wait! *Alors*! Be reasonable, will you. For God's sake, you know well that it was never about the money."

Osiris plays deaf, and Maurice gives up and returns to the patio. The saucy arrogance he displayed at the bar is gone, replaced by frailty and gloom. "He didn't want to hear anything I had to say."

"Who can blame him? You got some tact. Pizza, my ass."

"Okay, forget the pizza!" The fellow frowns, then seats himself where Osiris was sitting.

"What do you want, Maurice?"

"A little company, that's all."

"What do you want?"

"I would not burden you, youngster."

"Fine. Then beat it."

Maurice doesn't reply right away, but neither does it take long before his usually unperturbed demeanor cracks. His gray eyes widen with tears. "It's Sonia, youngster. It was never about money. I swear it."

"Your word isn't worth a toothpick."

"Come on, don't hold it against me. My treasure's that girl. Everything I did, I did for her. I wanted her to have a decent place to grow up, a child of the country and not the child of some filthy housing project where they shoot their arms full of needles. My whole rotten life, I had nothing to show for it. Not

even when that no-account son of mine came along, because I
have never been sure he's mine and anyway he's long since ruined
and worthless. But my little Sonia, she's my angel, my sunshine,
my happiness, my reason for going on. I loved Osiris' kids, too,
I never lied about that! I loved them so much it kept me working
here. But Sonia is different. She's family."

"*Family*, Maurice? *Family*? Do you ever think about your lies
before spitting them out? Sabag isn't your son but Sonia is *family*?
Who are you trying to kid?"

"This has nothing to do with Sabag."

"Of course it does, he's the kid's father."

"Sabag isn't her father."

"Well, who the hell is?"

"I am, youngster."

Stone stares at him. Maurice hangs his head, abashed but
sincere. "I went sniffing around again. Okay, to say it like it is, I
have never stopped sniffing around her in years. I'm just a man.
I'm filthy and have cravings. Once, maybe I even loved her. Well,
La Suzon being her age and what, neither she nor I figured she's
going to end up pregnant again. But she did. And now that poor
child has grand-folks for parents and a brother six times her age
who can't tie a shoelace and must wear plastic loafers because of
it."

"You're full of shit, Maurice. If this were only about paternity,
you would have talked to Osiris and worked things out. This *is*
about money."

"No, *monsieur*! Well, yes and no!" The abrasive scratching of
his whiskers sounds like dormice chewing on wallpaper. Dead
skin drops like dandruff on the table. "For years I had known
about the treasure but didn't go down that tunnel because I wasn't
interested in money. I never craved material things. If I did, you
think I would have passed the last 40 years living in a sardine can?

"Then Sonia was born. That changed the equation, you
could say. I hunted for the cache, and yes, I even found some
loot, but not a lot. Osiris' mother hid money like Dora buries
her bones. Stashed in little amounts all over the place. Can't

imagine how she intended to find it all. Anyway, that's neither here nor there, because she up and died and took the secret with her. What little money I found, I stuck away for safe keeping for the girl.

"But those incest rumors started. And one day Osiris told me that La Suzon and Sabag were becoming an embarrassment for him, what with their living on his land. True, he never said he wouldn't renew their lease. But he didn't say he would either. You see, I couldn't risk it."

"Risk what?"

"Him chasing Sonia off the property."

"You should have told him the truth then and there."

"All right, maybe I should. But my sleeping around with La Suzon didn't speak in my favor, did it? He might have given me the boot, too. Either way, I lose my little Sonia. So, I hatched my plan and used what money I had to pay some folks to come down here at night and paint those pictures. I bribed a fellow in Public Works to dig a hole in town, and I got the gold rumors going and paid Jean-Jacques and the Brouhaoui Boys to kick up a fuss."

"And run me off the road."

"I was real sorry about your ankle, but you were between me and my Sonia."

"Why are you coming clean with all this now?"

"Because she wants nothing more to do with me. You chased her from me."

"If you believe that, old man, take your pizza and keep walking."

"Okay, youngster, settle down. It came out all wrong. All I meant to say was—"

"You lied to her about me, you used her to your own ends, and your scheme got her pig killed. She's just a kid, but she knows."

"You're right, it was my fault. I ruined everything!"

Stone looks at him, and despite his loathing, he feels some pity for the man. "Are you going to tell me why you're here or not?" Maurice feigns innocence, but his shifty expression gives him away. "Go on, a guy like you is always after something. You scheme like you breathe and you can't breathe if you aren't scheming. So, let's have it."

"The girl likes you."

Stone finally understands what the man is after, and smiles bitterly. "You have some nerve, Maurice. You expect me to intervene on your behalf, after what you did? Where's your shame, man?"

"Come on, youngster, don't be triumphant. She respects you and would listen to you."

"You must be pretty desperate."

"It's killing me!"

"Then you won't mind writing Osiris a letter of apology."

Maurice scoffs. "Are you a lawyer?"

Stone isn't amused, and waits for an answer.

"I never write anything down on paper."

"First time for everything. That's my sine qua non. Otherwise, forget it."

"All right, damn it. You drive a hard bargain. I will write what you want, so long as you get her back to me."

"No, Maurice, no preconditions. You write the letter. Then, I will *talk* to Sonia. But she will have to decide for herself to see you or not."

Maurice agrees and tries to grab his hands in gratitude. Stone withholds the handshake. "And one other thing. You get that bar asshole to telephone Osiris tomorrow night and take back everything he said about Osiris' ancestors."

XI

Dear Penny,   *June 16th*

> *Greetings from the farm. Weather's been funny lately. Mornings and evenings are mild and soft. But*

in the afternoon, a hot wind rises and dries you out. It's asparagus season, so Osiris and I are eating a lot of them and every time one of us pisses you can smell it all over the house.

Maurice's reconciliation with the little girl took place yesterday at the Grand Oak. She didn't want to go and asked me not to force her. To get her to agree, I took a snapshot of her. When she asked me why, I said it was for the old man because without at least a photo he would die of a broken heart. A shabby trick, but I guess you know why I wanted this so much. For two years now I've been looking for a chance to give someone back a child.

Maurice was very gentle and remarkably contrite for him. Yes, he's a rat, but he adores that little person. Unlike La Suzon or Sabag, Maurice would never lay a hand on her. He even took the extreme step of getting himself washed and groomed!

I went with him, to help him with his hair. We followed the brook 400 yards downstream to a concrete basin built by Osiris' father 70 years ago. Maurice said it had been his "private bathroom" for the past half century. He stripped naked and waded in. The surface was mossy and leafy and, personally, I didn't think it much cleaner than him (looked like ditch juice). But he got himself bathed and shaved and we washed his hair with a thick brick of lard. I'd brought some scissors and got busy hacking off his barbs of tangled hair. I even clipped his toenails. He felt lots better afterward.

I wish I could say the same for Osiris. He's going down the tubes faster than flushed dust. That written apology I had Maurice write him had no positive effect whatsoever. I doubt he even read the letter. He hung up on the bar man, too. I certainly haven't been able to cheer him up. It's too bad you aren't here. You worked wonders on the man. Reawakened his libido or something.

I can't see myself abandoning him right yet, but as soon as he is better, I'll be on my way. Don't know where, but I'm thinking more and more about what a fool I am, letting you get away. Penny, the last time we saw each other, you said you would wait for me, if I asked you to. So, I'm asking. Penny, can you give me—

Give him what? Five months, five years, five minutes?

Stone throws down the pen. Selfish bastard, you will not do that to the woman. You will not break up her wedding when you know damn well that you love someone else. She's better off getting married. You have no future back in Los Angeles. No one ever goes home. End of story.

He crumbles the letter and throws it in the wastebasket. The kitchen clock reads 5:12 a.m. "Time to slay a giant."

Outside is dark and cool and a light breeze stirs in the acacia trees. If his fears are confirmed and it's a north wind aloft, this will prove a hell of day to attack Mont Ventoux. Tough shit, he's up and ready to get it done!

Daybreak is at least an hour away, and nothing, not Osiris nor the rooster nor sparrows in the eaves nor the dew point, has risen. He bikes through the morning murk, managing the road by moonlight, with the stars and nocturnal beasts for company, toads croaking in the ditches, field rodents relaying high-pitched danger signals, winged predators whistling above, and bugs swarming all around. The air carries a bite to it, and Stone has stuffed yesterday's *La Provence* newspaper under his shirt, a biker's trick for staying warm the time to get warmed up.

He reaches the summit of the Pointu Pass before six a.m., no automobile in sight, but a few rabbits, a hedgehog, and even a bushy tailed fox. A swift drop on the backside brings him into the waking village of Apt, and his first traffic light in over 40 kilometers. The outdoor market is only just setting up. He pulls over to a garbage container and tosses the soggy newspaper.

The Murs Pass is long but not too difficult. A deep blue morning breaks over the scrub hills, crags and deep gulches. Ahead, the waking giant cracks an eye with the first light, yawns and throws a shadow over the open plains of Mormoiron. The wind stiffens.

Three hours after the start of the ride, he bikes into the village of Bedouin, on the southern flank of the Giant of Provence. The beanstalk starts here. The Bedouin route up Mont Ventoux is legendary for its difficulty, for the toll it has taken on professional riders over the years, even killing one, bursting his overtaxed heart. The road starts parallel to the mountain, giving Stone a full and intimidating view of what's in store: 18 miles long, 6,000 feet high and 13 miles straight up a 9% gradient. Two hours of incessant undiluted physical distress.

Stone drops his gears and seeks to develop a rhythm. Having nothing to do but suffer, he can, paradoxically, relax. He can throw off the world and attain a form of peace through pain. He is Sisyphus, rolling himself up Hades' hill and finding liberation in the task itself.

Yet, his trance offers up not freedom and tranquility, but a reel of images from another hot June day two years ago in Los Angeles.

Blood on the swing sets. Children crying, screaming, some injured from shards of exploding glass, most scattering across the playground, running for cover with their teachers. An adult woman lying slumped in a pool of her own blood in the hopscotch court. Hostages in the classroom windows, human shields forced to look out, miserable and sobbing behind glass, little kids and their teachers, in shock. The perpetrator pushing a loud speaker out of a window, yelling anything that comes into his head. A one-way ticket to paradise, 50 million dollars, a meeting with a certain actress. A killer in shock, and too dangerous to bargain with.

Hawk One, the minute he makes a clear target, you take

him out. Roger. A crack of a weapon, the brisance of shattering glass, the killer disappearing into chaos. Hawk Two, report! Negative on that, Home, not a clean hit, I repeat, not a clean hit, I repeat, not a clean hit! Subject still alive and going berserk!

Stone sees him jump over a school desk, dragging a shredded useless arm like a broken tail. The killer is popping hostages. Hawk Two, fire! Do it, Stone! You, the Watchman with the power of life and death. Get the man. In the crosshairs again and squeeze. Then the boy. Peter. Pete Terrell. Crossing his field of vision like some . . . some . . . messenger.

The road lifts like a ladder heavenward. There are precious few bends to relieve the psychological pressure of seeing suffering approach, the straight-aways are long and steep. What's nice is the tree-cover. The first 16 kilometers pass through a lichen— and shade-covered forest of pines and cedars, with a silence as profound as time, protected from sun and wind.

Mistakes happen, whispers the commander in his ear while pinning the medal on his uniform. The official report makes no mention of what he had done. The boy's death is filed under murder, his name listed with those of the other victims. Protecting one of their own. Protecting the service.

There he is, sitting on his bed, watching the needle of his wall clock spin like a weather vane in a gale, his insides twisted in an Osiris-like funk, useless to himself, completely undone by nuances, poisoned by a lie pounding a last nail in the coffin of his innocence.

There he is, getting out of his car in front of their weedy lawn. Mailbox says Terrell. Standing at their front door, a faded brown door with scratch marks in the corner, dog-pawed so often that both paint and finish are gone. The kid had a dog. Knocking. Dreading it will open, or *not* open. Hello, Mr. and Mrs. Terrell, my name's Russell Stone and I must tell you something about young Pete's death.

No, they are too afraid of being hurt again, Save it, man, save it for yourself! Mr. Terrell says go, go now, we don't want to relive it again. Stone understands that his admission is intolerable for them, that his latent confession only manages to add absurdity to their misery. They excuse themselves and close the door in his face. Stone repeats that he understands. He isn't there for them. But now he is alone, talking to a dog-clawed door. *Save it for yourself.* It is the maximum sentence, the worse punishment that they could give him, that he could give himself. But, it is right.

He reaches the end of the tree line and the beginning of the final climb, an 18,000-foot ascent through a lunar landscape to a summit wearing a skirt of pale sand. The road veers left at the Chalet-Reynard ski lodge and bends sharply up and into the wind. From here on he will be totally exposed to the elements. The worst thing is that he can see the final 6 kilometers stretched out in front of him, teasing him to quit. The summit, crowned with an observatory and a television antenna shaped like a cartoon rocket, seems to get no closer despite all his effort, draining his energy and sapping his will to grind on. Now he knows what it means to be the Watcher. It is when you see sure suffering mapped out before you and your only wish is for the bliss of ignorance.

Aeolus grows more violent. The wind and the grade together almost bring him to a standstill and he fears he might fall over. Worse, he heard that a good Mistral could blow a rider off the hill. Stone leans into the side of the mountain and works against the heat reverberating off the wind-blasted stone, and his own exhaustion. The gradient slants, the climb gets only worse. Fucking hell, it is like trying to pedal up a buttress! Why are you doing this to yourself, Stone? Because you deserve it, you prick!

Each pedal thrust becomes a struggle he must win. He is reduced to seeking shelter in the smallest lapse of time and space, in the dead-zone as it is called, that section of the pedal's revolution where the foot reaches the ebb of the rotation. He stands *en danseur*, melds back into the saddle feeling his ass weld. He begins to do 8's, swerving into the great paradox of both seeking and hiding from wind. His arms are shaking. The back of his neck is taut as cable. He has barely the strength or will to raise his water bottle, much less himself.

But the peak gets no closer. Progress is an illusion, a sly trick like drawing extinct creatures on someone's cave wall. But he must not give up. The struggle is for control of the mind, for the proper perspective. The summit will come. To bolster his weakening spirits, he turns his head around to seek satisfaction in his accomplishment thus far. He has ascended out of a fertile valley 13 miles down and 100 miles across. He leans over the handlebars. His sweat peppers the bike frame. Starting to cramp and gag, he reaches the final bend and finds resolve in the knowledge that the end nears.

At the summit, as he tries to dismount, his legs and back falter and Aeolus gives him a last jolt. Stone topples and scrapes a knee and elbow. He gets up cursing himself and destiny itself, but suddenly stops and takes notice of the view.

Osiris once told him that the Giant offered an unparalleled panorama. « On a clear day on top, one can make out almost a quarter of France. » Stone wrote it off as typical Provencal hyperbole. He sees that he was wrong. Mont Blanc, the highest mountain in Europe, seems within touching distance. To the west he can make out the Canigou Peak in the Pyrenees. The vista stretches from the Dauphine Range and the Massif Central to the Gulf of Lions, and from the Ardeche River to the Mediterranean Sea. Three hundred square kilometers at his fingertips. A quarter of France.

And thus he turns in his badge, leaves Penelope, comes to France, resigns himself to the life of a watcher, finds a farm, falls in love, climbs the Ventoux, stands before an observation tower, and breaks down weeping the tears of a repentant killer. Fatigue, exhaustion, jubilation. Confronting the ogre holding reign over his miserable heart.

That evening he pulls out a bottle of champagne. Osiris asks what the occasion is, and he says it is his victory celebration. "Today, I vanquished the Ventoux." Osiris answers that it is a piss poor reason to crack open a bottle of champ. Stone laughs and agrees that it is stupid all right, but does one really need an excuse to drink chilled champagne on a mild June evening on a farm in Provence, specially named after a mythological paradise?

"Of course, paradise," grumbles Osiris.

The phone rings. Osiris steps inside, but isn't gone but a minute. "*Roussel*, you are wanted on the phone."

Stone stumbles into the kitchen, half-drunk with bubbly, exhaustion, and accomplishment. He makes a querying gesture to Osiris, but the smartaleck lets him dangle like the receiver.

"Hello, Penny?"

"Afraid it is only me. Mathilde."

He needs a moment to consider how to handle the situation. "What can I do for you, Miss Mathilde?" he asks, starting to break out in a nervous sweat.

"Is everything all right? You sound different."

"Fine. We're having a ball."

"It's Papa's birthday tomorrow."

"I didn't know."

"Well, it's not he who would tell you. I thought I would bring a cake by after work, if you are there."

"What difference does it make if I'm here or not? It's for him, not me." During her silence, he wonders why he is pushing for a fight. But she comes back gently:

"It would be good if you were present, too."

"Good for whom?"

"Still the detective, I see."

"Just tired of being used, is all."

"Russell, I was hoping we could talk again. I thought tomorrow would be a good time to do that."

"Did you square this *fête* with him?"

"Papa is not real big on birthdays, especially his own. But if you're there, it will work better."

"He's pretty down, your father. Do you think this is a good idea to surprise him like this?"

"Do you think it is a good idea to do nothing? Look, he hasn't had a proper celebration in years."

"Celebration is a big word. It is just him, you and me, right?"

"That's all he's got."

"What time?"

"6:30."

"I'll be here."

XII

Osiris is positively allergic to parties. "More nuisance than necessary, if you ask me! Not those plates, these plates. Not those spoons, either!"

Despite his bossiness, a strange sort of détente holds together over cake and champagne. Osiris is unwilling to stir up any real controversy with his daughter, and she has checked her sword and shield at the door. Mathilde is in one of her light-hearted moods. She lights the birthday candles, whose flames pale in comparison to her complexion. Stone has never seen her more radiant than tonight. She is the Madonna in all her sad glowing beauty.

They raise their flutes, toast the occasion, slice the cake, and somehow manage to avoid talk of the farm, its disappointments, feuds, estrangements, gold, cave paintings, accidents, deaths, betrayals, incest, or leases.

By the third glass, the one neutral subject left seems to be Stone himself. He finds himself trapped in a nightmare rendition of *This Is Your Life*. After 11 months, his employer suddenly finds an interest in his background. "Where were you born, *Roussel*?" (On the road, somewhere in Indiana.) "What was it like, your childhood?" (Chaotic.) "And your parents, what were they like?" (Normal, I guess, for a mixed-culture union.) "What part of France did she come from, your mother?" (I never told you? . . . it must have been Maurice . . . Avignon.) "Where did you go to school?" (The University of California at Los Angeles.) "What did you study?" (Political science.) "And what brought you to France?" (The stones, of course.)

Only Mathilde laughs. But Osiris seems satisfied. Stone sighs. He's off the hook. Or so he thinks.

"Don't I get a few questions?"

He shrugs. "Ask away."

"What drives you?"

"Osiris, occasionally." He chuckles weakly. "Hey, the subject of the evening should not be me. It's Osiris' moment in the spotlight."

"*Bof*, what do I care for spotlights, me!"

She persists. "Do you plan to go back to the States and get married?"

Stone looks at Osiris whose crooked back suddenly straightens with interested in the answer. "If I didn't know better," responds Stone with false gravity, wagging a finger at them, "I'd say you two have been planning this ambush for months!"

But not even that admonition, dressed up as burlesque, stops Mathilde.

"Do you see yourself, one day, with a family of your own?"

"Why not?"

Harmless enough. This time he thinks he's home free. She pours another round of the bubbly and there is a spell of silence. He takes a deep hit, closes his eyes, and lets the liquid settle slowly. When he opens them again, she has him fixed in a determined snare. "Come on, Russell, one more question, okay, and if you give me a serious answer, I promise to take my claws away."

"What's the question?"

"Why do you bike so much?"

She's done it. Immediately, the answer gets away from him, and once it is out running free, he has no hope of stifling it. "Because it beats *this*," he blurts out angrily, holding up his glass. "Drinking. It beats waking up in your own vomit 1000 miles from your house with no idea how you got there."

Mathilde stares at him, molten. Osiris, who was only half listening and deaf the other half, catches his daughter's frozen expression and gives Stone his good ear.

"You were an alcoholic?" she asks.

"No, but I had the nasty tendency of thinking that each sip of hard liquor could remove a thought, and I had plenty of thoughts to drown." He sets his glass on a silver tray older than any of his problems and those of his parents and their parents' parents, and turns to Osiris. "You asked me why I came here. Like Penelope, I, too, was a *flick*. A California State police officer."

Osiris turns to his daughter. "What did he say about *flick?*"

"He said he was one in America," she informs him, obviously having kept the information to herself up till now.

"*Eh beh,*" he says, leveling a look at Stone, "you should have said so from the beginning!"

"I didn't want to. I was running away from all that."

"Running away?" asks Osiris. "Why running away?"

"I belonged to a special team, a rapid intervention force."

"A what?"

"He says he was a member of the G.I.G.N., Papa!"

"The G.I.G.N.! So how come you don't know how to shoot?"

Stone glances at Mathilde who rolls her eyes and smiles apologetically. "Papa, listen to what he has to say and stop interrupting!"

"Osiris, one day we were called to a primary school under siege. I shot someone by mistake. I killed a seven-year-old boy."

She flinches, a sound of shock escapes her. Osiris is both stunned and critical. "How could you do something like that!"

She comes to his defense. "Papa, it's a terrible thing to have to live with." This night there is not a hard bone in her face. Conversely, Osiris' jaw tightens and he stops considering Stone. His mustache is dull, a deadened patch in a miserable mien. He grabs a smoke. The poor man, he has a lot of pent up anger and frustration and disappointment, and he just doesn't know how to deal with his watchman's weakness.

"I came to France to get away, Osiris. I was finished with stands, involvement, and interventions. My penance would be watching, looking and listening."

Osiris exhales a spiteful puff of nicotine. "And you thought you could do this penance here?"

Stone's grin is self-deprecatory. "It was the plan."

"Bah, I'd say you failed miserably!"

"Of course he did, Papa. That's the whole point."

"The whole point of what!"

"No one can hide for long from his own life."

The defensive farmer interprets her point badly. "And I suppose that would be another jab at me!"

"Papa, I'm not talking about you."

"I have never hidden! And I at least did not shoot a boy!"

"Osiris . . . ."

But this is the farmer's chance to have a whack at him and he takes full advantage of the situation. "He comes here and sticks his nose everywhere it does not belong and even has the gall to moralize and lecture to me, he who steals a 7-year-old's life! *Bon*! I have heard enough nonsense for one evening. I'm going to bed. Leave everything. I shall take care of it in the morning."

"I'll take care of it," offers Stone.

"Leave it, I said!"

"Osiris, I'm sorry to disappoint you."

Osiris swats at the apology as he might a bad odor and climbs the stairs.

That leaves just the two of them. She reaches for the bottle and starts to top off his flute, but he covers his glass with his hand. "I've had enough."

"Russell, I'm sorry. I didn't mean to push you into that."

"I think you did."

"Yes, but not to do you one better."

"It doesn't matter. If it hadn't been said tonight, it would have been said another time."

"Don't let what he said get to you. He never speaks to the real subject."

"I know what he was saying."

"Well, what did you expect, absolution?"

"Maybe just a little understanding."

"I think it's you who doesn't understand. Don't you see he's shitting in his britches? He's scared that you're going to leave soon."

"You're all of a sudden attuned to his fears, are you?"

She takes the blow in step. "Well, for what it's worth, I'm scared too."

He shoots her a sideward glance. "You're not very consistent, Mathilde, so maybe you had better explain that one to me."

"You're not very trusting, Russell, so maybe you should open your eyes a little."

He settles back in his chair. "I'm sick of this tug-of-war. My parents were the same. They tore each other down with arguments that were somehow never about what they were really saying. She was obsessed about the big picture, about principles and values, and was terrible with the nuts and bolts of daily living. He was Mr. Organizer, everything done by the book, but incapable of tenderness and understanding."

"How did they meet, your parents?"

"I don't know what crazy wind threw them together. She was bumming around America and he was back from a tour of duty in Vietnam and was driving along with no destination and their lifelines connected on some dot in the middle of nowhere. I doubt they were ever happy as individuals, much less a couple. Their fights were never physical, only verbal, and constant."

She makes a nod to recognition. "One acquires a tolerance for poison by taking small doses of it."

"While cancer was killing her, she talked to me a lot about her childhood in Provence. Maybe my doing penance here has something to do with bringing some part of her home to rest. Or maybe it's about putting an end to my parents' arguments, so that in my head they can shut up for eternity."

He finishes his glass and picks up the tray. "Screw him. I'll do the dishes if I feel like doing the dishes."

As the kitchen sink fills with water and soapsuds, she sets a hand on his shoulder, to make him finally look at her, which she apparently thinks he has not done this evening.

"Our last talk was not very agreeable, was it?"

"That's French understatement if I've ever heard it."

"You said some things to me. Things that have made me do some thinking. Is what happened between us, that night you stayed at my house, was it just a couple of 30-year-olds playing at an old pretense?"

"I wasn't playing, Mathilde. I don't know what your game was, but I wasn't pretending."

"But take away the sex and what have you got? A divorcée unable to get over her bitterness, and an aloof foreigner without working papers. Have you given the situation serious thought?"

He turns off the water and slides dishes into the foam.

"Please, Russell. Answer me."

He knows the look he gives her is full of bile. "Look, if you're telling me we have no future together, save your breath. I got the message a while ago."

She takes his hands out of the suds and holds them. "I'm pregnant."

He slips out of her grasp, takes the dish towel and methodically starts drying his hands as if the importance of the moment were all about the drying. Her face, its newfound rapture, he can now put in context. "What are you telling me, that I'm the father?"

"Yes, of course you are. There has been no one else, not for a long time." She leans her back against the counter, hands behind her, as if to expose the truth of what she is saying. "Russell, I demand nothing of you."

"Then why are you telling me?"

"So that you know that I plan to keep the baby."

"Fine. You have my blessing."

"And I prefer to raise it alone, not with a stand-in father whom I don't love."

"Look, your forthrightness or whatever you want to call it . . . ."

"I want it to be with you, Russell. You, me, and our child."

He cocks his head, trying to understand. "You're an enigma to me."

"For a watchman, you miss a lot."

"What," he reacts testily, "was I supposed to catch?"

She regards him in a way he could only dream about earlier. "I'm in love with you!"

"Damn it, I'm no clairvoyant! How was I supposed to know that?"

"Do you only see with your eyes? Has your heart lost its sight?"

"You pushed me away."

"I was feeling bad about myself. I was confused. You weren't the only one who had lost his way."

"You didn't give me a chance to help."

"You are right. But it does not change the fact that I fell in love with you the first time I saw you."

"You hated me the first time you saw me."

"Yes, that too."

The kitchen clock pursues its relentless ticking into the middle of the night. The dirty plates float in a film of chill dish water. Stone and Mathilde are seated together on the kitchen counter, where she used to sit alone, conversing, or not, both as indifferent to time passing and the undone dishes as those things are to them. He has his hand on her abdomen and she has hers over his.

"I dropped this on you," she apologizes.

"No more than it was dropped on you. It's true, it'll take some getting used to. God, you're. . . . soft."

"You don't regret . . . ."

"Mathilde, this is what I think. I think I will always remember your father's birthday for the presents *I* got! It's the greatest birthday I never had."

"And Papa? Who is going to tell him."

"I will."

OCTOBER 19TH

Mrs. Stone lies in panties and a bra on the consultation table, eyes glued to the monitor, as the midwife slides a gooey scanner back and forth over her meringue-white belly, commenting on such and such hump or curve on the sonogram screen. "Heart, kidneys, good, and, there, the spleen. Here, I'll increase the volume." The room fills with the pounding cadence of the baby's heartbeat. "Normal seventh month. All looks very well."

Mathilde gives his hand an encouraging squeeze. "Go ahead and ask."

Stone looks at his prone wife, who gives him a smile and a nod. "We'd like to know our baby's sex."

At the verdict, Stone covers his face and cries.

He drives Mathilde in her car back to the town hall and accompanies her to her office and spends a moment hugging her from behind and caressing her tummy. It creates the illusion of being inside her, of *being* her.

She kisses his neck and says go on now and let me get done what I need to get done.

"I'll be back at five."

"It's so nice having one's own chauffeur."

"Next pregnancy I get the belly and you get the keys."

It is a bumpy ride onto the property. The bridge is caked with cleated mud clods. And, the tracks of heavy trucks continue into and beyond the front yard. Through the autumnal light, a fine cloud of dust and exhaust rises in the west. The incessant din of machinery fills the environment, the distant racket of backhoes, bulldozers and cement mixers.

Stone calls into the house for Osiris, with little expectation of finding him there. Sure enough, he isn't home, meaning he's gone out to the site to pester the builders. The man just won't leave well enough alone. His new battlehorse is keeping the construction crew honest.

An earthmover comes down from the west fields, and Stone halts it. "My father-in-law, is he out there?" The driver gives a nod. Stone follows the embedded grooves to the construction site, where the cave and tunnel used to converge. Osiris is there, among the workers, leaning on a cane, his chin jutted forward and his big behind pointing just as poignantly in the opposite direction. He is leveling orders like a foreman and being a general nuisance to everyone. "Jesus Mary and Joseph! You'll need to dig the foundations deeper! We aren't planting onions here!"

"Take a break, Osiris," suggests Stone, coming up on his left shoulder.

"They're mucking it all up, I tell you. Those foundations must be dug deeper! But what do I know, I'm only the OWNER!"

"All right, I'll have a word with the supervisor. Listen, I have something to tell you. Can you come with me to a quieter spot?"

Reluctantly, like a watchdog being called away from something suspect, Osiris leaves the site. The poor besieged bulldozer driver gives Stone a relieved and grateful thumbs-up.

They walk to the Grand Oak, with his father-in-law still griping in high audio. "Even I know how to read a blue print, for crying out loud!"

Stone feigns a grimace of agreement. He allows the man his moment to calm down. All the farmer wants is to be involved. He criticizes, therefore he exists. "Will you listen to that, Osiris!"

"To what?"

"Why, the noise. The sound of activity. Was this what it was like when Marcel was boss? Motors running and lots of guys shouting sun-up to sundown?"

"Yes, except then at least we were producing something, not chasing a fool's dream. What do we need with another house? And a swimming pool to boot!"

Stone gives the malcontented fart a fair grin. "I've done my homework, Osiris. We won't regret any of it. Bed and Breakfasts in Provence are big business today. It's not even that. It'll give us all something to do and pay for improvements on the farm."

"It's madness. We are not making anything. I don't understand any of it."

"Look, you just practice your English and Japanese," he teases.

"And you think people will come from all over to be served breakfast? And how much will we charge?"

"Relax."

"You'd better be right, *Roussel.* This project of yours is costing me plenty."

"Aw, come on, most of it is being financed by the sale of your daughter's house."

"And the sale of my land!"

"Once again, what have you lost, my friend? The northern property? It was the least attractive part with its headlands and Sabags. Now that they've bought it, you don't have to worry any more about the electrical company throwing you in jail because Sabag is pilfering energy."

"Fantastic! Selling off land in exchange for money that was already mine!"

Yes, thinks Stone, the irony is undeniable. It *was* Sorbin money originally, dug up by Maurice and bequeathed to Sabag when the octogenarian peasant died that summer. Maurice was not carried off by a "good farmer's death", seizing up in a field and being transported by winged tractors into the heavens. Instead, the old hand met his maker in Pertuis hospital, losing a fight with pneumonia. His fear of revolting the daughter/ granddaughter who had become his reason to go on, had gotten him to take one too many baths in the chill water of the dirty basin.

"So, what is so important that you had to drag me away from surveying those scoundrels?"

"I just thought you'd like to know, you're going to be a grandfather."

"I know that, knucklehead."

"What you don't know is the baby's sex."

"Of course I don't. Neither do you."

"But I do."

"Then you must be like my Aunt Francine. She could tell a child's sex by the way a mother bent for a coin. Or what the moon was like at conception."

Stone laughs. "Times have changed. Today, they have machines to tell you."

"Are you having me on?"

Stone's enigmatic expression drives the farmer to fits. "Good God, are you going to tell me or not!"

"It's a boy!"

The farmer does not react right away, and though Stone knows it is unnecessary, he repeats it anyway, for the sheer pleasure of hearing himself say it. "It's a boy!"

"O *fatcha*! I heard you!" Osiris' wan face expands into a grin, and his mustaches pop like autumn crocuses. "And these machines, they do not make mistakes, you are sure?"

"Not in this case."

The farmer does something that takes Stone by surprise. He kisses Stone on both his cheeks.

That afternoon, once the workers have turned off their machines and the countryside has returned to its habitual calm, the two of them sit outside under the mulberry tree, sipping Pastis. Osiris speculates about his future grandson, how vigorous he shall be, and no milquetoast, *pardi*! Then, he takes a trip into the past to expand on other babies, namely Jean Horace and Mathilde, and even about his own infancy, rather what was told to him by women now long gone who held him in their arms and offered him affection and protection. Stone has never seen Osiris more serene or forthcoming.

"I admit," says Osiris, "this past year I thought that my life was over. I had nothing to look forward to. I stopped wanting to get up in the morning and I was afraid to go to my bed at night. I did not want to die alone. I think I put that ad in the newspaper as much for company as a helping hand."

"I know, Osiris."

"Ha! I understand now what motivated that wily fool of a Maurice, may his soul rest in peace. A grandchild is a new lease on life for an old bastard. I intend to teach my grandson how the land works. I will put a photograph of him next to Jean Horace's, and I will talk to him as never could I talk to my own son. You see, I was too afraid of failure back then, too afraid to be a proper father. I was too busy being proud to enjoy my child. But I tell you, I will not fail as a grandfather, no *monsieur*!"

"Osiris, I thank you."

"Thank me? For what?"

"For sharing all of this, your farm, your family. I have been reborn and my debt to you can never be repaid."

Osiris hoots, his livening spirit springing into his expression. "Who would have thought it, eh? The Yank and the Frenchie, stumbling and bumbling around and still managing to come out okay. Good fortune as they say comes on the wind."

Stone lifts his glass. "Here's to wind."

"To wind."

"And mother nature and renewal!"

"*Pardi*!"

A gentle breeze turns the high rising aspen trees silver and gray. Osiris pushes himself up and takes his cane. "Where are you going?" asks Stone.

"Last inspection."

"Damn it, man, they're on schedule and to specifications! Sit down."

Osiris regards him with compassion and compunction. "Listen, *Roussel*, you know I am a man for whom saying sorry does not come naturally. I wanted to say it though, to you. I regret putting you through everything that I have put you through."

"Osiris . . . ."

"Go get my daughter, so that I can make my peace with her now."

*   *   *

Stone is not late. Thus, Mathilde's being there on the curbside, waiting for him, gives him a start. She looks peaked. "What's wrong? Are you ill?"

"I don't know. I feel anxious, that's all. Let's get home."

They descend the hill into the valley and she sees that he is bemused. "What's so funny?"

"What's the last thing you would expect your dad to do?"

She raises her shoulders. "Buy a new truck?"

Stone scoffs like Osiris. "Bah, no! He made me an apology."

"About what?"

"How tough he's been this year. I should have recorded it! What's more, he intends to make his peace with you."

"*Eh beh*, hold your hat because I figure we're due for an earthquake! What did he say about the baby?"

"Oh, about what you'd expect, he was pretty disappointed but prepared to live with the fact."

"Very funny." He can tell, however, that she is not well, her light is dim, her smile, though brave, is forced.

"Come on, something's wrong. Tell me."

"I'll feel better when we get to the farm."

He knows not to push her. She is very much like her father in that respect, having difficulty getting out what's troubling her. But if her anxiety were personified, it would take the form of a little girl and an old hound. Because those are the two figures he sees from the bridge and through the trees, strange messengers performing a dance of pain in the front yard. And, dancing with them is the ghost of Peter Terrell. It is Stone's first haunting in almost half a year.

"Oh my god, what are they doing here?" cries Mathilde.

Stone throws on the brakes and jumps out. The girl and the dog are both whining in front of the locked kitchen door. "Sonia? What is it? Hush, Dora! Sonia?"

The girl babbles, her eyes, like frightened rodents, darting away beyond the barn to the west field. "He can't breathe."

"Who! Osiris?"

She nods, spilling tears the size of coins.

"Oh, God!" Mathilde moans.

"All right, don't panic. Mathilde, go in and call the paramedics. Sonia, you take me to him."

Osiris is lying on his side behind a bulldozer. Stone turns him over and lifts his eyelids. Eyes dilated. No pulse. He gets astride him and pumps his chest, squeezes his blue-veined nose, does mouth-to-mouth. Osiris' pursed parched lips. The needles of his mustache, shrunken like petals. Stone gropes for a pulse, locates one. "Got it, Sonia!" The little girl stares on numbly. Stone swats a bug dead against his sweaty neck. "How long ago did this happen, Sonia? What, five, ten, fifteen minutes? When did he tell you that he couldn't breathe?"

She shrugs, stupefied. "I heard him talking."

"What did he say, Sonia?"

"He was crying. He was saying, oh no God no not now."

Behind her, in the distance and beside the barn, Stone sees Mathilde approaching, holding her belly and having great difficulty to put a foot in front of the other. "You go on back home, sweetheart. I promise to let you know, okay?"

Sonia takes off running for home. Poor little thing, he thinks, to have to watch something like this at the age of 7, his age, days upon days of the same thing, watching his mother fade out gram by gram. He adjusts his pity. This is better, he decides, like losing your pig fast and gone and not chopped up a piece at a time by machines.

Stone retracts Osiris lids again. Pupils still terribly dilated, not a good sign. "Come on, Osiris, come on!" Stone gets a grip under the farmer's back and legs and lifts him and starts back to meet Mathilde making her way across the plain.

"Is he . . . . ?"

"No," he says.

A siren calls over the darkening wood. A formation of birds overflies the house. The fateful day follows its ineluctable course, heedless to misery, waiting for no one. Stone carries Osiris to the yard, and the ambulance screams across the bridge. He holds the farmer in his arms to meet them. Two paramedics hop out before

their truck has stopped moving and rush to him and relieve him
of his load.

"His heart is up and beating again, but I cannot tell you how
long he went without oxygen."

They set Osiris on a stretcher.

"His pupils are dilated."

Mathilde attaches herself to his arm. She's shaking.

They follow the ambulance to the hospital that had given
them such pleasure earlier in the day. In the emergency ward,
they take seats and wait. And wait. The room is hot, malodorous,
and Mathilde cannot sit still. Neither can she speak. Her jaw
seems wired by an incapacity to deal with the sound of her own
voice, to manage her growing irritation and panic. Stone's
suggestion that she go home just worsens the climate.

Finally, a doctor comes out to speak with them. Mathilde
clutches for Stone's hand.

"Your father's heart is strong, but his brain was deprived of
oxygen for a long time, probably due to hypertension."

"What are you telling us?" she asks shrilly.

"Your father is in a coma."

"Will he come out of it?"

"We're getting precious few impulses. The prognosis is not
very optimistic, I'm afraid."

The doctor takes them into a long room of beds partitioned
from one another by thin screens. Osiris lies in bed number 4.
He looks peaceful, reposed on his back, wearing only a light blue
bib the color of his eyes. His naked white farmer's legs. The
gnarled knees. Mathilde breaks down weeping and has to lean on
Stone to remain standing. "Why now!"

Stone says to the doctor, "You're keeping him alive artificially,
is that it?"

"That, in sum, is correct." The man addresses Mathilde.
"I know how tough this is for you. But you might want to
ask yourself if it is worth it to him and to you, to keep the
machine turning." The doctor leaves them alone to make their
decision.

Stone picks up the farmer's hand, presses it, and gives the man a kiss on his forehead. He calls Mathilde, but she is heading in the opposite direction. "Mathilde," he says again. "Please. Talk to him."

"Talk to him? He is dead!"

"Yes, but not yet gone. His heart is still beating."

"What is a heart, without a mind!"

"Maybe much more than the contrary. Come say goodbye. It is not too late."

She moves sideways towards the bed, her brilliant eyes full of pregnant tears. A first attempt at touching her father's flesh, fails. She bites her finger, and collapses on top of him. "Oh, Papa, I'm so sorry! Please forgive me for being late!" She cries over him a good while and then takes his flask hand and presses it between her own and her belly. "Your grandson loves you!"

She lays her head down on his chest and closes her eyes. Within the clammy enclave of a coma, father and daughter embrace at last. She does not yet know how united they finally are, nor how infinite will be the separation.

The End